Slocum slammed the

"Moseley!" he yelled.

The wiry little outlaw's gaze snapped toward Slocum, surprise and a touch of disbelief flickering in his eyes. "You!" the outlaw barked. "Slocum, you bastard! I thought I'd put you down to stay up in Kansas!"

"You didn't get the job done, Moseley. Now it's pay-back time . . ."

The two men stared at each other for several heart-beats, both with handguns drawn and cocked. "Think you can face a man eye to eye, Moseley?" Slocum's words were steady, the tone cold as the ice outside. "You're sure enough a hoss when it comes to gunning down women and kids."

"You bastard." Moseley's voice tightened; his face flushed in rage, his knuckles whitened on the grips of his handgun. Slocum kept his concentration on Mose-ley's eyes; that was where the tipoff came, the split-second flicker before muscles went into action.

JAKE LOGAN

SLOCUM AT HELL'S ACRE

JOVE BOOKS, NEW YORK

SLOCUM AT HELL'S ACRE

A Jove Book / published by arrangement with
the author

PRINTING HISTORY
Jove edition / November 1998

The Penguin Putnam Inc. World Wide Web site address is
http://www.penguinputnam.com

ISBN: 0-515-12391-9

A JOVE BOOK®
Jove Books are published by The Berkley Publishing Group,
a member of Penguin Putnam Inc.,
375 Hudson Street, New York, New York 10014.
JOVE and the "J" design are trademarks belonging to
Jove Publications, Inc.

PRINTED IN THE UNITED STATES OF AMERICA

10 9 8 7 6 5 4 3 2 1

SLOCUM AT HELL'S ACRE

1

Slocum's mood was as bleak as the flat gray, lead-sky land rushing past the soot-stained window.

He didn't like trains.

Trains were cramped, stuffy, noisy, their joltings and lurchings unpredictable. Trains were no place for a man who liked the wide expanse of the frontier. The prairies or deserts with land that went on as far as the eye could see, until it smoothly blended into the sky. Or the mountains, where the sky and the land crashed together in a frayed edge of ragged, snowcapped peaks. Country where the air tasted fresh and clean, even when it was hazed with dust, blurred by rain, or flickered through the latticework of blowing snow.

Out in the open, on horseback, a man could settle into the easy motion of the saddle, feel the controlled power in the muscles of a good horse through the reins and stirrup leathers.

There was no way to catch the rhythm of a train.

Even as the thought formed in Slocum's mind, the Texas & Pacific passenger car lurched across a particularly rough stretch of track. The unexpected jolt nudged his ribs into the unpadded armrest. Slocum winced. Not from pain. From growing aggravation.

The irritation had started when he'd boarded the T&P at Trail City hours ago, with the disapproving scowls cast at him and the Colt Peacemaker holstered at his left hip. Three of every four passengers in the car were Quakers. Slocum didn't give a particular damn what a man's religion was, as long as he didn't try to push his theology onto Slocum. But the Quakers were a different breed. No violence, no weapons, and an unspoken scorn for men who carried guns.

The concept didn't make sense to Slocum. Turn the other cheek out here and somebody would rip it off.

But most of the reason for his growing aggravation with trains in general, and this one in particular, swayed heavily against his right shoulder at the sudden rocking of the car.

The trip had been bad enough to begin with, and it had gotten noticeably worse at the Santa Fe stop. The drummer had waddled down the aisle and plopped down in the seat beside Slocum, and his double chin had been flapping ever since.

If silence truly was golden, Slocum grumbled inwardly, this man was stained copper.

Slocum shifted his weight, shoving the fat man's shoulder away from his upper arm. The drummer ignored the not-so-subtle push. He put chubby fingers on Slocum's forearm, determined to impress his fellow traveler with the particular value of a certain pharmaceutical in the satchel beneath the seat.

The touch raised Slocum's blood pressure another notch. He glared at the fat man, feeling the throb at the base of his own skull that held the seeds of a full-blown headache, the kind that only fresh air and freedom could cure.

"Yes, sir, partner," the fat man babbled on in his earnest pitchman's voice, "I can tell you right now, and with a full guarantee, that these new scientific developments can cure all manner of ails, from dropsy to shin splints—"

"Move your hand, mister," Slocum said, interrupting, his tone low and hard, "or *I'll* remove it. From your shoulder."

The fat man jerked his hand away as if he'd just touched the glowing wood stove at the forward end of the car.

"Sorry, partner," the drummer said. "Habit of mine."

"Habits can get a man hurt," Slocum growled. "I don't like people pawing me. And quit calling me 'partner.' "

"Sorry. Just trying to be friendly. Didn't mean to offend, part—mister." The fat man's eyes, set deep above puffy cheeks, were bloodshot, piggish, the pupils little more than black pinpoints. Slocum figured the man had been sampling some of his own wares; he had seen that look before, in the eyes of people far gone on opium or even its little sister, the painkilling extract called laudanum. He had also seen what happened when they tried to back off from the stuff. It wasn't a pretty sight.

"Didn't catch your name, part—mister?" The pasty flab of the drummer's jowls swayed as the train wheels clacked across another uneven stretch of track.

"I didn't throw it," Slocum said tightly.

"Headed to Dallas myself," the drummer yammered on, missing the warning in Slocum's tone, either from his drug-fogged state or general inability to take a hint. Beads of sweat blossomed on the man's forehead, turned into trickles, then into rivulets along the flesh folds rolled across the collar of his shirt. "Where you bound?"

"To wherever I get off this train," Slocum said, his words soft but the tone hard in warning.

"Well, part—mister—you get into Dallas, you look me up." He fished a rumpled, clammy square of heavy paper from a shirt pocket and thrust it into Slocum's hand. "My card. You want anything—anything at all—you just ask for Wood-row W. Weatherby, dealer in medicinal pharmaceuticals. As I said. Good field to be in when you get tired of drifting, friend. I'm assuming you can read and write? Why, a man can make more money in pharmaceuticals in a month nowadays than Jesse James and his boys made in a year robbing banks and trains."

"Woodrow," Slocum said, "let me explain something to you very carefully. Pay attention, now." He paused for a cou-ple of heartbeats. "Are you paying attention? Really listening? Good. What I want to explain to you is this: Shut the hell up. Savvy?"

The drummer seemed to comprehend. He settled back in his chair, wiping a dirty handkerchief across his brow.

The silence lasted a blissful nine seconds before an infant in a woman's lap two rows up let out a howl. Other babies took up the wailing chorus. Slocum sighed heavily. He knew from painful experience the babies would be screaming for at least an hour, and the coach was full of them. Maybe Quakers weren't fighters, Slocum groused inwardly, but they were damn sure lovers.

He felt a touch on his arm.

Woodrow W. Weatherby's pudgy fingers locked onto Slocum again. "Look, partner, I didn't mean to offend—"

That does it, Slocum thought. He bunched his left fist.

"Mister Slocum?"

Slocum glanced up. The conductor, a big, beefy man with a florid face and wide-set brown eyes, stood in the aisle beside Slocum's row. Slocum nodded.

"A.J. McDonough would like to see you, if you can spare a moment, sir?"

Slocum lifted a mental eyebrow. He had heard of A.J. McDonough, one of the owners of the Texas & Pacific. Slocum didn't like to be summoned to an audience anymore than he liked being stuck in the heavy, hot, smoky air of the T&P car. He hesitated—and made up his mind when the drummer opened his mouth to speak.

Slocum would welcome a visit with the Devil himself or a band of mad Apaches to get away from the talking machine beside him and the squalling babies all around. At least maybe A.J. McDonough enjoyed a bit of silence from time to time. It couldn't be worse than this.

Slocum nodded to the conductor, stood, retrieved his Winchester .44-40 rifle from its nest between his seat and the railcar wall, swayed a bit as the train lurched again, pushed none too gently past the fat man, and stepped into the aisle. He realized he still had Woodrow W. Weatherby's business card in his hand. He wadded it, dropped it, and followed the conductor.

The trainman didn't speak, a blessing for which Slocum's noise-numbed ears were dutifully grateful, as he led Slocum through the door at the end of the car. On the open platforms of each of the three cars they passed through, the conductor breathed deeply, his nostrils flared.

Slocum also breathed deeply inhaling the sharp February air, tainted with fly ash, cinders, and woodsmoke from the locomotive ahead, but still fresh and welcome after the stuffiness of the passenger cars. The steam of his breath whipped away on the wind. An occasional snowflake or weak flurry blurred past the platforms.

"Chilly, but not too thick to breathe," the conductor said with a knowing glance at Slocum as they reached the open platform of the fourth car.

Slocum nodded his silent appreciation. He knew they had reached their destination. They stood at the heavy, thick hardwood door of an ornately decorated private car built almost entirely of mahogany with rosewood trim. Small carved figurines plated in gilt flanked each side of the doorway, each figure holding globed but unlighted kerosene lamps.

The conductor tapped on the heavy door panel.

"Wallace here," he called. "I have Mr. Slocum with me."

"Come in," a woman's voice replied from inside.

The conductor swung the door open and silently motioned for Slocum to step inside. The trainman didn't enter; he closed the door behind Slocum.

Slocum stood for a moment, vaguely aware of the faint scent of tobacco smoke tinged with the faintest hint of expensive perfume in the plush interior of the private car. He barely sensed the aura of money because his attention was, at the moment, entirely on another object of class.

The woman leaned against a wing-backed chair at the side of the car, her hip cocked against the brocade covering. She was taller than most women Slocum had met, maybe five feet seven; she barely had to tilt her head back to look into Slocum's eyes.

It was those eyes that hit Slocum in the gut.

They were the deep gray of the backstrap on his revolver.

The gunmetal-gray eyes were emphasized by the sweep of black hair that fell in gentle waves past a dark-skinned, oval face, then past bared shoulders, and almost to her waist. The deep-gray eyes lay between the arch of trimmed brows and sweep of long lashes. She wore a low-cut green gown, obviously expensive. The gown exposed an interesting amount of light brown skin that was almost Spanish in its coloration. The deep valley between her full breasts lay in the shadow cast by the golden light from oil lanterns flanking each end of the car. She could have been in her late thirties or early forties; Slocum couldn't tell. And didn't care. Altogether, she was a hell of a package.

Her waist was nicely trim, but not pinched into hourglass shape by corset stays. The floor-length gown beneath yards of petticoats concealed her hips and legs. Slocum suspected her legs would be long, firm, well-muscled, not overly thin like those of many women who had large breasts.

She smiled at him, aware that he was sizing her up, and at the same time unabashedly sizing *him* up. The smile creased smooth cheeks, formed dimples above a strong jawline, and emphasized the fullness of her lips. Tiny crow's-feet wrinkles softened the tempered-steel eyes. Her expression somehow seemed mischievous, Slocum thought, and at the same time solemn. With a tint of curiosity.

She was aware of her impact on men, Slocum sensed, and she wasn't the least bit embarrassed or self-conscious about it.

She stepped toward him and offered a hand.

"Mr. Slocum, I'm delighted you could see your way clear to come, despite the somewhat abruptness of the invitation." Her voice was firm and a bit husky, with a musical touch, like the ripple of a mountain stream over stones.

"My pleasure, ma'am," Slocum said with a slight bow. He realized he still wore his hat, and swept it from his head. He took the offered hand. Her long, elegant fingers were dry; she didn't offer the limp back-of-the-hand-up, kiss-it-if-you-wish greeting favored by most society women. It was a firm, straightforward handshake that hinted at a surprising physical strength. His hand seemed to tingle at her touch.

"I hope you don't perceive me as too forward, sir," she said as he reluctantly released her hand. "But you seemed somewhat, ah—uncomfortable, shall we say—in that cramped car."

Slocum half smiled. "The courtesy of the invitation may have stopped a killing, ma'am," he said. "I was about ready to throttle that drummer and stuff him out the window."

"So Anson told me."

"Anson?"

"Anson Wallace. My conductor."

Slocum noted with curiosity her reference to the conductor as "my," not "our."

"I do believe I owe that man a drink, then, ma'am. A full quart." Slocum let the faint smile fade. He finally tore his gaze from those tempered-steel eyes and glanced around. "Is that why your husband sent for me? To stop a killing on his train?"

Confusion flickered in her eyes for a moment, to be quickly replaced by a knowing glint. "My husband? I doubt that, Mr. Slocum. There is no such creature in my life."

Slocum glanced at her left hand. A plain gold band circled the third finger, the only jewelry she wore.

"Oh, that," she said with a smile. "A woman's ploy. Sometimes it helps keep unwanted attention at bay."

Slocum nodded in understanding. A woman who looked the way she did would draw plenty of unwanted attention wherever she went. "I believe you have me at a disadvantage, ma'am."

"Sorry. My manners seem to have abandoned me for a moment." She smiled and inclined her head. "I'm A.J. McDonough."

Slocum's brows went higher. "You're A.J. McDonough? I'm sorry, I thought—I expected . . ." His voice trailed away.

Her chuckle was deep and throaty. "No need to apologize, Mr. Slocum. Many people make the same mistake. But I *am* A.J. McDonough. The A.J. stands for Anita Julienne. I feel it much simpler to conduct business by my initials alone. Most men seem hesitant to enter into business dealings with a woman—until they've signed on the dotted line and it's too late for them to realize they have been had."

"Then this *is* your railroad," Slocum said.

"Lock, stock, and locomotive. Or at least forty-nine percent of it, soon to be more than half. I would take it as a compliment if you called me A.J., as do my friends."

Slocum nodded, a wry smile on his lips. "What do your enemies call you?"

" 'Bitch' is the most common term," she said with a wink. "There are other words, some more colorful, depending upon the situation and the gender of the person who has just been screwed without benefit of a kiss in a business deal. Many of them have wound up calling me 'yes, ma'am, Miss Mc-Donough,' if they've not yet worked their way out of my bad graces. By the way, you may store your rifle in the rack behind you, if you wish.''

Slocum realized with a bit of a start that he still held the Winchester in the crook of his left elbow. His attention had wandered a bit when he stepped into the car. He eased the weapon into the rifle rack she indicated, noting in satisfaction that the cutouts that supported the stock and fore end were padded in green velvet. No weapon would be scratched or marred by the jostle of the train in that rack.

When he turned back, A.J. McDonough lifted the lid of an ivory-inlaid mahogany humidor. ''Would you care for a cigar, Mr. Slocum? I'm told they're quite good. Fine Cuban to-bacco.''

Slocum shook his head. ''If you don't mind, ma'am . . .''

''A.J.''

''A.J. If you'll drop the 'mister' and just call me Slocum.''

''Agreed.''

''Thanks for the offer, but I prefer my own. Do you mind?'' He pulled a thin Mexican cheroot from his breast pocket.

''Not at all,'' she said, ''if I may join you. Some people don't approve of a woman smoking. Or drinking.''

''I assure you I don't mind in the least,'' Slocum said sincerely. ''Just out of curiosity, what do you tell those who do object?''

''To mind their own damned business.'' She lifted a thin, ivory holder from a round table beside the brocade chair, fitted a factory-rolled cigarette into the end, and nodded her thanks as Slocum thumbnailed a match into flame and lit her smoke, then his own.

She waved a hand toward a chair facing the brocade one. ''Have a seat. I think you'll find this one more comfortable than the one back in the car.''

Slocum settled into the armchair, which seemed to be more a man's throne than was the smaller brocade wing-back. It was comfortable, covered in thick but supple leather, and not padded so heavily that he sank so far into it he couldn't come to his feet in a hurry if need be. He shifted the cross-draw holstered Colt at his left hip to a more comfortable position.

"Would you care for a drink, Slocum?" A.J. McDonough asked. "I have all manner of liquor here, from wine to vodka. I believe you prefer rye? Straight, no water?"

He nodded. "You seem to know an awful lot about me." It was a question as much as it was an observation.

"We'll get to that in a moment. I figure we have an hour and a half, at least, so there's no particular rush." She made no effort to explain the time reference. Slocum didn't ask. "I'll join you in that drink," she said, stepping behind a four-foot-long bar made of polished teak. A moment later she strode to Slocum's side, a squat, heavy crystal glass in each hand. "I believe you'll find this satisfactory," she said.

Slocum took the drink with a nod of thanks. He waited until she settled into her brocade chair, noting with interest that instead of wine or some fancy liqueur, she drank whiskey straight. He lifted his glass in a silent salute. She answered the gesture, took a swallow from her glass, and sighed in obvious pleasure.

"The finest money can buy," she said. "It's perhaps not normally something that would be considered a woman's drink, but what the hell—I'm a big girl. I'll drink what I want when I want it."

Slocum sipped at the amber liquor. It was the smoothest he could remember ever having had. Easy on the throat, a savory aftertaste that let a man know he'd been drinking. And a nice, warm glow in the gut when the liquor hit bottom.

They drank and smoked in comfortable silence for a few minutes. Slocum listened to the rustle of the wind past the railway car, the sound muted by thick, heavy walls, the clack of wheels over rails barely audible, and studied the woman across from him.

She sat casually, her legs crossed at the ankles. She wore high-topped, lace-up black shoes; nothing fancy, but stylish. The soft suppleness of the leather hinted that the shoes were handmade. So the woman had common sense to go along with the money. Shoes or boots that fit right were worth the investment. It seemed a long way from those trim, leather-clad ankles to the hips in the chair. Slocum couldn't shake the feeling that she just might have the finest pair of legs he'd seen in years beneath those yards of petticoats.

A complex woman, Slocum thought. And she certainly didn't fit the image that came to mind when he pictured the owner of a railroad.

He became aware that she was sizing him up with the same analytical gaze he had turned on her. When a man looked at him that way, Slocum's hackles went up. They stayed down now.

That he wasn't especially dressed to impress a woman was of no concern. He was comfortable in his worn but clean Levi's that were faded from sun and frequent washings, the pale blue cotton shirt, and brown cowhide boots that were comfortably broken in but still new enough to hold a polish. Slocum didn't figure this was anything resembling a courting call anyway.

The look in those gunmetal-gray eyes across from him seemed, at first glance, as cold as the raw north wind outside. Yet there was a smokiness to them as well, a softness. And more than a hint of interest.

"Slocum," she finally said, "I suppose you're curious as to why I asked you to come to my car. I don't normally invite every man I see for a drink and a visit."

Slocum tapped the ash from his cigarillo into a cut-crystal tray on a table beside his chair. The ashtray was recessed into the top of the table, which in turn was bolted to the floor. It would drive a woman who liked to rearrange furniture crazy, he figured, but it certainly wouldn't turn over during a wild lurch or sway of the car. "The thought had crossed my mind," he told her.

She flicked the ash from her cigarette into a stone hollowed into a bowl by years of Indian women grinding corn on the coarse surface. It looked to be genuine, not the fake Indian stuff from back East, where such artifacts fetched a decent dollar on the market these days. Or so Slocum had heard.

"I recognized you when you passed my car to board the train," she said. "You aren't a difficult man to notice."

Slocum had to nod in agreement. A man who stood six-one with jet-black hair, green eyes, and the lean build of a mountain cat, and who carried his revolver in a cross-draw rig, wasn't hard to spot. Slocum got noticed a lot. Most of the time it was an aggravation. But he seriously doubted that A.J. McDonough intended to pull a gun on him. She didn't need a man-kill to make her reputation.

"I believe your destination is Fort Worth?" she said.

Slocum nodded, his curiosity piqued even more. She knew a lot about him and his business. But since she owned a chunk of the railroad, she probably could find out most anything about most anybody, he figured.

"And you have no plans until you reach there?"

"None except to keep my sanity. Trains can be boring."

She smiled. "You don't have the look, or the reputation, of being a man who enjoys being crated up like a Longhorn steer on the way to market." She paused to drag at her cigarette and let the smoke trickle from her nostrils the way men often did. "I suppose you'd like me to get to the point?"

"In your own time," Slocum said pleasantly. "It's a long way to Fort Worth, and I'm enjoying the company. But yes, I am a bit curious."

The expression in the tempered-steel eyes seemed to harden for a moment, then quickly reverted to normal.

"The point is, Slocum, that I have a problem looming. Rather soon. A problem that requires the attention of a man of your experience and particular expertise." She paused for a sip at her drink, noticing his raised brows. "Hear me out, please. You may accept or decline when you've heard my story, and I'll not argue with your decision should you say no. You have nothing against money, I trust?"

Slocum shrugged. "I've been flat and I've been flush. I prefer flush." At the moment he was somewhere in between, with Colonel Wes Connally's travel expense money and half the pay for the job ahead in his pocket. It wouldn't hurt a thing to hear her out.

A.J. McDonough smiled back. "I agree, Slocum. I too am somewhat fond of money. I am, as you say, flush. Enjoying life to the fullest. And I would like to keep things just as they are.'' She snubbed out her smoke. ''And that brings me to the point, finally. You've heard of the Moseley gang?''

Slocum's smile abruptly faded; a muscle in his jaw tightened. He pinned a steady gaze on A.J. If she knew so much about him, did she also know of the long-standing blood feud between him and Caleb Moseley? That the next time they met, only one would walk away? That Slocum had wanted for years to get the son of a bitch in his sights just one more time? He didn't ask. He merely nodded. ''I've heard of them. Tough bunch.''

''They, Slocum, are my problem.'' Her eyes turned as hard as the tempered steel they resembled. ''At the last stop, I received a message from one of my confidential sources. A very reliable source. The Moseley gang plans to raid this train. I'd like to hire you. To stop them.''

2

Slocum sat for a moment in silence, staring at the woman seated across from him.

She was asking a lot. Especially of one man.

Caleb Moseley and his bunch—seven of them altogether, the last Slocum had heard—were not exactly amateurs at the owlhoot trade. They were hardcases. Shooters with a trail of bodies behind them across six states and two territories. More often than not, they killed people just for the pure hell of it.

Slocum became aware that the ash on his cigarillo had grown to more than a half inch, and tapped the residue into the crystal ashtray on the table beside his chair.

"Before you answer, Slocum," A.J. McDonough said calmly, "I am very much aware that you don't make a practice of hiring out your gun. I admire standards in a man—a man who has the moral principle not to exploit his talent for pure monetary gain." She snubbed out her cigarette and leaned back in the chair. "Ordinarily, I would take care of problems like this without seeking outside help. I mostly stomp my own snakes. But I'm also smart enough to know when I'm in over my head. And there is more at stake here than money."

She paused for a moment to finish off her drink. Slocum waited patiently.

"This train," she said, "is carrying less than two thousand dollars in cash—a sum I could easily afford to write off as an expense of doing business. But Moseley is no fool. He knows where the *real* money is. They'll empty the safe, of course. After all, that's found money. But what they really want, Slocum, is me.''

Slocum's brows lifted. ''Ransom?''

''Precisely. My board of directors would, I think, pay a hefty reward for my return.'' A wry smile touched the corners of her lips. ''On the other hand, they might not. Some of them still harbor a bit of resentment over a woman holding most of the power. At any rate, even if they did pay, I fear I'd be slightly the worse for wear.''

No doubt about that, Slocum thought. Even more than robbery or murder, the Moseley bunch liked a good rape. And Anita Julienne McDonough was the type of woman they would play with until she died. Or lost her mind.

''So you see, Slocum, I have a *very* vested interest in not letting that happen,'' she said. ''And there's one more reason I'd prefer to have their efforts thwarted.'' She gestured toward the end of the car where heavy damask drapes separated the living area from what Slocum assumed were sleeping quarters. ''There is a small safe beside my bed. In that safe are bearer bonds, negotiable shares in the Texas & Pacific Railroad. Not a large amount in terms of dollars, but enough to increase my forty-nine-percent ownership in the company to fifty-one percent. If those bonds fall into the wrong hands before they are duly registered, I will lose the opportunity to gain controlling interest in the T&P.'' She reached for another cigarette and fitted it into the slim holder.

''Do any others on the board of directors know about those bonds?'' Slocum asked as she lit her smoke.

''Possibly. I don't know that for a fact, but normally when a block of shares becomes available, everyone with a stake in the company knows of it.'' She blew a perfect smoke ring. It drifted lazily toward the ceiling. ''Are you perhaps thinking that someone within the company is behind this planned robbery?''

Slocum shook his head. ''I don't know. It always pays to look at the whole deck before sitting in on a poker hand. I don't believe Moseley himself is smart enough to know—or really care—about bearer bonds. He's more of a gold-and-greenbacks man.''

''It seems you know his thinking rather well, Slocum.''

''I know him some.'' Slocum didn't add that he too had a personal interest in seeing that the Moseley bunch didn't manage to get aboard this particular train. Caleb Moseley would shoot him on sight. As he would Moseley. If it were just the two of them—he and Moseley—Slocum would welcome the chance. But it wasn't going to be *mano-a-mano*. There were others involved, innocent people who would die as sure as it rained in Oregon.

Slocum finally nodded. ''I understand the problem.''

''Would you consider a fee of five hundred dollars in cash an adequate price for your services, Slocum?''

It was a lot of money. Ten months' top-hand wages on any reputable ranch. Slocum snubbed out his cigarillo. ''Before I say yes or no, I'd like to have some more background. Did this warning you received come by telegraph?''

She shook her head. The movement sent ripples of light dancing over the glossy black hair. ''A note, hand-delivered. Telegraph operators sometimes forget their oath of secrecy. You never know whose payroll they might be on.''

''Then we have the advantage in information.'' Slocum realized with a bit of a start that he had used the plural. And he hadn't agreed yet to take the job. At her nod, he continued. ''The disadvantage we face is that I doubt there's five men on this entire train who can, or will, handle a gun. Most of the passengers are Quakers. Those who aren't are mostly drummers, farmers. Not shooters.''

''Which is why I asked you to come here.''

''How many reliable men do you have on the crew? Men you would trust with your life?''

She sighed. ''Not that many, I fear. Some of them are new and unfamiliar to me personally. My conductor, Anson Wallace, is loyal to the core. A good man, but no shootist. He's fair, at best, with that little snub-nosed .38 Smith & Wesson he carries in a shoulder holster.''

Slocum nodded. He had noticed the shoulder rig the first time he'd seen the conductor.

"My engineer is a top railroad man, but he isn't a gunman. Old Charles, the porter, is as loyal as anyone's dog, but he's never owned or fired a gun. The shotgun guard in the baggage car is young and untested. It's his first run." She paused, a faint worry line forming between her eyes. "He has no criminal past. On the other hand, according to my investigators, he seems to have no past at all—and that troubles me, Slocum."

As it should, he thought. If she knew as much as she seemed to know about *him,* she should have been able to uncover at least something about the new man.

A.J. opened the drawer of the small table beside her chair and pulled out a handgun. It wasn't the cute little silver-plated, pearl-handled derringer or cloverleaf rimfire .32 he'd expected to see. This wasn't the kind of weapon most women carried. It was a Sheriff's Model Colt .45, four-inch barrel, gutta-percha grips, and it showed signs of having been used. It was a handgun that meant business.

"Nice weapon," Slocum said.

"A tool, Slocum. But a good one. It gets the job done, and I know how to use it. Does that surprise you?"

It was Slocum's turn for a wry smile. "As a matter of fact, no. I've known many women who were excellent shots, better than most men. And where you're concerned, A.J., I'm past the point of being surprised at anything."

"Have you reached a decision yet?" She stowed the weapon back in the drawer.

"What do you know, if anything, about their plan? I have a habit of liking to know what I'm riding into before I saddle up."

"Good habit."

"It's saved my hide a few times."

A.J.'s brow wrinkled in thought. "There are two of Moseley's men on the train at the moment. They boarded at different stations. My source says they'll make their move when we stop to take on fuel and water at the Sour Lake siding."

Slocum frowned. "Perfect spot for a train holdup."

"You know the place?"

"It's been a while, but I've been there. The railroad hadn't been built at the time. In fact, they were surveying the route

then.'' He ran the lay of the land through his memory. Sour
Lake was in a stretch of rough, arid, almost desert country.
The logical place for the water tower was in a swale of sorts,
flanked on the north by a low, sloping bluff. To the south, the
land fell away abruptly into a deep ravine.

''I know what you're thinking, Slocum,'' A.J. said after a
moment. ''If I had in mind hitting this train, that's where I'd
do it.''

''Can we just barrel on through without stopping?''

She shook her head. ''If we don't take on water, we'll
blow the boiler before we get twenty miles. There's one constant in the railroad business, Slocum. Locomotives have to
be fed, watered, and oiled regularly, or they quit running.''

''And a constant in the holdup business is that a stopped
train's a lot easier to take than one on the move.''

A.J. lifted an eyebrow. ''I doubt you've held up any trains
yourself, but you seem to know a bit about it.''

''I know outlaws and how they think. How much time do
we have?''

She plucked a heavy pocket watch from the table beside her
and flipped open the gold case. ''An hour, give or take eight
minutes.''

Slocum nodded. ''That should be long enough. Now, what
else do you know about Moseley? The last I heard, he had six
men with him.''

''Two of them are on the train now,'' A.J. said. ''If they
do the same with us as they did with the Santa Fe and the
Great Northern, one of the men on the train will take control
of the locomotive—the engineer and fireman. The second will
take care of the conductor and brakeman. Which, I presume,
would mean four of my employees would be killed.''

Slocum nodded solemnly. ''It's their style. After they elim-
inate the crew, the rest of the gang will ride up. A couple of
them will rob the baggage car. The others will line up the
passengers outside, relieve them of any valuables they happen
to be carrying, kill three or four for fun, then take their pick
of the women. They take the women with them.''

The picture of Caleb Moseley's face snapped into sharp
focus in Slocum's brain. It brought a warmth, an ember of

rage, to his gut; he forced the emotion away. Angry men made mistakes. A mistake here could get him, and many others, killed. Or worse.

"We'll be outgunned, A.J. I'll need one good man."

"Where will you find him?"

"Two cars back. He got on board at Trail City."

"Then hire him. A hundred dollars. Go to two hundred if necessary. There's too much at stake here to worry about a bit of loose change."

Loose change to this woman, Slocum thought, was a fortune to most men on the frontier. He became aware that her gaze was locked on his, a knowing expression in the gunmetal-gray eyes.

"You're going to kill him, aren't you? Moseley, I mean."

"If I get the chance, yes. And if I do get that chance, this time I'll finish the job." He didn't expand on the statement. She didn't push for an explanation. "We've got a deal, A.J. I assume you know what the Moseley men on the train look like?"

"Down to the hair in their ears."

"Okay, tell me about them, and I'll go to work."

Slocum grabbed a handrail as the T&P locomotive leaned and lurched across a trestle over a dry creek, the sleet-laced wind tugging at his hat on the platform between cars.

For a moment, this particular spot was free of woodsmoke and cinders from the locomotive. Slocum paused for a couple of deep breaths of the frigid, bracingly clean air, then reached for the handle of the car before him.

It didn't take long to spot his man.

He was in his aisle seat, third row from the front on the left, just as A.J. had said he would be. He was young, little more than a pup, probably just out of his teens. He leaned back in his seat, a new and expensive plainsman-style leather hat tipped forward over his eyes.

Slocum strode to the seat and stopped alongside. There was no doubt this was the man. Pimpled face, blue chambray shirt, black leather vest, shoulder-length brown hair, and a Smith & Wesson Schofield .45 in a holster at his right hip. Slocum tapped the kid gently on the shoulder. The young man's eyes popped open.

"Red wants to see you, Charlie," Slocum said casually.

"Who the hell are you?"

Slocum raised his hands as if to ward off an attack, and forced a weak grin. "No need to shoot the messenger, Charlie. I was headed up this way, Red asked a favor, that's all. I did my part. Whether you go see what he wants or not is up to you. Wouldn't want that big fellow mad at me, though. You know how it is with redheads. Bad tempers. Blow up over nothing."

Charlie snorted in disgust, but he rose, snugged his hat down on his head, and started for the door Slocum had just come through.

Slocum followed silently.

Charlie stepped out on the platform, shivered slightly at the blast of cold wind, and turned to close the door.

He never finished the turn.

Slocum's right hand snaked out, whipped the Schofield from the kid's holster, and tossed it away in one motion. His left hand locked into Charlie's long hair and yanked his head back. Slocum rammed his right knee into Charlie's lower back and heaved. A startled squawk was the only sound as the young man's body hurtled clear of the fast-moving train. Above the clack of wheels, Slocum heard the dull thud as Charlie hit the ground.

Slocum leaned out a bit, caught a quick glimpse of the kid bouncing and rolling down the cinder-covered slope of right-of-way, and grunted in satisfaction.

If Charlie lived through that, Slocum thought, he was going to be banged up bad enough to be out of action for a while. One Moseley man who wasn't going to be a worry any longer. The young guns were the dangerous ones. They were also a tad dumb, most of the time. Hadn't learned to never trust a stranger. Things like that got them thrown off trains or shot dead.

Slocum wiped Charlie's hair grease from his hand and went into the next car.

The man he now sought still rode in the seat he'd settled

into at the Trail City stop. The man's shaggy gray hair, unkempt beard, and worn, rough clothing marked him as a plainsman. So did the .45-70 Springfield trapdoor rifle leaning against his shoulder. Pale blue eyes in a deeply lined face the color of old saddle leather watched with interest as Slocum stopped alongside.

"You look bored, mister," Slocum said.

"Reckon I am. Don't like trains."

"You have the look of a man who knows how to use a Springfield," Slocum said, his voice low. "Scout?"

"Some. Buffler, back when we still had some shaggies about." He pinned a hard stare on Slocum. "You ask a lot of questions, feller."

"Got one more. How'd you like to earn a hundred dollars?"

"Who you want killed?"

Slocum glanced around. No one seemed to be eavesdropping, but on a train a man couldn't be sure. He nodded toward the door at the end of the car. "Come out on the hitch platform with me, have a smoke, and I'll tell you about it. In private."

"Don't smoke. Could use a chaw, though. Reckon it won't hurt to parley some." Slocum stepped aside as the weathered frontiersman rose from his seat a bit stiffly. Slocum noticed he kept his thumb on the hammer of the Springfield. Slocum nodded toward the door.

The old-timer nodded back. "You first."

Smart man, Slocum thought as he led the way onto the small platform outside. Which was why this gent was still around and young Charlie wasn't. Slocum waited until the frontiersman pulled a plug of tobacco from his pocket and bit off a chunk. His pale blue eyes settled a steady gaze onto Slocum.

"Lay 'er on me, friend. What's this all about?"

"Ever shoot a man before?" Slocum asked.

"Here and there. We gonna talk maybe shootin' somebody, I like to know who I'm workin' for."

"Slocum's the name."

"Heard of you." The old-timer held out a knuckle-scarred hand. "Go by the handle of Stanky myself." The man's grip was firm. "Got stuck with the moniker back in my skinnin' days. Smelt a tad ripe most of the time. English feller I skinned for didn't know how to say a man stinks. Said I 'stank.' " He released Slocum's grip. "What I got to do to earn this hundred?"

"Help stop a train robbery." Slocum filled Stanky in on what lay ahead at Sour Lake. The expression in the old man's blue eyes never changed.

"Five of 'em, you say?"

Slocum shrugged. "Best guess. Could be more. Could be less. You game?"

Stanky spat a stream of tobacco juice—to the downwind side, Slocum noted with relief. "I'll play. What's the plan?"

Slocum told him what he had in mind. Stanky nodded. "Sounds good enough to me. You sure they'll come in from the north once the train's stopped?"

"Would you charge across two hundred yards of open ground uphill into the teeth of a north wind, when you could have half that distance to cover and the wind at your back?"

"Reckon not."

"Speaking of wind, it might get a little chilly for you up there on top of the baggage car," Slocum said.

"Hell, son, I been through winters in the Dakotas and up Wyoming way. This here's shirtsleeve weather." Stanky took a deep breath of the chill air rushing across the platform. "Man can't hardly breathe in them damn coach cars nohow. Nice out here. Deal me in."

Slocum pulled the gold coins A.J. had given him from a pocket and handed them to the frontiersman.

"You a trustin' soul, Slocum, payin' in advance. How you know I won't turn on you when the time comes, throw in with them Moseley boys?"

"You're not the type," Slocum said. "One thing I've learned is how to read men. Do you have a watch?"

Stanky shook his head. "Never had to be no place a man couldn't judge by the sun or the season. Folks has got in too big a hurry these days, seems to me. Never met no man was such a bigwig his time was worth more'n his hide. Met a few thought they was, but they had a damn sight higher opinion of theirselves that I had of 'em."

"Good point. Anyhow, you won't need a watch. When the

train passes through a deep, rocky cut on the downgrade, then over a short trestle, it will be just over a quarter hour to the Sour Lake stop. Plenty of time from there for you to get in position.''

"I'll be there." Stanky spat again. "Only thing bothers me is, can that conductor handle the big fella—the one called Red?"

Slocum nodded. "He has to. Or we're all in trouble."

Slocum crouched behind the cold steel wall of the locomotive tender, the screech of wheels against iron rails grating against his ears as the train braked for the Sour Lake siding a couple of hundred yards ahead.

He glanced at the wooden water tower standing alongside the tracks, hoping Caleb Moseley hadn't had the foresight to station a sharpshooter on the catwalk of the tank. One good rifleman up there could make it hot for anybody on the train. The old military idea of holding the high ground was just as true in outlawry as it was on the bloody battlefields of Gettysburg. It was a chance Slocum had to take.

The stinging sleet pellets driven on the freshening north wind had given way to light, swirling snow flurries in the last few miles. The air had the smell of a full-blown snowstorm, maybe a blizzard. But it wouldn't hit for a couple of hours, Slocum figured, and by then this mess would be over. One way or another.

Slocum was satisfied with his defenses, such as they were. Stanky lay atop the baggage car, the Springfield at the ready, two extra cartridges clamped between his tobacco-stained teeth. Anson Wallace had gotten the man called Red out of the way with quiet efficiency. Something about having a snub-nosed .38 stuck in his ear made even a big man turn meek. Red was tied up like a steer for branding in the caboose, a nervous brakeman holding a shotgun on him. Red wouldn't be any problem.

Slocum had only two worries, aside from the possibility of getting killed when the lead started flying. That idea didn't worry him all that much. He lived with the possibility most of the time. His main concern was that he didn't have a man stationed in A.J.'s private car at the rear of the train, just in front of the caboose. She wouldn't hear of it; she'd just loaded the sixth chamber of the Sheriff's Model .45, looked him straight in the eye, and said, "I'll handle things here, Slocum."

His other worry was that innocent passengers might get hit. It was up to Wallace to see that the women and children got down and away from the windows when the firing started. The soft-spoken, broad-shouldered conductor probably could handle that, but you never knew with civilians. Sometimes they were just flat out dumb enough to look up to see what was going on. And look right into a slug.

Slocum shrugged the thoughts aside. There was no need fretting on it now. What would happen would happen.

The locomotive clanked and screeched to a stop before the water tank and coal bin, sparks flying from the near-side drive wheel. The outlaw gang would be coming any minute now, spurring their horses over the ridge to the north. They had to cross almost a hundred yards of open ground before reaching the train.

Slocum knew he was taking a chance.

If Moseley decided to attack from the south, everything would be screwed up; it would take a few seconds for Slocum and Stanky to react, and in this game a few seconds could get a man killed. Or maybe several men, women, and children.

It was a chance, true enough, but the odds were in Slocum's favor. No raider wanted to charge into a north wind across two hundred yards of open ground. Not if he could come with the wind at his back and only have less than half that much exposed terrain to cover.

Slocum heard and smelled the raiders before they came into view; the distinct scent of horse, the clank of curb chains and bits, the creak of saddle leather carried on the north wind. Slocum cracked the action on his Winchester for one final check to make sure a round was chambered, then eared back the hammer.

The sounds were closer now, hoofbeats picking up speed behind the rise. The hoarse call of a man's voice sounded from just beyond the low bluff.

Slocum barked a curse as the horsemen topped the rise at a lope, a Rebel yell and whoops splitting the sharp air, handguns already drawn or shotguns resting on hips, bandannas pulled above their noses.

Moseley had picked up reinforcements somewhere along the way.

There were nine of them. . . .

3

Slocum's biggest worry wasn't the unexpected men.

What brought the explosive curse from his lips was that the man he wanted most was on the far end of the line from Slocum's post—a small man, looking even smaller in an over-sized peacoat atop a big, rangy bay.

Caleb Moseley.

And Moseley, along with two other men, were headed for the end of the train. Directly toward A.J.'s car.

Slocum couldn't spare the time for a shot at Moseley. The other outlaws were closing fast. A few more seconds and they'd reach the train. He lined the Winchester's sights on the nearest rider and stroked the trigger. The crack of the .44-40 sounded an instant before the rider jerked erect, dropped his handgun, and sagged in the saddle.

Slocum levered a fresh round into the chamber as the throaty blast of Stanky's Springfield reached his ears. A rider near the center of the line seemed to rise into the air, hang there for an instant as his horse ran out from under him, then fall heavily onto the hard-packed ground. Midway down one car, a handgun barked, then another.

The outlaw band's charge faltered for a heartbeat at the unexpected gunshots; the line slowed as men instinctively pulled back on the reins. But the line didn't break, even when Slocum's second slug brought an audible grunt from the next rider in line. The man rocked back in the saddle and reined

25

aside, the fight knocked from him by the slug. An instant later
a horse squealed and went down under Stanky's .45-70 round,
spilling its rider.

The odds were thinning fast. Slocum winced as a volley of
lead spanged from the wall of the locomotive tender; one slug
whipped over the steel plate, ricocheted from the metal on the
far side, and whined back past Slocum's ear. The shot had
come from a higher angle than the men on the ground could
manage. Slocum glanced toward the rim of the bluff a hundred
yards away, and caught a glimpse of powder smoke wisping
away on the stiff north wind. He slapped a quick, unaimed
shot toward the rim, not expecting to hit anything—just give
the sharpshooter something to think about.

He ignored the buzz of a slug past his ear, glancing toward
A.J.'s car. His heart skipped a beat. Moseley and two of his
men were within a few feet of the car; a few more seconds
and they'd reach the platform—

A puff of gunsmoke rolled from a partly opened window
of the expensive car; the man at Moseley's right spun from
the saddle and went down. Slocum lost track of Moseley then
as the raiders, now within a few yards, loosed a volley of lead
from handguns. Slocum ignored the spang of slugs against the
tender, and aimed and put one more down as a blast from the
.45-70 knocked another from the saddle. The odds were narrowing rapidly.

Over the crackle of gunfire, Slocum heard a grunt and a
curse from atop the baggage car. It sounded to him as if Stanky
had taken a hit—Slocum caught a quick glimpse of wispy gun
smoke from the ridge above, and levered three quick rounds
toward the rocks where the sharpshooter had taken cover. He
knew he had hit nothing, but at least it would keep the rifleman's head down for a few seconds.

Two cars back, an outlaw skidded his horse to a stop, bailed
from the saddle, and reached for the platform handrail. Slocum
put him down, then thumbed fresh cartridges into the Winchester's loading port.

The attack wavered and broke. The surviving outlaws
whirled their mounts about and spurred back toward the ridge.
Slocum winced as a round from the sharpshooter clanged off

steel barely a foot from his head. He slapped another unaimed shot toward the rocks, convinced now that Stanky had been hit; he hadn't heard the .45-70 blast for a minute or two.

Slocum forgot the man on the ridge, the fleeing horsemen. He had to get to the back of the train, hope he got there in time to help A.J. And the quickest way to get there was along the nearly flat top of the cars, hurdling the gaps between them. He could only hope the man on the ridge had trouble hitting moving targets.

Slocum drew a quick, sharp breath, scrambled up the back of the tender, and leapt atop the first passenger car. He ran, crouched low, concentrating first on keeping his footing on the narrow flat catwalk, slick with ice and a light dusting of snow. A missed step would send him tumbling to the cinders at trackside. Another slug from the ridge gouged splinters of wood and shards of thin ice almost beneath his feet.

Two more jumps, a skidding sprint, and he was atop the end of the baggage car. Stanky lay on his side, his back toward Slocum; Slocum at first glance feared he was dead. Then he realized that Stanky was working the blade of his hunting knife into the chamber of the Springfield. Slocum barely checked his stride, yelled Stanky's name, and tossed his Winchester to the frontiersman.

"Ridge!" Slocum called. "Son of a bitch up there may learn to shoot sooner or later."

"I got 'im," Stanky said, then whirled on his belly, lined the Winchester, and loosed a round. Slocum forgot about the man on the ridge; either Stanky would keep him pinned down, or the rifleman up there would get a slug into Slocum. It was out of his hands now. And there were more important things to worry about—

It was only a few yards more. Finally, he was above the coupling platform. Slocum slid down the brakeman's handrails, landed lightly on his feet, and paused to gasp air back into his lungs as he listened. To go charging into the car might get him shot—if not by Moseley and any of his men inside, then by A.J. His pounding heart seemed to tighten in his chest; through the heavy wooden door, he heard a voice from inside. Moseley's voice.

"Forget the damn baggage car, Joel," Moseley said, his words slightly muffled by the wood. "Grab the bitch—she's what we come for."

Slocum pulled his Peacemaker, eared back the hammer, and put a hand on the doorknob. It turned silently beneath his grip. He cracked the door a couple of inches, peered inside, and his heart sank.

A big man in a heavy buffalo coat stood directly between Slocum and Moseley, a Merwin Hulbert revolver in an oversized fist. A.J., her face pale but composed, stood behind the wing-back chair, her hands and arms out of sight.

"Let's go, lady," the man called Joel said, his voice surprisingly high-pitched for a man of his bulk.

"I don't think so," A.J. said.

"Listen, dammit, I don't want no trouble from you." Joel lowered his handgun and took a half step toward A.J. She whipped her right hand up from behind the chair. The report of her Sheriff's Model .45 rattled the coach interior. Joel's head snapped; the big man toppled backward, dead before his body bounced off the overstuffed chair where Slocum had sat earlier.

Moseley squawked, starting to swing his handgun toward A.J.

Slocum slammed the door open.

"Moseley!" he yelled.

The wiry little outlaw's gaze snapped toward Slocum, surprise and a touch of disbelief flickering in his eyes. "You!" the outlaw barked. "Slocum, you bastard! I thought I'd put you down to stay up in Kansas!"

"You didn't get the job done, Moseley. Now it's my turn." At the edge of his vision, Slocum saw A.J. draw down on Moseley. "No, A.J.," Slocum said calmly, "it's between him and me now."

"Then take the son of a bitch, Slocum," A.J. said.

The two men stared at each other for several heartbeats, both with handguns drawn and cocked. "Think you can face a man eye to eye, Moseley?" Slocum's words were steady, the tone cold as the ice outside. "You're sure enough a hoss when it comes to gunning down women and kids."

"You bastard." Moseley's voice tightened; his face flushed in rage, his knuckles whitened on the grips of his handgun. Slocum kept his concentration on Moseley's eyes; that was where the tipoff would come, the flicker before muscles went into action.

Slocum saw the flash in the hazel eyes half a heartbeat before Moseley's handgun came up. Slocum stroked the trigger. The slug hammered Moseley back a half step, but the little man didn't go down. Slocum twisted to the side as fire flashed from Moseley's handgun, felt the tap of a slug against his coat sleeve. He didn't fight the recoil of his .44-40, cocked the weapon as the muzzle dropped, and let his thumb slip from the hammer as the Peacemaker fell into line. Slocum's shot took Moseley at the base of the throat.

Moseley still didn't go down, despite the wallop of the soft-lead .44 slug. He stood, blood pulsing from the hole in his neck, shock and disbelief spreading across his face. He tried to bring his revolver into play, but the weapon sagged downward as strength drained from his fingers. He went to his knees.

"You—bastard—never thought"—Moseley's voice carried a slight gurgle—"you'd ever get lucky—twice in a row—" The hazel eyes glazed. Moseley shuddered and pitched forward. His boots crabbed weakly at the floor of the passenger car as he tried to get back to his feet.

Slocum strode to the dying man, toed Moseley's handgun aside, and stood looking down at the outlaw for a moment. The harsh, gasping gurgle of a man drowning in his own blood seemed loud in the sudden silence.

"Go—ahead—Slocum." The words were barely audible. "Finish—the job."

"It's finished, Moseley," Slocum said calmly. "You only have a few minutes left. I'm not going to deny myself the pleasure of watching you die, and I'm sure as hell not going to make it easier for you."

Slocum cut a quick glance at A.J. McDonough. A strand of black hair had worked loose and plastered itself to the sheen of sweat in front of her left ear. A smudge of powder residue darkened the curve of her cheekbone, but her fingers were steady; the muzzle of the Sheriff's Model didn't waver. Finally, she shifted her gaze from the dying man to Slocum.

"I'm going to leave you to your fun now," she said, "and go check on my brakeman. I heard a gunshot from the caboose. I hope Garland's not hurt." She stepped over Moseley and went out the back door. Slocum became aware of the chill spreading through the car from the open door behind him, the heavy, acrid scent of burnt powder, and the coppery smell of Moseley's blood. Moseley managed to raise his head once, glare at Slocum, and mutter something that sounded like curses through the pinkish froth of blood on his lips. Slocum couldn't tell. The words were weak and gurgly. Slocum nodded casually.

"Love you too, you miserable bastard," he said.

Moseley shuddered once and died. Too damn bad, Slocum thought; he would have liked to have seen it take a lot longer and be a lot harder. Moseley had gone too easily to suit him. He felt neither elation nor remorse over the outlaw's death, just a calm satisfaction that it had finally ended—and that Caleb Moseley had died knowing damn well who'd killed him.

Slocum was wondering what to do with the bodies when a slight scuffling noise at his back brought him whirling about, the Colt in his hand.

"Slocum? You all right in here?"

Slocum breathed a sigh of relief at the familiar, gravelly voice. "Couldn't be better, Stanky," Slocum called. "Come on in."

The frontiersman stepped inside, Slocum's rifle in one hand, the .45-70 in the other. Stanky shook his head by way of greeting. "The feller up on the ridge won't be botherin' nobody else." He handed Slocum the Winchester. "Shoots good for a little gun." A touch of embarrassment flickered across his weathered features. "Sorry I couldn't be no more help up there. Damn cartridge case separated on me. Brass stuck in the chamber. Happens more'n a man might think on these damned Springfields. The lady okay?"

"She's fine. Or at least she seems to be."

"Might be she'll fall to pieces once it dawns on her what happened," Stanky said. "Can't tell about females. Lived with one a couple years. Never did figger out what the hell she was thinkin' or how come she done or didn't done somethin'. Was I you, I'd stick close to that one for a while, just in case she gets the shakes and blubbers.''

"I'd planned to do just that," Slocum said solemnly.

The grizzled old-timer cocked a knowing eyebrow. "Fact she's a looker don't have nothin' to do with it, o'course."

"Course not, Stanky. Mind giving me a hand cleaning up this place? Seems to be a bit of trash accumulated here."

"Slocum," A.J. McDonough said, the hint of a twinkle in her gunmetal-gray eyes, "you're not much of a businessman."

Slocum lifted a quizzical eyebrow. "What makes you say that?"

"I would have paid you twice as much."

He lifted his glass in salute. "From one poor businessman to another. I'd have done it for free."

A.J. chuckled, raised her glass, and said, "Then I suppose it worked out to everyone's satisfaction. Down that one, Slocum. I've got plenty in the cabinet and the evening's still young." She finished her own drink in two swallows, rose, and took Slocum's glass. A moment later it was back in his hand; Slocum noted that she hadn't skimped on the bourbon.

"Are you trying to get me drunk, A.J.?" he asked.

"If that's your pleasure. I'm working on getting drunk myself. Haven't gotten there yet, but I'm working on it." She lit a cigarette and leaned back in her wing-back chair, eyeing Slocum curiously. "It's none of my business, I know. But would I be too far out of line to ask why you wanted to kill Moseley?"

Slocum shrugged. "He did something I didn't like to a friend of mine."

"Which was?"

"He killed her."

A.J. nodded. "I understand." She didn't push the point, just accepted the statement. Slocum was grateful for that. It had been years, but the memory still pained a bit. He forced his mind not to dwell on it. It was over now between him and Moseley. Accounts were squared.

Slocum sipped at his drink, then nodded toward a roll tied with heavy twine leaning against the far corner of the rail car. "Sorry about the rug."

"Don't be. I didn't like it much anyway. The Persian seemed like a good idea at the time, but once I got it in here, it turned out to be a bit too gaudy for my tastes. Even if I had liked the thing, it would be cheaper to replace it than try to get the blood out." She dragged at her smoke and shook her head. "I didn't realize two men could have that much blood in them."

Slocum didn't reply. He had to admit he was still trying to figure out A.J. McDonough. For a woman who had been through a close-quarter gunfight, just shot a man, and narrowly escaped with her own life, she seemed remarkably composed. As though this sort of thing happened all the time. Most women Slocum had known, with a few exceptions, would have broken down into a quivering mass when it was over. She did look just a touch frazzled on the outside, which Slocum had to admit made her even more attractive. But if her belly was churning, it didn't show. A remarkable woman, he thought. In a lot of ways . . .

"Where's Stanky? I expected him to jump at the chance to have a drink with us," she said.

Slocum half smiled. "Stanky, believe it or not, doesn't drink. He's back in his seat, sound asleep."

"A strange man."

"A good man, A.J. And a tough one."

"Where's he bound?"

"He never said."

She merely nodded, again accepting the statement at face value. She knew something about Western men and their ways, Slocum thought.

Slocum asked, "How's your brakeman?"

"He's fine. A little mad, because he's never been shot before. Bullet nicked his neck just below the ear. Barely broke the skin, but he'll have enough of a scar to show his grandkids when he tells them the story of the big Texas & Pacific train holdup he single-handedly foiled."

Slocum had to grin. "I expect most every man on this train

will have stopped Moseley's gang all by himself after a few years. Human nature.'' The slight smile faded. "How about the big man, Red?"

A.J. tapped the ash from her smoke. "Dead. Slug came through the wall. Hit him in the chest. Fitting end for an outlaw. Killed by accident by his own gang. I can see the epitaph on his tombstone now: 'Ah, shit.' "

Slocum chuckled. "A good epitaph for a lot of us, maybe," he said. "So we didn't lose any of our people?"

"Not a one. A job well done, Slocum." She snuffed her cigarette in the stone ashtray and sat for a time in silence, a serene expression in her tempered-steel eyes, outwardly relaxed and content. Slocum inwardly marveled at her self-control. He had known grown men, tough men, whose knees would have been jellied under the circumstances.

A.J. glanced at the watch beside her on the table. "Not too bad," she said. "We'll be back on schedule by the time we reach the edge of the post-oak belt."

"I noticed the crew didn't waste any time taking on fuel and water."

"They always work fast. And they wouldn't admit it, of course, but they might have been worried—just a wee touch—that the outlaws were going to come back."

Slocum shook his head. "They weren't. Not as hard as they were hit. The Moseley gang is done for. And good riddance."

"Amen, brother. How's your drink?"

He tossed back the last swallow from the crystal glass. "Gone."

She rose and nodded toward the small bar. "Help yourself. Whiskey's on the shelf under the bar-top. Pour me one, if you don't mind. I need to freshen up a bit. Be back in a minute."

Slocum nodded, and watched as she strode toward the heavy damask drapes that curtained off a quarter of the car. She paused and flashed a quick smile at Slocum before slipping behind the curtain. After a moment, he heard the rustle of cloth and the soft splash of water, and tried not to imagine what she was doing in there.

•   •   •

Slocum was halfway through his drink, A.J.'s glass beside him as he leaned against the bar, tired of sitting. He pulled a cigarillo from his pocket, licked a stray leaf back into place, lit the smoke—and paused with the match between his thumb and index finger still burning. His breath caught in his throat.

"Got my drink poured?" A.J. McDonough said. She stood at the corner of the curtained area, head held high, one hand raised above her shoulder and resting on the damask drapes, one hip slightly cocked, a smile on her full lips.

The heavy formal gown and the yards of petticoats were gone. In its place she wore a clinging satin ankle-length dress. The warm ivory color emphasized the darkness of her skin and hair, caressed her tall, lush body. And she wore nothing beneath it. The quarter-sized dark pigment at the tip of each full breast was clearly visible. Erect nipples pushed outward against the wispy cloth.

"You're going to burn your fingers," she said.

Slocum started, aware of the growing heat of the flame, and quickly shook out the match. The lucifer wasn't the only thing heating up. The warmth in his groin grew as she strode toward him. Her breasts didn't flop or sway from side to side as did most full-chested women's; her nipples barely jiggled as she walked. She had closed only a few of the small buttons of the dress. Lamplight danced over the sheen of dark skin from the valley between her breasts to a handspan above the knee. The exposed lower thigh showed firm, but smooth, muscle.

The warmth in Slocum's crotch spread, became more intense. He had seen his share of women. He didn't remember ever seeing one who had the overall impact of A.J. McDonough. It was like a .45-caliber slug in the gut.

She stopped at Slocum's side, a smile toying with her lips and deepening the crow's-feet wrinkles at the corners of her eyes. She didn't speak as she plucked her glass from the bar and downed a swallow, her gaze still on Slocum's face. The expression in the steel-colored eyes was sultry, but at the same time coltish, more than a touch mischievous. Slocum felt the warmth from her body, smelled the faint scent of rosewater and woman, as she half turned and propped an elbow on the bar. The ivory cloth of the dress fell away. Her right breast was fully exposed to his gaze, the smooth, full swell of flesh tipped by a dark brown circle and a perfectly formed, erect nipple. Her nipple wasn't the only thing erect now. The swelling in Slocum's crotch had almost reached the painful stage.

A.J. sipped at her drink again, making no move to cover her exposed flesh. "In case you hadn't guessed by now, Slocum," she said after a moment, "on rare occasions, I can be a real slut. Totally shameless." She lifted a finger to his lips to cut off his protest. "I'll lay it straight out for you. I haven't had a man in two years."

Slocum swallowed, his mouth dry. "That shouldn't ever be a problem for a woman like you."

"It wouldn't be, except it's been that long since I've even seen one I wanted. Until now." She reached out, plucked the cigarillo from Slocum's fingers, and stubbed it out in the ashtray. "I'll buy you a pocketful of them when we get to Fort Worth. That won't be for a while." She put a hand on Slocum's shoulder, turned him toward her, and came into his arms. Her breathing quickened against his neck. She kissed him, lightly at first, then deeper, her lips moist and warm; her tongue teased its way between his parted teeth. After a moment she broke the kiss, breathing heavily, her body still pressed against him.

Then she turned slightly to her left, opening a space between them. She took Slocum's right hand and lifted it to her breast. She moaned softly as his palm and fingers cupped and gently stroked the pliant but firm flesh. She gasped audibly as Slocum's fingers brushed across her nipple, then shuddered as his thumb and forefinger closed on the erect bud of tissue. Her breath came in short, shallow gasps as she slid her free hand down his belly. The heat from her palm and fingers quickly penetrated Slocum's Levi's. She gently stroked his tightened scrotum, caressed his engorged shaft. A half whimper, half moan escaped her lips. Slocum could feel the rapid thumping of her heart against her ribs, a counterpoint to his own.

She abruptly pulled back. "We can't do this properly out here, Slocum," she said, her words forming in quick, broken gasps. She picked up the two glasses. "Bring the bottle and come with me," she said. She led him toward the heavy damask curtains.

4

A.J. McDonough's sleeping quarters were small but well appointed.

The bed, a four-poster with the uprights most likely bolted to the floor and ceiling, the covers neatly turned down, took up most of the space. Above the bed, soft gray light filtered through tied-back window curtains. Beside the bed stood a table holding a cut-glass ashtray, alongside a padded wooden chair. A gilt-framed mirror above a shelf holding a water pitcher, bowl, and folded cloths rounded out the furnishings.

"It's a bit cramped, but I'm sure we can make do," A.J. said, still breathless. She put the two whiskey glasses on the small table, took the bourbon bottle from his hand, and placed it in a ring holder fastened to the edge of the table.

"So much for the housekeeping." She turned to face Slocum, her hands slightly behind her as she leaned against the table, elbows crooked. The pose, planned or not, had a greater impact on Slocum than seeing most women stark naked. The soft, diffused gray light from the window was enough to reveal the dark circles tipped with erect buttons at the center of her breasts, to paint smooth strokes along her exposed thighs where the thin dress parted. The light seemed to enhance the tempered-steel color of her eyes, which now reflected a smoky, sultry, yet somehow still mischievous glint. A smile played at her full lips, dimpling her cheeks.

This is no girl, Slocum thought appreciatively; this is a

woman. A real woman. He let his gaze linger on her for several heartbeats, enjoying the sight despite the urgency growing in his crotch. And it was obvious that she didn't mind his staring. A.J. McDonough *knew* she was a woman. And she wasn't ashamed of being one. After a moment she straightened, her fingers moving to the few still-fastened buttons of the filmy dress.

"I hope you like your women hairy, Slocum," she said, "or you're out of luck this time around." The dress fell away. At the junction of long, smoothly muscular thighs, a thick triangle of black spread in a V halfway up to her belly button.

"Well," she said huskily, "what do you think? Do I pass inspection?"

Slocum swallowed, trying to work some spittle into his dry mouth. "I think I should throw myself to the floor. I've never been this near a goddess before."

Her laugh was throaty, husky. "I'm no goddess, Slocum. I'm a depraved—and long deprived—wench with absolutely no modesty. Under the current conditions, of course. But you have me at a disadvantage, sir. I seem to be the only nude in here. And we can't do a hell of a lot as long as you've got your clothes on." A lecherous grin further dimpled her cheeks. "Besides, it is a policy of mine never to bed a man who's wearing a gun."

Slocum didn't need a second invitation. Moments later his clothes were draped across the chair beside the bed. Despite the urgency in his groin, the ache in his testicles, he still took the time to place his Peacemaker atop the clothing, the grips of the weapon turned toward the bed and within easy reach. Then he stood, naked, his shaft erect, scrotum tight, aware that she had been watching him the entire time.

"It's your turn now," Slocum said, his cheeks warming; he wasn't accustomed to displaying himself like a stud horse standing before a potential buyer. It was a bit embarrassing, but at the same time stimulating. As if he needed more stimulation. "What do you think?"

Her breath was raspy and quick in her throat. "I think you'd better get your ass on that bed, Slocum, before I rape you standing up."

They lay side by side on the bed for a moment, staring into each other's eyes. She reached out, drew him close, and kissed him. Gently, almost tenderly, at first, then with growing urgency. Slocum had one arm beneath her head; with his free hand he caressed her shoulder, let his hand slip slowly and gently down her rib cage to the distinct narrowing of her waist. His palm rested for a moment against her hipbone.

Finally, she broke the kiss, her breath now coming in quick, sharp gasps. "My—God—Slocum." Her words puffed against his neck. Her left hand slipped from his shoulder, down his ribs, its warmth building a small fire where it came to rest against his buttock.

Slocum, also breathing heavily, flicked his tongue against her earlobe and the sensitive skin just beneath it. She whimpered softly. Already, he could taste the pleasant, salty flavor of her sweat. Her hand slid from his buttock around to his crotch. Warm fingers cupped his tight scrotum, then closed around the base of his shaft as Slocum lowered his head to her breast. His tongue toyed with the smooth skin, moving first in wide circles around, but not yet touching, her erect nipple. Her chest heaved in growing excitement; she shuddered, deeply, as his lips and tongue closed about the dark, firm nipple. He flicked his tongue across it, then drew it between his lips. She shuddered again; her breath seemed to catch in her throat, her head tilted back, lips parted.

Her hand began to move along his shaft. Her touch further engorged his already swollen erection. Slocum stroked her nipple with the flat of his tongue as he ran his hand down her hips, along the outside of her firmly muscled thigh, then to the inside of her knee. She moaned softly and parted her thighs as his hand flowed to the dense thatch of hair between her legs. The upper inch or so of her thighs was damp; when his hand reached the heat of her labia, Slocum knew the wetness was not from sweat. It took him a fumbling moment before he found the slit between her labia and stroked a finger upward to the swollen nub of flesh between them.

She shuddered again at his touch against her clitoris, pressed her pelvis against his hand. Her hips began to move against his fingers. After only a few seconds she moaned aloud, arched her back, shuddered deeply, every muscle in her body convulsed. For an instant she didn't breathe, her head back, eyes closed. Then her breath burst from between her clenched teeth and closed lips. She raised his head from her breast, kissing him deeply, urgently, her fingers again stroking his shaft.

"Now, Slocum," she said, pulling him atop her as she spread her legs wider. "I want—you—inside me."

For an awkward moment, Slocum tried and failed to find the opening below her clitoris, the tip of his swollen shaft nudging against her wet heat. She slipped her other hand down, parted the thick hair, spread the lips of her vulva, and guided him to the opening.

Slocum feared for a moment that he wouldn't be able to enter her. Despite the flow of juices from inside her and the slickness of his own shaft head, she was almost too tight to allow him entry. Then the first couple of inches wedged into her, triggering another burst of air from her lips. Slocum slowly eased himself into her, and gasped himself as her wet heat and tight muscles clamped against his shaft.

Slocum almost lost control then. It took every bit of willpower he possessed not to explode on that first entry. He lay still for a moment, aware of the pulsing of her vaginal muscles against his aching shaft. The fit was the tightest Slocum had encountered, so snug she might have been an adolescent virgin.

After several heartbeats, when he was reasonably sure he could last long enough to give her some enjoyment, Slocum began to move his hips, sliding his shaft almost from her, then slowly entering her again, all the while softly rubbing the swollen nub of her clitoris with the tip of his finger. He concentrated on her, trying to ignore the threatening swelling of his shaft. She began to whimper, then moan, and her hips moved in time to his still-cautious thrusts. Then she abruptly cried out, convulsed, grabbed his buttocks, and shoved her pelvis hard against him, forcing every inch of him into her; and every muscle in her body shuddered. Her convulsions sent waves of contractions through her vaginal muscles; each ripple was as a hot, wet, stroking of his shaft—

Slocum could hold back no longer.

He exploded into her, an almost painful throbbing and jerking, as his testicles emptied with a force he hadn't really expected. The urgent pulsing gradually slowed, but several convulsions followed, like the aftershocks that followed the earthquakes of California. Finally, after what seemed an eternity of almost excruciating ejaculations, Slocum became aware that at some time during the coupling she had wrapped her legs around his buttocks, using her thigh muscles to pull him deeper into her. The legs about his hips were strong and firm.

He also became aware that in the aftermath of his orgasm, he had collapsed onto her. She bore most of the weight of his torso on the slippery sheen of mutual sweat between them. Still, Slocum lay still for a moment, his muscles weak, failing to respond to his will. His shaft begin to wilt inside her. Finally, he was able to muster the strength to raise himself on his elbows—and noticed the tears trickling down the smooth, dark skin of her cheeks. His heart leapt in his chest in fear that he had hurt her.

He lifted a thumb and gently wiped the tears from her face. "I'm sorry," he said.

She opened her eyes. "What for?"

"You're crying. Was I too rough? Did I hurt you?"

She smiled wistfully. "No, you didn't hurt me. Quite the contrary. Women sometimes cry when—afterward—if it's been especially—rewarding."

Slocum sighed in relief, kissed the salty tears from her lids, and started to lift his body from her.

"Just a minute, mister," A.J. McDonough said, "you're not going anywhere. I'm not through with you yet."

He smiled ruefully. "I'm afraid I'm out of commission for a while—" His protest ended in a short gasp as her vaginal muscles clamped down on his wilting shaft, then relaxed, then tightened again. Even through the slippery wetness of their combined juices, he felt himself slowly stirring to life within her. Moments later he was fully erect again.

Slocum's second explosion was even more intense than the first; it disconnected the muscles and tendons in his knees, almost burst his heart, squeezed the air from his lungs. And even as he softened again—this time, he knew, for good, or at least for a half hour—he realized that she had climaxed again. Not once, not twice, but three times more.

Slocum knew the many orgasms she had reached were not faked. He had been with enough women in his travels to know the difference. The realization brought him even greater contentment, if that were possible. With prostitutes, it didn't matter. With a woman like A.J., it mattered a hell of a lot.

They lay for some time afterward, exhausted, totally spent, unable to move even if the train had caught fire. Her thighs and his were slick, their crotch hairs wet and matted, as he finally mustered the energy to roll off her. Then they lay side by side, gazing at each other; this time, no tears rolled down her cheeks. Strands of her black hair were plastered against her forehead and chin.

Her face muscles were relaxed, her eyes dreamy, her nipples no longer erect, as she weakly smiled at him. "Son of a bitch," she muttered softly, but the curse was an expression of wonder, not anger. "This time, by God, I picked the right one. I never thought a man could make me feel this—contented. Slocum, you are a talented stud horse in bed. An artist."

A wry smile touched Slocum's lips. "Any man could be an artist with a canvas like you to work with."

"No, Slocum. You're wrong there. Not that I've had all that many men, but if you were any damned better, my heart would have exploded."

"Just trying to do my job, ma'am," he said, teasing.

"You damn sure did." Her voice turned solemn. "I don't spread my legs for just anything that comes along wearing pants. I'm not a so-called loose woman, Slocum. I'm a picky bitch."

Slocum's grin spread. "I dispute the bitch part, but you're sure as hell not loose. How do you do that?"

"Do what?"

"Work your muscles like that. The ones inside. It's enough to raise the dead, or at least the mortally wounded. If I'd been a lazy man, I wouldn't even have had to move."

Her smile grew into a low, throaty chuckle. "I have no idea how I do it. It just happens." She glanced down at her crotch.

"Jesus, Slocum, you pack a hell of a load—loads. I'm over-flowing. If I stand up now, I'll gush."

"It had been a while for me too. But it isn't entirely my fault. You started it, if you recall. You're full of surprises, A.J."

"Not to mention something else at the moment." She sighed and stretched languidly. "I'm like one of those lizards I've read about. The kind that can change color. I can be as prim and proper as any preacher's wife, raise my little finger ever so daintily as I sip my tea at a Lutheran lady's social, be as mean and hard-assed as any man in a business deal. But deep down, and usually kept under tight rein, what you see now is the real me, Slocum. A wanton, earthy slut."

Slocum heard no tinge of remorse, regret, or self-reproach in her words. A.J. McDonough was a rarity among women, he decided. She didn't play games, and she told it straight. He admired her for that even more than for the body stretched out beside him.

"Now," she said, "which one of us has the energy to fetch the other a smoke and a drink? The table's a bit out of reach. Poor design on my part, putting it that far away."

Slocum stirred, testing sapped muscles. "I can give it a try. It'll be hard to do with no knee joints left." After a moment, he was able to stand. He reached for his trousers.

"Don't bother," A.J. said. "If you get dressed, I'd have to get dressed, and that would take too much effort. In addition to being a shameless slut, I like to look at naked men, Slocum. Besides, I may not be through with you just yet."

A bit self-consciously, Slocum shuffled the couple of steps to the table and fetched the glasses, the bottle, the ashtray, her cigarettes, and the long-stemmed holder.

They sat on the edge of the bed, A.J. having tucked a towel beneath her to absorb the drainage. For a time they smoked and sipped their drinks, sated and content.

Finally, A.J. sighed. "Slocum, may I ask a question that's obviously none of my damned business? You don't have to answer it, of course."

"Ask away."

"Granted, I should know better than to pry into a man's

affairs. But you know how it is with women. We're curious creatures. Descended from the cat side of the cave, some say. So, my question. What takes you to Fort Worth?''

"I'm looking for a girl," Slocum said. "A prostitute."

He couldn't read the expression in her eyes; it could have been confusion, disappointment, hurt, even a touch of anger.

"Well, you sure as hell won't have trouble finding one. Fort Worth's full of them."

Slocum raised a hand. "Wait a minute—it's not for the reason you think. I'm looking for one girl, and one girl only. To take her back to her father and mother. As a favor to a friend." He breathed an inward sigh of relief as the ever-so-faint chill faded from her eyes. "And for a fee."

"Oh." She paused for a sip of her drink, her brow wrinkled in thought. "How did she come to leave her home? By force or by choice?"

"She left of her own will. Sort of. It's more complicated than that, of course. Not black or white, but shades of gray all through."

"Suppose you find her and she doesn't want to go home."

Slocum shrugged. "I'll take her anyway. What she does after that is between her and her parents. I promised her father. I took his money. For that, he gets his daughter back. If she's still alive."

A.J. held out her glass for a refill, still frowning. "If you care to tell me about her, maybe I can help—if, of course, you want help. I can't promise anything."

Slocum sipped at his drink. "It's a long story."

"In case you hadn't noticed, we're trapped on a train with nowhere else to go. And it's still a long way to Fort Worth."

Slocum's natural caution led him to hesitate for moment. Then he sighed. Maybe it would do some good to talk it out; he wasn't sure exactly what he would do once he reached the city. And the girl might not even be there.

"I can give you the short version," he said, "but first, you have to promise you'll keep it just between us. The fewer people who know of it, of her background, how this all came about, the better. For her, her parents—and for me."

A.J. nodded solemnly. "Agreed. Please, go on."

"Her name is Mary Connally, the daughter of Colonel Wesley Connally. I've known the colonel for years. Since the war. I spent a few months working with him and his outfit, the Fourth Georgia."

Slocum paused to snuff out the butt of his cigarillo. It was his last one. "After the war, we went our separate ways. I hadn't seen him since, until about a month ago. I had heard of him occasionally—from mutual acquaintances from the war years—and knew that he had built a successful ranch up in the Crooked River country in Oregon. Apparently, he'd also heard stories about me from time to time. I was a bit surprised when his letter finally caught up to me in the Jackson Hole country."

"How did he know where to find you?"

"I wondered about that myself, until he told me he had sent letters to any place a drifter might show up, in hopes that one of the messages got to me." Slocum paused to top off his own glass. "What surprised me the most was the tone of the letter. The colonel was accustomed to giving orders, not asking favors. And that note was almost begging me to come. It read like a letter from a desperate and hurting man, totally unlike the colonel. I wasn't doing much of anything at the time, so I went.

"Before I give you the short end of the story, you should know something about the colonel. He was a West Point man, stern, unyielding. Some called him a martinet. Most of his men disliked him, a few hated him, but they all respected him, and not because he demanded it. He earned that respect. He was a soldier's commander. His men were always well fed and equipped, or at least more so than any other Confederate outfit at that stage of the war. And his command took fewer losses and won more battles than any other."

Slocum paused for another sip from his glass; so much talk in one bunch had dried his throat. "He was just as stern and unyielding with his daughter—his only child, by the way—as he had been with his men. She could do nothing to please him. He always demanded too much of her. So finally, she ran away from home. That was five years ago. She was fifteen at the time, and she eloped with a young cowboy."

Small furrows had formed between A.J.'s thick eyebrows. "That must have enraged him, if he was such a domineering man."

"He was, and it did. It wasn't until he began to mellow somewhat, to think about it, that he even spoke her name aloud again. But it hurt him more than he ever let on. Finally, he came to realize that it wasn't any weakness in his daughter that had caused her to run away. He had to admit that *he* had driven her away. Now he wants to try again, to make amends. So he hired me to find her and bring her back."

A.J. nodded solemnly. "I can understand her feelings, and to some extent his." She flicked the ash from her cigarette. "You said she eloped. How did she wind up as a prostitute?" She offered him one of her ready-rolls, lit it from the end of her own smoke, and handed it to him.

Slocum dragged at the cigarette, pulled the smoke deep into his lungs, and glanced at the slender tube in surprise. It was extraordinarily good tobacco. He let the smoke trickle from his nostrils, and continued.

"As I understand the story, which the colonel managed to piece together from a rumor here and there, less than a year after she ran away from home, her young husband was killed when his horse fell on him. Mary could barely read and write. The colonel was of the old school. He didn't believe in wasting education on a mere girl. So she had little education, no salable trade, no family to turn to, no friends. She did the only thing she could to survive. She spread her legs for money."

"A sad story, but not without precedent," A.J. said after a moment. "I would think a man like the colonel would be in a towering rage if he found out his daughter had become a common prostitute."

"At first, he was. Then he had to admit it was his doing, not hers." Slocum tapped the ash from his cigarette and sipped at his drink. "It took a hell of a lot of courage for him to face what he had done. Most men couldn't do that."

"And now she's in Fort Worth?"

"Possibly. The last the colonel heard of her, she was believed to be there. She never wrote, not even to her mother. Colonel Connally found out from a passing cattle trader that a woman who *might* have been Mary was seen in a saloon in Hell's Half Acre.''

A.J. winced visibly and shook her head. ''The worst section of the worst part of town, and a misnamed one at that. It's more than a half acre. It should be called Hell's Acre.'' The expression in her eyes softened almost to the point of pity. ''Why didn't he go after her himself?''

''Because he's convinced that she wouldn't come with him. That she hates him for what happened to her.''

A.J. nodded. ''Understandable. Even possible. Slocum, if she's there—and if you find her—you may wish you hadn't. Terrible things happen to prostitutes in the Acre.''

''Another reason the colonel hired me for the job. He was afraid of what he might find.''

A.J. sat silently for a moment, then sighed. ''You said you hadn't seen the colonel since the war. That means you haven't seen his daughter. How will you know her if you see her?''

Slocum leaned across the bed, rummaged in his pile of clothing for a moment, and produced a thin gold folder, hinged on one side. He flipped it open to reveal a faded tintype. The picture was barely larger than a quarter, faded with the passage of time. ''This, and a physical description of her at age fifteen, a year after this was taken, when she ran away with the young cowboy. It's all I have to go on.''

A.J. studied the tintype for a moment, then again shook her head. ''She may not even resemble this picture now, Slocum. The passage of years, the ravages of poverty and her trade—and God knows what else—may have changed her so much her own parents wouldn't recognize her. Provided she's still alive. And I hate to say it, but the odds are against that. Disease, suicide, even disfigurement and murder are commonplace among the girls of the Acre.''

''I know that, A.J.,'' Slocum said softly. ''I've never been to Hell's Half Acre—or Acre, if you say so—in Fort Worth, but every town has one. I've been to some of those others, and they seem to be all alike. But I made a promise. I took the colonel's money, and I have to give my best effort to find her. To take her home.''

A.J. handed the tintype back. Slocum briefly studied it

again. The young girl shown there was round-faced, almost plump, blond hair tumbling to her shoulders. Pretty, but not beautiful. It was the eyes that gave away Mary Connally's inner torment. Even in the small tintype, Slocum could see the hurt, the sadness and despair in her eyes. He closed the gold folder and replaced the tintype in his shirt pocket.

"I'll do what I can, Slocum, but I may not be able to help much," A.J. said. "I have connections, sources, throughout most of Fort Worth. I don't have many in the Acre, because I don't do business there and have no need for such information."

"Anything you can find out would be a great help," Slocum said. "The best place to start is by telling me where I might find a decent hotel or boardinghouse."

The expression in A.J.'s eyes brightened. "The very best. My place. It's on the far side of town from the Acre." She leaned back, stretched her arms over her head, and arched her back. The motion emphasized the fullness of her breasts, which of themselves were a source of wonder to Slocum. "You're welcome to stay there. With me."

Slocum had to admit the offer was one of the best he'd ever had, and he said so. "But," he concluded, "it wouldn't be the smartest way to go about it. I'll be coming and going at all hours of the night. I'll have to spend most all my time in the Acre until I find her. Or find out she isn't there."

The flicker of disappointment quickly faded from A.J.'s gaze. "You could still come to visit me, though? Especially when you get the urge to—well, I'd hate to see it wasted on some dollar whore."

Slocum leaned over and placed a finger across her lips. "I could and I will, A.J. Unless it could cause embarrassment for you. I mean, the gossip and all, about a woman of your status."

She chuckled softly. "Another nice thing about being rich, Slocum, is that I don't have to give a fuck what other people think." She snubbed out her cigarette and leaned back across the bed. Her nipples had come erect again. "Speaking of which, come here, mister. I think I'm a virgin again. . . ."

5

Slocum's knees were still a bit wobbly when he stepped from the Texas & Pacific train. He wasn't sure if the weakness was because of A.J. McDonough, or simply the fact that the ground was once again steady beneath his boots.

He had been the last to disembark from the train, letting the main crush of humanity thin out from the aisles before he finally headed for the wooden steps placed at the door. He left through the car nearest the tender, as far away as possible from A.J.'s private car—not to spare her any embarrassment, but to draw as little attention to himself as possible.

A.J. got plenty of attention. Porters were still loading her trunks and bags into the back of a black curtained surrey drawn by a matched pair of dappled gray horses. Four men in expensive woolen topcoats and tall hats clustered around A.J. Slocum idly wondered how many of them were there on business and how many of them were simply trying to ingratiate themselves to the striking brunette, some to get into her purse, others to get under her petticoats. Or both. A.J. was the sort of woman who would draw a crowd no matter where she went. Even if she didn't have money.

Slocum was in no particular hurry. He stood for a moment, getting his bearings along with his first look at Fort Worth in many years.

What had been a mostly drowsy frontier outpost in those early days after Appomattox had gone sour, at least as far as

Slocum was concerned. People were everywhere.

Houston Street, which angled northwest away from the depot, was almost shoulder-to-shoulder. Pedestrians, horsemen, farm wagons, surries, and big freight haulers with their six- and eight-horse hitches jostled for space on the wide but crowded thoroughfare. And the noise was almost deafening.

Shouts of greeting or an occasional curse of anger rose from the throng, mingled with the yells and oaths of teamsters, the cries of streetside vendors, and the barely muted notes of pianos and banjos from the row of saloons and other establishments along Houston. The constant yap of dogs, the mournful howl of hounds that somehow sounded like the wail of the locomotive whistle, and the frequent nickering of horses added to the landslide of noise.

The smell alone was enough to give a man a headache.

The scent of horse droppings wasn't so bad. Slocum was accustomed to that, even found the sharp, slightly sweet scent rather pleasant. It was the rotting garbage, the acrid stench of human waste mingled with the sharp odor of coal and wood-smoke and cooking that made his nostrils rebel and his eyes itch. Fort Worth represented just about everything Slocum despised in a city. He fought back the urge to climb back on the train and head for someplace where a man could turn around without bumping into somebody.

The snow hadn't reached this far south yet, but the skies overhead were a flat gray and the north wind held a bit of a bite as it eddied and swirled among the buildings, tossing paper and other trash and eddying dust along the street as it whipped past. The locals, Slocum noted, were bundled in heavy coats, gloves, scarves wrapped around their necks, some in fur caps, as if slogging through a blizzard. If they thought this was cold, he mused, they should spend February in Montana. Then they'd recognize real winter when they felt it.

The change in Fort Worth carved a slice from Slocum's mostly pleasant memories of the town. When he had first passed through here on his way west, the settlement had had a population of maybe three hundred people tops. First the cattle drives, and then the railroad had turned it from an enjoyable little town into a city with more than five thousand permanent residents. Or so A.J. had told him. Looking over the teeming street, Slocum had to agree with her. There were at least that many, and they all seemed to have picked today to go outside.

He found himself again wishing he had turned the colonel down. Finding one girl in a town this size—he forced the thought aside. He had a job to do. He'd do his best to get it done.

He finally decided the depot crowd wasn't going to thin out much; as soon as one man or woman left, another arrived to hand over bags to the porters and wait for the conductor's "All aboard!" call. For every passenger who stepped down, another waited to take his place. Slocum pitied the poor bastard who had the misfortune to draw the seat next to Woodrow W. Weatherby.

The crush and the racket were at least good news for A.J. McDonough. The Texas & Pacific was doing a booming business.

A sudden jolt against his side set Slocum's teeth on edge. He glowered at the fat, sputtering, middle-aged lady who had jostled him as she'd shouldered past, dragging a screaming kid in each fist, screeching for "Harry!" at the top of her lungs. Apparently, she soon irritated someone else, because all once she stumbled as if she'd been tripped, and went down face-first into a puddle of stagnant, muddy water. When she regained her footing, with the help of a couple of men standing nearby, she came up looking like a Comanche harridan. On her, Slocum thought with satisfaction, the mud looked good. The black muck on her cheeks and forehead could just as well have been war paint. It matched her temperament.

The incident lifted his spirits a bit. He did feel a twinge of sympathy for the poor bastard named Harry she apparently was coming home to. He idly wondered what Harry ever did to bring the wrath of the gods down on him in the shape of that woman.

When the shoving and grabbing momentarily slowed, Slocum strode forward and picked up his small travel bag. He shouldered his saddle. He had brought no horse. He could always buy or rent a mount if needed, but good saddles were hard to come by. He stood for a moment beside the depot, wondering which of the hotels and boardinghouses A.J. had recommended he should try first.

"Need a ride, friend?" a gravelly voice asked from beside the depot platform.

The speaker was a gnarled, weathered man not a hell of a lot bigger than the wheel of the worn buckboard he stood beside. The rig was pulled by a swaybacked sorrel mare that looked to be as old as the man. But the mare was considerably fatter and better groomed. There was no sign of a buggy whip, quirt, or stick in the buckboard. Anybody who took better care of his horse than himself had to be all right. Slocum noted that the old-timer, unlike others on the street, wore only a light denim jacket, a faded red bandanna knotted loosely below his shirt collar. He had no gloves, and his hat was battered and shapeless, the brim fluttering in the breeze.

"How much?" Slocum asked.

The old man shifted his chew and spat. "Depends on where you're headed. Fifteen cents for a five-block ride. Two bits'll get you any place in town."

Slocum thought the price seemed a bit steep, but he didn't haggle. "Looking for a place to stay a few days. Friend of mine recommended the Commercial Hotel."

The old-timer nodded. "Good pick, if it ain't full. Clean. Passin' fair grub. Expensive, though."

Slocum swung his saddle and bag into the back of the buckboard, then climbed onto the seat. A gust of breeze flipped open the left side of his unbuttoned jacket. The old man nodded casually toward Slocum's gunbelt.

"Might want to be careful the laws don't see the hogleg," the old man said casually. "Supposed to be agin the law to pack iron in Fort Worth. Don't nobody pay it much mind, though. Every ranny in town's haulin' iron. They just keep it out of sight."

"Thanks," Slocum said as the mare leaned into the harness at the old man's gentle tongue cluck. "I'll keep that in mind." He settled back to study the town as the old mare moved along at a steady walk. The banjo and piano music grew louder, then faded, as they passed the Palace Saloon a block from the railway depot. The buckboard made a right on Fourteenth Street, crossed Main after a bit of a delay waiting for an opening in the traffic, and turned back north on Rusk.

A man wouldn't have a bit of trouble getting drunk—or anything else, including robbed or dead—in Fort Worth, Slocum thought. It seemed there was a saloon or whorehouse every half block, and a row of prostitutes' crib shacks stood every couple of hundred yards along Rusk.

Slocum's muscles tensed as a woman, gripping the arm of a man dressed in the range garb of a cowboy, strode toward one of the crib shacks. Even though her back was to Slocum and she wore a heavy, ankle-length coat, he could tell that she was slightly built and blond. He was about to tell the driver to rein up a moment when the woman stopped and turned sideways as she opened the crib door. That long, humped nose couldn't have belonged to Mary Connally. In the tintype, Mary's nose was little more than a perky, upturned button.

Slocum sighed inwardly, but he wasn't all that disappointed. Nothing ever came quite that easy in life. As his gaze swept the teeming streets, noting the number of saloons, pleasure palaces, and rows of crib shacks, he realized a lot of work lay ahead. It would be easier to track down one man in the Sonoran Desert than to find one small girl in this mob of humanity. He *could* get lucky and find her by sundown, but he wouldn't bank on it. A man who counted on sheer luck turned gray in the hair and stooped in the shoulders before he found what he sought. Slocum believed in making his own luck. It simplified life.

The crush of people on the streets wasn't Slocum's only concern. Towns were dangerous. Every window, every alley provided a perfect ambush site for any would-be shooter. On top of that was the chance to catch a stray slug that wasn't even intended for him. A bullet, once fired, didn't know or care what it hit.

"None of my business, friend, and I ain't pryin', just makin' an observation," the old-timer holding the reins said. "You got the look of a wild-country man about you. Used to be one myself, back in my flat-belly days. That was a spell back. Been in Fort Worth nigh onto ten years and ain't got completely used to town livin' myself yet.''

Slocum half grinned. ''You pegged me on that one, mister.'' He pulled the tintype from his pocket and showed it to the driver. ''Ever see this girl before?''

The old man took his eyes from the road, trusting the mare to get them through traffic on her own. He took the faded picture, held it close, then at arm's length, and finally at a spot in between. He studied the portrait for a considerable time, then shrugged.

''Can't be sure. Looks kinda familiar, but not enough I could say for sure. This was took some time back?''

''Six years or so,'' Slocum said.

''Then she'd of changed.'' He handed the picture back to Slocum and shook his head. ''Sorry, friend. Wish I could of been some help. Well, here we be. Commercial Hotel.'' He tugged lightly at the reins. The mare stopped.

Slocum sat for a moment, studying the three-story structure on the northwest corner of Fifth and Rusk. It had been around for a time and showed some wear and tear—including a few bullet holes—but it sported a reasonably fresh coat of paint and the windows were intact. He handed the weathered driver a quarter and stepped down.

''I'll stick around till you find out if there's a room,'' the old man said. ''This place and Mansion House most times are full up.''

Slocum nodded his thanks. He left his bag and saddle in the buckboard, trusting the old-timer not to drive off with them.

The Commercial, Slocum thought as he strode through the spacious lobby, would have rivaled the most expensive hotels in Denver or Cheyenne in its prime. A glass chandelier, only slightly stained from years of tobacco smoke, dominated the lobby. Slocum noted the gaslights sprinkled liberally about the room, and the shelves lined with books and newspapers flanking the fireplace.

He noted with less approval the three men who stared at him from overstuffed brown leather chairs around a mahogany table. Two held fat cigars. A third cigar was smoldering in a cut-glass ashtray. He ignored the curious or even suspicious glares. But he kept the three men at the edge of his vision as he stepped to the polished mahogany desk. The middle-aged, balding man behind the desk greeted Slocum with a courteous nod.

"Help you, sir?"

"I was hoping you'd have a room available," Slocum said.

The clerk glanced briefly at the registry book, thumbed through a stack of cards, and said, "Yes, sir, we have one left. It's not our most luxurious—a second-floor corner room overlooking Fifth and Rusk. I'm afraid it's a bit noisy during the most boisterous nights." He ended the sentence with an uplilting note, as if in a question.

Slocum nodded. "It'll do fine."

"And how long will you be needing the room, sir?"

"I'm not sure. Maybe two nights, maybe two months."

The clerk cleared his throat. "The charge is one dollar per night, or six dollars a week, sir." His brows lifted as if to ask if Slocum, dressed in range clothing and now sporting more stubble than he felt comfortable with, could afford such luxury. Slocum didn't think the colonel would mind unless the search went on more than a couple of weeks, in which case Slocum would find cheaper accommodations.

"I'll take it. On a weekly basis."

"We, uh, require payment in advance, sir. From those who don't have an established account with us, that is."

Slocum merely nodded, paid the man, and took the offered key to Room 206. He retrieved his saddle and bag, thanked the old man who had driven him there, and a quarter hour later was settled into his room.

Room 206 was neither spacious nor small. It held the basics: a bed, two chairs, small tables, a stand-alone cabinet to hang his clothes, water pitcher, basin, two glasses, and an ashtray. A gas lamp near the bed and another beside the door would give plenty of light after sundown. A window on each side of one corner overlooked the busy streets below.

Slocum stood at the Rusk Street window for a moment, studying the crowd below. The clerk was right. Street noises did penetrate the upstairs corner room. But he also had an unobstructed view of a long stretch of both Rusk and Fifth streets. He could watch the comings and goings of people below. It would be a decent exchange.

He watched for ten minutes, saw nothing much of interest, and turned away from the window. He poured himself a drink from the bottle in the travel bag, rolled a smoke, and spent the next half hour carefully cleaning and reloading his weapons. He cleaned only one at a time; only a fool would leave himself defenseless by having all his guns out of action at once. He checked over the spare .44-40 Peacemaker he carried in his saddle back, wiped it down, and tucked it back into the pouch.

Slocum half smiled at the wall card listing the "Rules of the House"—drinking was permitted, but no drunks allowed; no discharging of firearms in the room; and no female visitors unless a man happened to be married to them. They were pretty picky about things, he thought, considering some of the places he'd stayed in in the past.

Satisfied with the condition of his weapons, Slocum made his one concession to the Fort Worth law. He stripped the gunbelt from around his waist, pulled the shoulder holster rig from his bag, fiddled with the fit for a moment, put his jacket back on, and glanced into the half-length mirror on the far wall.

To the trained eye, there would be no mistaking the fact that he was armed. The sheer bulk of a .44-40 Peacemaker with its six-and-a-half inch barrel left an obvious bulge beneath his left arm. Slocum didn't worry much about that part of the situation, but he did fret about getting shot when pure habit sent his right hand crossing to his left hip instead of to the shoulder rig. He unloaded the handgun and spent almost an hour trying to retrain his instincts, practicing his draw from the shoulder rig.

He was considerably slower with the hideout holster than the hip rig, Slocum conceded, but each practice draw seemed a touch faster than the one before. Finally, still not satisfied but at least a bit more comfortable, he shucked the jacket, donned an ankle-length canvas duster lined with cotton ticking, and left the hotel.

Within three blocks of the Commercial, Slocum found most

of the things he needed: a barbershop with a hot bathroom, a "gentlemen's apparel" store that happened to have his size in stock, a decent cafe that knew how to cook a steak properly, a tobacco shop that stocked the right brand of cigarillos, and a saloon where he picked up a bottle of Old Overholt.

He didn't enter the cost of the new suit in the small notebook he carried in a vest pocket, but did jot down the amount spent for the bath, meal, and bottle. The suit was a luxury, the three other items necessities.

Slocum kept accurate records of his expenses, not because the colonel would question his word, but because Slocum had no intention of charging the man a penny more he spent doing the job.

The sun had dropped below the eastern skyline an hour before Slocum made his way back to the hotel. He left the door to his room open long enough to locate and light the gas lamp by the bed. After tonight, he'd know instinctively where it was.

The gas lamp seemed to sizzle instead of flicker, and its light was too white and harsh, not comforting like the reddish gold illumination from a gently crackling campfire. Some of the things done in the name of progress, he thought, were an affront to nature. And to man.

Slocum took one drink from the new bottle before the walls started closing in on him. He decided he might as well go to work.

He thought for a moment about putting on his new suit, then decided against it. He'd bought that for one reason—A.J. McDonough's invitation to visit the big house on Bluff Street overlooking the Trinity River, "whenever you have the time or the urge," as she'd put it.

Besides, he didn't think it would be especially bright for a man to look too prosperous in a part of town where anybody who had a few dollars in his pocket would be a target. And he didn't want to draw attention to himself any more than necessary. He knew that eventually, word would get around. He just wanted to put off that eventuality as long as possible.

He rechecked the fit of the .44-40 in the shoulder holster,

slipped into his duster, turned off the gas lamp, and headed into the mass of humanity on the streets.

Slocum took his time, strolling casually down Rusk in the general direction of the prostitution and shady saloon district known as Hell's Half Acre a few blocks from the Commercial. He studied the faces in the crowd as carefully as he noted potential ambush spots—a habit he had no desire to break. He saw no one who resembled Mary Connally. Or *might* resemble her, depending on how much she had changed.

A half hour later he crossed Third Street, paused for a moment before a weathered one-story saloon with its faded sign proclaiming it as "Mike's Place," and stepped inside.

A single glance told Slocum he wasn't going to find Mary Connally in Mike's. It was a drinking establishment, no more, no less. Kerosene lamps flanked a stained bar. The odor of tobacco, spilled beer and whiskey, and faint man-sweat mingled pleasantly with the rich scent of sawdust on the floor. Slocum saw at a glance he had stepped into what could best be described as a workingman's watering hole. There was no expensive mirror or painting of a reclining nude behind the bar, only a crude stack of shelving with a limited selection of bottles, mostly whiskey, gin, and tequila. The coats and jackets hung from pegs along a wall showed signs of wear.

A crudely lettered sign behind the bar cautioned simply, "If you got a urge to fight, go outside. Mike."

The place was only moderately crowded. Most of the customers at the bar and the five small tables bore the stamp of teamsters and railroad men, with a smattering of tradesmen. There were no cowboys in Mike's. Conversations were subdued, occasionally broken with a hearty laugh at somebody's joke.

Slocum stepped to the bar, aware that the man behind the pine had been watching him. Beetled black brows almost met above equally dark eyes in a broad, ruddy face.

"Get you something, mister?" the barkeep said.

"Rye. Old Overholt, if you've got it."

The man nodded, turned away, and a moment later placed a small tumbler before Slocum. The glass was clean. The hands that held it were big and broad, the knuckles scarred, the little finger of the right hand ending in a stub where the first knuckle would have been. The barkeep showed Slocum the Old Overholt label and poured a couple of shots into the glass.

"Two bits," the bartender said in a gravelly but cordial baritone. "Boiled eggs at the end of the bar there come with the drink."

Slocum put a half-dollar on the bar and shook his head. "Just wrapped myself around a half a beef. I'll pass on the eggs." He sipped at the drink. The rye wasn't watered, and it was what the label said it was. He reached for a cigarillo as the bartender took his half-dollar and replaced it with a quarter. Slocum left the two bits on the bar-top.

"Been a while since I was in Fort Worth," Slocum said. "Town's changed."

The beetle-browed man frowned. "That it has, and not all for the better. When I first opened this place, it was a nice, quiet little town. At least we had honest thieves, card sharps, shooters, and outlaws back then."

Slocum flicked a match with his thumbnail and lit his smoke. "Times change. You'd be Mike?" At the man's nod, Slocum said, "Maybe you could help me, if you're of a mind. I'm looking for a girl."

Mike snorted. "Won't find one in my place. But all you got to do is walk around the corner. Any corner in this part of town. When it comes to prairie peaches, the Acre's an orchard."

Slocum pulled the gold folder from his pocket and flipped it open. "I'm not looking for just any woman. I'm looking for this one. Seen her around, by any chance?"

Mike peered at the tintype, then shook his head. "Not as I recall—wait a minute." He carried the tintype closer to the kerosene lamp behind the bar, slipped on a pair of half-moon spectacles, studied the picture intently for a couple of minutes, and returned shaking his head.

"Wouldn't swear on it, but she *might* have been in here a few months back. If it's the same girl. One who came in here was skinnier, like she hadn't been eating regular, and it'd been a spell since she'd washed up. She asked for a job whoring. I told her the same thing I told you. I don't run a stable. Told her to check out Miss Esther's between Ninth and Tenth on Houston. That's two block over.''

Slocum nodded. "Thanks. I'll take a look over there."

The bartender's bushy brows lowered even more. "I got to tell you something, friend. Even if I had been running whores, I wouldn't have hired her."

"Why's that?"

"Her eyes. Didn't look right. You notice the light in here's not all that bright, but her pupils were so small you couldn't hardly see 'em. And the way she looked at me—well, it was like there wasn't anybody there behind those eyes.'' He sighed. ''That's why I sent her to Esther's. Esther isn't all that picky about the type of women she runs. Like I say, I'm not even sure it was the same girl. Anyhow, hope you find her.''

Slocum pocketed the tintype and sat for a moment, thinking. He had no reason to doubt Mike's judgment or question his observations. What the barkeep had said about Mary's eyes bothered him, though. It could be she'd gone around the bend; maybe, as Mike said, there was no longer anyone there behind those blue eyes. Slocum had seen women—and men—lose their minds when life got too tough to handle. With some folks, it didn't take much to push them around that bend in the road.

Slocum tossed back the last of his drink and stood. "Thanks again, Mike. You've been a big help."

Mike nodded toward the quarter on the bar. "Don't forget your change."

"Buy yourself a drink on me."

"Quit the stuff ten years ago." He dropped the coin in a wooden cash bar behind the counter. "Next time you're in, your first drink's paid in advance."

Slocum nodded and left.

At least now, he thought as he settled his hat against the breeze outside, I've cut a trail. A cold trail. Or maybe even a false trail. But it's a start.

Wandering into Mike's Place had been a stroke of luck more than any intuition on his part. Slocum didn't count on luck, but when it came along, he embraced it.

He idly wondered how long his luck would hold.

6

Slocum had been in classier whorehouses than Miss Esther's Boarding House for Young Ladies.

At least, he thought, it made no pretense at being anything other than a whorehouse. A cheap one. And business was good tonight.

The customers lounging at the bar, knocking back drinks as they ogled the women, were mostly low-wage types. Young cowboys still in dusty range garb, burly freight handlers, callused railroad-spikers and tie-wranglers, and several men who looked to be nothing but toughs and footpads. The weight of the .44 in the shoulder holster felt reassuring as Slocum surveyed the place.

On a torn sofa leaking horsehair against one wall, an obviously drunk cowboy sat with a plump red-haired woman in his lap, his hand up her dress. Her squirming and giggling were obviously forced, but the cowboy seemed to think he was the world's best lover. Whiskey confidence, Slocum figured. At the other end of the couch a thin brunette with a pinched face nursed an infant.

Two women came down the stairs, one on each side of a tall, heavily muscled teamster. A man with a few quirks in the sack. Slocum dismissed the thought with a mental shrug. Different men had different notions.

What wrinkled Slocum's nose and dampened any feelings he might have had was the odor of the place. The dominant scent was that of sweat, cheap perfume and unwashed sex, with an underlayer of stale liquor, tobacco smoke, and the acrid reek of vomit where drunks had downed one too many and lost their suppers.

"Hi, big fellow," a voice at his elbow said. "Buy a girl a drink?"

Slocum glanced at the woman beside him. She stood barely five feet tall, her dishwater-blond hair plastered in ringlets against her face. She might have been reasonably pretty at one time, he figured, but for pocked scars on her cheeks and narrow, thin lips. And the smell of her. It was early in the evening, but Slocum's nostrils told him she'd already serviced her share of customers. He wondered if Esther's girls had ever been told they should at least make a swipe with a wet cloth after doing their business.

"Sorry, miss," Slocum said softly, "I'm looking for Esther."

The dishwater-blonde pushed a small breast against his elbow. "Esther doesn't work the floor. Just counts the take from the rest of us." Her voice held a faint New England tinge. "You're looking for a good time, I'm the gal. Name's Hanna. How about that drink?"

Slocum sighed inwardly and nodded.

Hanna led him to the bar, where a big, broad-shouldered man with knuckle-scarred hands growled a question.

"Gin for me, Dan." The woman lifted an eyebrow at Slocum. "You, honey?"

"Whiskey. Rye, if you've got it."

"Four bits for you and the lady."

Slocum put a half-dollar on the counter. The whiskey came in a glass that was less than clean, and the drink was at least a quarter water. The woman tossed back her "gin" in one shot. Her breath didn't smell like juniper when she leaned close to Slocum. He'd just paid two bits for her shot of water.

"Well, handsome," the brunette said, "you're looking for a good time, I'm your gal. Dollar for straight, anything—anything at all except pain—for three."

Slocum gently lifted her hand from his forearm and smiled. "Sorry, miss," he said again, "but I'm not looking to get my rope pulled tonight. Like I said, I came to see Esther.''

The blonde sniffed in either disgust or disappointment and started to turn away.

Slocum said, ''Hanna, maybe you can help me, in a way.'' He showed her the tintype. ''Do you know this girl?''

Hanna's pocked skin blanched even whiter and her breath caught in a slight gasp. Then she shook her head—a little too emphatically, Slocum thought. ''Never saw her before.'' She wouldn't look Slocum in the eye. He knew she was lying through her teeth. The picture had obviously jolted her. He didn't know why, but he didn't press the point.

''Thanks anyway, Hanna,'' Slocum said. He watched as she strode away, a bit hurriedly, as if anxious all of a sudden to leave his company. Slocum decided he'd keep Hanna in mind for a private talk later, and turned to the bartender. ''Esther in tonight?''

The bartender bristled. ''Miss Esther don't work the floor, mister,'' the big bartender said, a barely concealed warning in his tone.

''So the young lady told me, Dan,'' Slocum said amiably. ''I just want to talk to her. Won't take a minute.''

The bartender's voice took an even harder edge. ''You hurt her, you're dead meat.''

Slocum raised a hand. ''I have no intention of harming Miss Esther, Dan.'' He eased a sliver dollar onto the bar and shoved it toward the bartender. ''All I want to do is ask her a couple of questions. Just talk, that's all.''

''You ain't the law.''

''Not hardly.''

Dan pocketed the silver dollar. ''Wait here.'' He barked, ''Hold your damn horses,'' at a cowboy clamoring for a refill, disappeared through a door at the near end of the bar, and came back a moment later. ''Go on in. You got three minutes before I come after you.''

Slocum stepped into the small office, removed his hat, and nodded a greeting to the gray-haired woman behind the cluttered, cigarette-scarred desk.

''Miss Esther?''

''Yeah? Dan said you wanted to see me. Make it short and

sweet, friend. If you're looking for young boys, you come to the wrong place. I run women, not Greeks.''

Slocum's face flushed. He bit back the anger. He didn't have that much time to waste, and he'd as soon not tangle with the big bartender if he didn't have to. Or Esther, for that matter. He didn't have to look to know that she'd have a gun of some sort within easy reach. This was one tough woman.

"It's not that, Miss Esther, not that at all. I'm looking for a girl.''

She glanced at him in disgust, her green eyes hard. "Shit. You walked through a whole damn herd of them outside. Why bother me?''

"The girl I'm looking for may have come to you some months ago," Slocum said. "I'm trying to find her. As a favor to a friend, not for anything else.'' He showed her the tintype.

For a moment, the woman who called herself Esther didn't look at the picture. The disgust slowly faded from her gaze and her expression seemed to soften as she looked him over, head to boots. "Damn me, if I hadn't retired from the business, I'd be tempted to take you on myself, mister.''

Slocum forced a smile and a gentle lie. "And I'd be more than willing, Miss Esther. But we both have other things on our minds. The picture?'' Esther glanced at the faded tintype. Her eyes went wide, her face paled, and the thin lips parted in a quick intake of breath. The she tossed the tintype back.

"No. Never saw her.''

"I think you have, Miss Esther." Slocum's tone tightened. "Tell me about her.''

Esther's gaze flicked nervously around the room. Her shoulders slumped. "Well, it could be her, I guess. The girl who came to me looked older than this. And thin. Not hardly any tits.'' She fell silent.

"And?'' Slocum prompted after a moment. "Tell it straight, Esther. You know her a damn sight better than you let on.''

She couldn't seem to meet Slocum's steady gaze. "All right, I'll tell you what I know.'' Her voice was little more than a whisper. "She called herself Melissa. She wasn't here long. Wasn't much of a whore. I ran her off after three, four days. Too many complaints. She didn't put any effort into satisfying the customers. The end of the line for her came when a cowboy cornered me and said he'd rather fuck a sheep than that bitch. You know how cowboys hate sheep.''

Slocum nodded. "Yes, ma'am, I surely do. Where did she go after you fired her?"

Esther shook her head. "Don't know. My guess is she wound up in one of the crib shacks. Girl like that couldn't keep a job in a nice whorehouse."

If Miss Esther considered this a "nice" whorehouse, Slocum thought in wry disgust, he hoped he never wandered into a disreputable one. He also knew he wasn't getting the whole story from Miss Esther. She knew a damn sight more than she let on. He also sensed he wasn't going to get another word out of her.

He nodded his thanks, left the office, and almost bumped into the bartender on his way out.

"Was just comin' to tell you you're time's up," the barkeep said in that grizzly-bear growl of his. He poked a thick finger against Slocum's chest. "Reckon you'll be leavin' now."

Slocum didn't smile. His eyes narrowed. "Dan, don't push your luck. Get that finger off my breastbone or I'll rip your nuts off and feed them to you. *Sabe?*" The surly look in Dan's eyes faded. Slocum held his gaze until the big man dropped his hand away. Dan obviously savvied. "And," Slocum said, "since you asked me stick around for a while, I'll stay long enough for one more drink. The real stuff this time. No water."

The drink wasn't watered. In the reek of the saloon and "meat rack," where the girls put their wares on display, Slocum took his time, sipping at the barely passable rye. The red-haired woman led the drunk cowboy up the stairs. Slocum figured the young man would wake up in the morning with a headache and empty pockets. And maybe something else he'd as soon not have. Slocum idly wondered how many different diseases were to be caught in Miss Esther's.

The thought deepened his frown. Maybe that was why everyone said Mary Connally, if it was her, looked older and thinner. The so-called social diseases were a hazard of the whore's trade. He pushed the thought from his mind. No need to fret over such things until he found her.

Slocum became aware he was being watched. He lit a cigarillo, half turned from the bar, and let his gaze drift around the crowd, finally settling on three men seated at a table not far from the door. He'd noticed them when he'd first walked in, all dark of face and broad in the shoulders, like three peas in a pod. He figured the trio for shoulder-hitters, probably in the business of rolling drunks and robbing anybody who might be packing more than a couple of bucks in his pocket. The footpads were paying a lot of attention to him, Slocum noticed. They spoke quietly, but all three stared in his direction until they realized he was staring back. Then they quickly turned away. Slocum doubted they had been admiring him as a dashing figure of a man. They might as well have had dollar signs tattooed on their foreheads.

Slocum decided not to make it easy for them.

He finished his drink and took his time working his way toward the front door. He left his duster unbuttoned. At the edge of his vision he saw the three men rise as one. They would be following him.

Slocum went out the door, immediately stepped to his right, and leaned casually against the wall, the ember of anger the bartender had lit growing in his gut. Slocum found himself anticipating the fight; he didn't know—and didn't care—if the anger inside him was due to what he'd found out about Mary Connally, or simply that he had no use for thieves. Especially when they ran in packs.

The door swung open. The three men emerged and stood for a moment, glancing about. The gaslight by the front door had been shattered, and the flickering light from a distant street lamp on the corner didn't penetrate the winter gloom much here. Slocum stood in the deep shadow cast by the big wooden sign marking Esther's place. The sign creaked in the swirling wind. Slocum noted with relief that the crowd in the street had thinned a bit. There was always a chance an innocent bystander would get hurt, but fewer people around decreased the odds of that happening.

"Where the hell'd he go?" asked one of the men. "Can't

let that jasper out of our sight, boys. I know a man packin'
cash when I see 'im.''

Slocum flicked the cigarillo. A trail of sparks arched high,
ticked off one of toughs' shoulder. The man the cigarillo hit
yelped in surprise.

"You gentlemen looking for someone?" Slocum asked casually.

The trio spun to face him, standing almost shoulder to
shoulder. That told Slocum they weren't shooters. Real gun-
men wouldn't be caught bunched up in a herd like that; they'd
spread out to get some shooting room and boost the odds one
of them could take him down.

One of the men, slightly taller than the other two, took a
step toward Slocum. "Yeah," he said. "You." A faint speck
of light flicked from the steel blade in his right hand. "Hand
over your money and you won't get hurt."

Slocum smiled. "Afraid I can't do that, gentlemen. It's truly
against my nature to do such a thing."

The man with the knife growled audibly. "You son of a
bitch, I'll gut you like a butcherin' hog!" He took a step
closer. "Now, hand over the money!"

Slocum's right hand snaked beneath his open duster. The
Peacemaker whispered from leather, the distinctive sound of
the hammer drawn to full cock loud even in the city street
noise. The bore of the handgun pointed straight at the burly
man's shirt pocket.

"You're one dumb son of a bitch, friend," Slocum said,
his words cold, eyes narrowed. "Nobody but an idiot brings
a knife to a gunfight—"

The man at the speaker's left stabbed a hand toward his
belt. Slocum shifted the muzzle and stroked the trigger. The
fire-bolt of the muzzle flash almost touched the man's shirt;
Slocum knew the soft lead slug had hit him squarely in the
breastbone. The close-range impact hammered the tough backward onto the splintery plank boardwalk. A small-caliber revolver flipped from the man's fingers as he fell. The other two
men broke and ran before the first startled yelp sounded from
inside Esther's.

Slocum let them go. Any second now, the drunker or less

intelligent of Esther's clientele would come boiling out the door to see what the shooting was about. Slocum had no desire to answer a bunch of fool questions from the law. He slipped into the dark alleyway between Esther's and the place next door.

"Jesus," somebody yelled, "somebody shot Bud Bannister!"

A voice shouted back, " 'Bout time somebody did! They get the other two?"

"Nope! Just Bud!"

"Shit! Can't count on nobody to finish no job nowadays!"

Slocum half smiled. From the tone and content of the yells, nobody was likely to worry too much about who had shot Bud Bannister. The law probably wouldn't be inclined to invest much time and effort into finding the killer of a common robber.

The smile faded as Slocum holstered the Colt. He wondered if he'd made a mistake in not downing the other two. If they were blood kin, and they *had* looked it, they might decide to settle the score. He shook the thought away. Cowards and bullies usually didn't want to face a dangerous man. Only those they could rob with little chance of losing hide or life. Which, come to think on it, was another reason he should have dropped the hammer on all three. But he hadn't seen the need.

Slocum strode unhurriedly toward the patch of light at the end of the cluttered alley. He was a block away from Esther's before the excited voices faded behind him.

He dismissed the incident from his mind. He didn't like killing, but he didn't whip himself with a cactus bush when it happened to some son of a bitch who'd deserved it. Bud Bannister had robbed his last pilgrim. One more wolf thinned from the Hell's Acre pack.

Back in his hotel room, Slocum bolted the door behind him, poured a drink, and placed his rifle on the table before setting about cleaning the powder residue from the Peacemaker. As he worked, he pondered his next move. The trail to Mary Connally was still cold, but it had warmed substantially.

The reactions of the whore named Hanna and the madam named Esther told Slocum that at least two people knew more about Mary than they'd let on. Hanna was the weaker of the two. He promised himself a quiet, private conversation with Hanna as soon as possible. He finished cleaning the Peacemaker and thumbed a fresh load into the fired chamber.

He finished his drink, tore a blank page from the back of the small notebook in which he kept track of his expenses, and wrote a brief report to Colonel Connally. It wouldn't say much. "Arrived in Fort Worth. Will keep you informed." He signed it simply, "S." He'd get it on its way to the Crooked River country when the telegraph office opened tomorrow. The wires ran nowhere near the isolated ranch, so it would take a week, maybe two, for the message to reach the colonel. By then, Slocum hoped to have some better news.

Or, he had to admit, worse news . . .

As was his habit, Slocum awoke well before daybreak. He lay for a moment in the pleasant comfort of the soft bed, listening. Even an all-night town like Fort Worth had to catch its breath sometime.

There were few noises from the street outside his second-floor corner window. A few muted voices of early risers, the creak of rough board sidewalks underfoot, and the occasional snort of a horse carrying a broke and hungover rider back to the ranch were the only sounds to disturb the still morning air. Noises carried well in the chill, but nowhere near the way they did in the dead cold stillness of the high mountain camps, where a man could hear a twig snap from two hundred yards away.

Slocum wished he was back in one of those high camps. He sighed the thought away. The mountains would still be there when this job was done.

He dressed, slipped into his duster, and left the still-silent hotel. Two doors down the street, a light shone through the window of a cafe. Slocum smelled the coffee before he eased the door open.

A slight, balding man tying an apron around his waist glanced up as Slocum stepped inside.

"Mornin', hoss," the aged man said. "Coffee's ready. Hot enough to make a man get religion, rank enough to make your eyes bug out like a goosed badger, and thicker'n the water on the Salt Fork of the Brazos.''

Slocum chuckled aloud. "Just the way I like it."

"Help yourself while I rob the settin' hens, butcher a couple hogs, and burn some biscuits, and we'll have breakfast." The voice was low in pitch, considering it came from such a thin chest, but softly cheerful. "Mighty nice day out. Just the right nip in the air to make a man feel like he was twenty again, full of piss and vinegar, wakin' up beside a cute Shoshoni gal and ready to whup the world." The little man lifted an eyebrow. "I get to talking too much, just tell me to hush up. Be back in a minute." He went through a door in the back of the serving area. Slocum noted that he walked a bit hunched, as if his back or hips bothered him.

Slocum helped himself to the coffee.

The cafe owner had pegged the brew. It was scalding hot and strong enough to float a cartridge. Slocum leaned against a wall, the heat of the heavy stoneware mug comfortable in his hand.

He studied the place as he sipped the coffee. It was small but clean, the tables and chairs stout and handmade, and it smelled of fresh coffee and sourdough. The scent set his mouth to watering. Good cafes were harder to find than good horses. Slocum sensed he had wandered into one of the best.

He had barely lowered the level of the mug when the wiry man came back, wiping his hands on a towel, poured himself a cup, and grinned at Slocum.

"Poked a few eggs out of that old hen. Biscuits are in the oven." He nodded toward a chair at a table near the small stove that held the coffeepot. "Set yourself down, hoss. You don't mind waitin' a couple minutes for breakfast, I'll join you." He extended a hand. "Name's Toucherman."

Slocum's brows went up as he took the small hand. "Not Jeremiah Toucherman?"

"One and the same."

Slocum stood in awe of few men, but if half the tales were true, this wiry little half-cripple was one of the top rank. "Slocum. Pleasure to make your acquaintance. Don't get to meet many legends." The slight man's grip was firm, a surprising strength in the thin fingers. Slocum released the hand.

Toucherman laughed, deep and full-throated. "I'll be damned. Didn't know anybody remembered the name."

"They still do, up in the Black Hills, Powder River, and Yellowstone country. Not just white men either. Every Shoshoni, Sioux, Cheyenne, and Blackfeet camp I've wintered in has its stories about Touchy Toucherman," Slocum said.

Toucherman's grin widened. The man still had all his teeth. That told Slocum a lot about the scout and mountain man who'd broken trails even Jim Bridger and Kit Carson hadn't known about. If the yarns were halfway right, Touchy Toucherman should have been dead years ago. He'd be in his late sixties, early seventies by now.

"Spotted you for a plainsman and mountain fellow right off, Slocum," Toucherman said. "Probably why I started running off at the mouth so much. Not many people around Fort Worth ever been that far north by west. Kinda nice, thinking those tall tales will outlast me." He pushed his chair back and stood. "I'll rustle us up a bait of greasy ham and overcooked eggs. We'll jaw some more over breakfast. It'll be an hour or more before these town loafers even roll out of the sack."

Slocum poured himself a second cup and mentally ran through the stories he'd heard told of Touchy Toucherman. A mountain man from the same tough mold, if not with the same bulk, as Jim Bridger and Liver-Eating Johnston. Trapper, Indian fighter, and then Indian ally, finally adopted into half-a-dozen tribes that had discovered it was a lot less trouble to befriend him than try to kill him. Wagon train scout during the gold rush years. Grizzly hunter, an occupation even more hazardous than fighting Indians. A white man who spoke for the Sioux and Cheyenne at the Laramie Council. Tracker without peer . . .

The yarns still spun through Slocum's mind when Toucherman returned, a heavy plate filled almost to overflowing in each hand. He set a plate in front of Slocum, fetched knives and forks, refilled both coffee cups, and sat down across the table.

Slocum stared at the plate before him in disbelief. Three eggs over easy, a half-inch slab—as broad as Slocum's spread fingers—of smoked Virginia ham, the rest of the platter piled high with fried potatoes and four sourdough biscuits.

"Honey and molasses to spice the soppin's, and there's more biscuits," Touchy said as he picked up his own knife and fork. "Dig in, hoss. Loses its flavor when it gets a chill."

Slocum dug.

A half hour later, he pushed his plate back, stuffed to the point that he thought his belt was going to give way and spang the buckle across the room like a rifle ball. Touchy had matched him bite for bite; for a little man, he put away the chow, Slocum thought. Slocum moaned softly.

"Best meal I've had in years. You always feed your customers like this?" Slocum asked.

"Only if they're high-country or big-plains folks and would do to ride the river with, Slocum. You fit."

Slocum nodded, accepting the compliment at face value. He leaned back, lit a cigarillo, and waited until Toucherman packed and fired an oversized pipe with a deeply curved stem.

"Touchy," he finally said, hating to disturb the comfortable silence, "it's none of my damn business, but I'd like to know what a man like you is doing cooped up in town running a cafe. It doesn't seem—natural."

Touchy dragged at the pipe, the blue-white smoke almost obscuring his features. "Most folks I'd tell to go to Hell, hoss, but I reckon you'll understand. Man's got to make some concession to the passing years, because they don't make none to *him*. I'm markin' time now, waiting for the wind to cut my sand dune down flat. There isn't much sand left to me, Slocum. When it's mostly gone, I'll sell this place, wipe the grease off my old Hawken, saddle a good mule, and ride off toward the mountains. And that's where I'll die, a happy man to the last."

Slocum nodded solemnly. "I can't think of a more pleasant way to go myself."

"Figured you'd know exactly what I was talking about. Now it's my turn to get nosy. None of *my* business either, but I read you for a hunter, hoss. Only one animal's track leads *toward* a town. Who're you hunting?"

"A girl. Her father asked me to bring her home. The last

he'd heard, she was in Fort Worth. Working Hell's Half Acre.''

"Name?"

"Mary Connally. Or at least that's her given name." Slocum produced the tintype and handed it to Touchy.

"Colonel Connally's daughter? From up in the Crooked River country?"

"The same. You know him?"

"Not personal. Know of him, though, and like what I heard." Touchy studied the picture closely, then shook his head. "I don't recall seeing her around, Slocum, but I'll be glad to ask around some if you want me butting into your business." He handed back the tintype.

"I'd appreciate it, Touchy."

The former mountain man glanced up in what might have been aggravation as footsteps sounded on the boards outside. "First customers coming. Must be getting on toward six o'clock. Damn. Just find somebody who talks my tongue, and these city folk butt in."

Slocum stood. "How much for the breakfast?"

"A handshake. And a couple of drinks some night. Maybe lead the mule for me if the sand blows flat before I get to the mountains, you happen to be around at the time." As he took Slocum's hand, worry flickered in the pale blue eyes. He lowered his voice. "Slocum, a lot of whores don't live long in the Acre. If you're going to find her, you'd better find her fast."

Slocum reached for his hat. "Thanks, Touchy. For the meal and the talk. Most of all, the talk."

"See you around. Keep your powder dry and your hair on."

Slocum strode—or, stuffed as he was from breakfast, waddled—into crisp, still morning air. The sky in the east had lightened. The overcast had moved on during the night. The day would be clear and colder. Good hunting weather.

And before nightfall, he planned to hunt up a thin, dishwater-blond whore. The more he'd thought on it, the more convinced Slocum had become that the woman called Hanna knew where Mary Connally was. Or had been.

7

Slocum leaned against the wall of the general store a half block down the street from Miss Esther's Boarding House for Young Ladies and worried the frayed end of a match stick between his lips.

The lowering sun had dropped behind the false front of the general store, leaving Slocum in shadow, but the winter air had turned almost balmy during the day. The temperature had risen to well above freezing; there was little breeze, only an occasional gentle puff. All in all, Slocum thought, a nice enough day for waiting.

Slocum was a patient man when the need arose. Many a time he had lain or crouched on a hillside or behind a bush without moving for a full day. Or longer. The most patient dog caught the most rabbits, and an impatient man could catch a slug or lance when he moved too soon.

Waiting did seem harder in the city.

He had been here only a few hours, but already his skin felt gritty from the haze of dust kicked up by buckboards, spring wagons, and heavy freighters that passed. With so little wind, the dust merely eddied above the streets and drifted around the buildings until it settled of its own accord back to earth.

Hell's Half Acre had started coming to life a couple of hours ago, but hadn't got its pulse racing yet. The wolf wouldn't hit full howl until after sundown. Slocum spat out the frayed match, pulled another from his vest, and idly whittled a semblance of a point on the small stick with his stockman's-style pocket knife. He watched as the pedestrian traffic thickened by the half hour.

Men who were obviously dealers and barkers drifted past, on their way to another night at the gaming tables of the Acre. Storekeepers swept the dust from crude plank boardwalks. A half-dozen cowboys rode in, laughing and joking, young faces eager and flushed with excitement. Their horses wore the T-Bar-6 brand. They'd come all the way from north of Denton to blow a month's pay in a night or two in the Acre. And now and then, a prostitute worked the streets, trying to entice her first customer of the day.

Slocum hadn't seen the two men who were with Bud Bannister when he'd shot him. He'd just as soon not see them. He didn't need any distractions or complications right now.

Slocum hadn't idled away the entire morning. He'd walked off the overfeed at Touchy Toucherman's place by prowling the Acre, getting a look at the lay of the land in daylight, mentally noting the gambling parlors, whorehouses, saloons, and opium dens along a dozen streets.

His wanderings had given him a better feel for Fort Worth. It was more than just a cowboy town, as it had been in the heyday of the trail drives. The population was a diverse one. He'd met a surprising number of Chinese on the streets; almost four full blocks on Eighth were filled with Oriental businesses—laundries, restaurants, opium dens. Slocum knew of the Chinese fondness for opium. It was as much a part of their culture as the peyote cactus was to the Apache or whiskey was to the white man.

There were more black faces in Fort Worth than he'd expected too, some on horseback on working cowboy saddles, some in the tough, rugged clothing of stevedores and freight handlers, a few in creosote-stained shirts that marked them as tie-handlers. A few looked to be former buffalo soldiers, veterans of the 9th and 10th Cavalry, but the majority seemed to be truck farmers. Their spring wagons, loaded with winter vegetables, fresh eggs, chickens, and other small farm animals, rolled past, an occasional pig trotting on lead behind the wagons.

Slocum had expected to see more Mexicans. There seemed to be few permanent brown-skinned residents. Aside from the occasional cantina or cafe, and a handful of women who looked to be housekeepers, maids, and cooks for the more affluent whites living north of the Acre, most of the Hispanic males were *vaqueros* or farmers. Like the Chinese and the blacks, they kept to themselves when not working.

Slocum had gotten another surprise during his brief stay in the Acre. One of every six whores was black. Slocum couldn't recall seeing many ebony-skinned prostitutes in the frontier towns further north and west. He'd always heard the fable that a man could change his luck by bedding a Negress. Slocum had run into some mighty fetching black women during his travels, but only a couple who were in the whoring business.

He'd also learned a lot about that part of Forth Worth north of the Acre from the old-timers of the local spit-and-whittle clubs gathered on benches in front of feed stores and cafes.

He knew where the high-stakes gambling went on. The White Elephant was noted for its honest games; the Pacific had lower-stakes tables of more questionable honesty. Among the better class of saloons were the Cattle Exchange, Merchants Exchange, and the Star, all "uptown." Slocum decided to drop in on one or more later on.

His musings came to an end as his gaze settled on the person he'd been waiting to see. The thin figure of the dishwater-blonde came around a corner a block away, and turned toward Esther's. Slocum threaded his way through the growing traffic.

"Afternoon, Hanna," Slocum said as he fell into step alongside her. She started visibly at the sound of his voice, glanced up with wide eyes, her pocked faced gone almost colorless, and abruptly stopped. Her gaze flicked about nervously, her fingers fidgeting with the straps of the small cloth bag hung over a bony shoulder.

"Go away," she half whispered, still glancing about. Her thin shoulders shivered, but not from the cold.

"I just want to talk, Hanna. I think you know more about Mary Connally than you've let on. I need to find her, and I may not have much time."

She stopped and grasped his forearm. Her fingers were cold.

Slocum felt them tremble against his skin. "I can't be seen talking to you. Word's got around what you're after. Bull'd kill me sure."

"Who's Bull?"

She dropped her hand from his arm. "Please—forget I said that. Now, leave me alone."

"I'll make it worth your while, Hanna. Give me some solid information, something I can use to find her, and I'll pay you fifty dollars. Cash. More than you can clear in a month at Esther's."

The look in her eyes reminded Slocum of a frightened doe. But the fear faded a bit as she pondered the offer. She dropped her gaze from his, glancing around. "Not here. Not in plain sight. Meet me in the Texas Wagon Yard. Sixth and Rusk. Two o'clock tomorrow morning." Her voice trembled so that Slocum had to strain to hear the words. "And for God's sake, please, *please,* don't say a word to anybody."

"I won't, Hanna. See you then." He strode quickly away from the blond whore. The woman was frightened half out of her mind. And, Slocum wondered, who the hell was this "Bull" she had mentioned? This was beginning to feel like more than a simple job of finding a wayward child for a family who wanted her back. The idea left a small, hard lump in his gut.

With nothing much else to do until two in the morning, Slocum drifted back to Touchy's place, hoping to find an answer or two. Or at least a cup of coffee.

He tried the door and found it locked; it wasn't until then that Slocum noticed the small hand-lettered sign tacked to the frame:

BREAKFAST ONLY
GET YOUR OWN DAMN SUPPER

Slocum chuckled aloud. That sounded like something a crusty old mountain man would write. He'd have to settle for a cup of barely passable and overpriced brew in the hotel restaurant. On the way, he bought a copy of the *Fort Worth Democrat*. As he sipped his coffee, he scanned the paper for any news of use or interest.

Local politics didn't interest Slocum a whit, but one small, two-paragraph notice at the bottom of an inside page caught his attention. The headline read:

ANOTHER SOILED DOVE
CROSSES THE RIVER

The story was a somewhat sarcastic report about a prostitute, a woman identified only as Prairie Jane, who had taken her own life with a massive overdose of morphine. The article concluded, "The last suicide of such nature was but one week ago."

Slocum folded the paper. It was common knowledge that a prostitute's life was anything but easy. A lucky few escaped the life, married, and went on to raise families. For each one who climbed from the crib to respectability, many went to unmarked graves. Disease claimed more than a few. Others drank themselves to death. Some died at the hands of clients, or disappeared when they fell into disfavor with the whorehouse operator for one reason or another. Still others, perhaps a majority, turned to drugs when such releases were available. Opium, morphine, and in growing numbers the new drug, cocaine, were the chosen escapes from a dreary and debasing life.

The whore who really enjoyed her work, who had chosen freely to sell her body instead of being forced into the life to survive, did exist. Slocum had known some of them. More than a few, in fact. His instinct for reading human nature had served him well when he felt the need for release. He chose his women, especially prostitutes, with care. He had collected no diseases and no scars as souvenirs from the women he'd bedded.

Slocum finished his coffee and stared out the window as he dragged at his cigarillo. Quite a few people he had shown Mary Connally's tintype to had said they "might have seen her," but that if it was Mary, she was now thin, drawn, with no life showing in the listless blue eyes.

Esther had said she was a failure as a whore.

Slocum began to wonder if the girl the Connallys called

Mary still existed. If she'd fallen into the trap of drugs and disease, it might be less painful for the Connallys to be told she had died of natural causes. That was a last resort, of course. Slocum couldn't lie to the colonel, even to save the aging man from an even more painful truth.

Slocum sighed, pushed back his chair, and stood. There was no need to fret over what might be—or might not—until he found her. Then he could worry about the rest. He paid for his coffee and ambled to the desk.

"Tsing Lo deliver my laundry this morning?" he asked the clerk.

"Yes, sir." The clerk reached beneath the counter and produced a neatly folded stack of clothing. In his room, Slocum decided he had at least found one good thing in the Acre. Tsing Lo did a fine job, and for a reasonable price. Slocum stowed the garments and stretched out on the bed for a nap. He knew it was going to be a long night, so he'd better get his rest while he could. At least at this time of day, it was reasonably quiet outside.

The racket from the street woke Slocum a couple of hours before midnight. He lay still for a moment, pondering what to do next. He had no desire to venture back into the Acre until his early morning appointment with Hanna. He had had enough of that part of town for a few hours. Right now, he needed a quiet place that served decent beer and good whiskey. He washed, shaved, and changed to fresh clothing—black twill trousers and a crisply ironed unstarched medium-blue shirt. The dark-gray wool hip-length riding coat concealed the shoulder holster rig adequately, and would be more than sufficient to ward off the chill. He eased the door open and glanced down the hall, more a force of habit than from any real concern, and strode downstairs into the busy street.

The White Elephant Saloon and Restaurant covered almost half a block of Main Street, uptown between Second and Third, an imposing two-story structure. An ornately lettered sign beside the door boasted a menu of fresh fish, oysters, and game, the finest wines, and a wide selection of cigars for gentlemen.

When he stepped inside, Slocum was glad he had taken the time to clean up and change into clean clothes.

The place was as elegant as the spit-and-whittle-clubbers had said. Crystal chandeliers hung from the rafters; the bar was long, of heavily waxed mahogany, the brass rail at its foot polished to a bright gleam. Most of the men wore suits and string ties. Others dressed more casually, but still neatly. There were a surprising number of women in the restaurant area, seated at tables covered with white linen cloths, a dazzling array of silverware and glasses at each place setting. Slocum could tell at a glance none of the women were soiled doves. They were elegantly dressed, many in formal gowns, all escorted. Mostly wives and maybe a few mistresses, Slocum concluded.

Waiters and waitresses, all dressed in white shirts and string ties, scurried among the tables, delivering drinks and steaming platters. The atmosphere was pleasant, almost subdued. Though the place was crowded, the various conversations were little more than a murmur in the room. The slight haze of tobacco smoke hugged the high ceiling, well above the level for comfortable breathing for the ladies.

An array of bottles of every conceivable type of liquor stood in neat order beneath the showplace of the establishment—a gleaming back-bar mirror, unmarked by cracks or bullet holes.

Slocum strode to the bar, and was instantly attended to by a middle-aged man whose towel and apron were clean, a black string tie knotted at the collar of his starched white shirt.

"May I get you something, sir?"

"A beer, please."

"Yes, sir. Dark, pilsner, local, or imported? We have some excellent Dutch pilsner, and the local brew is quite good."

"I'll try the local."

The beer appeared before Slocum only seconds later, served in a frosted mug that had been nestled while still wet from washing against a block of ice. The added touch was worth the extra nickel, Slocum thought. The beer was light on the tongue, with just the right aftertaste of hops and grain. He nodded his satisfaction to the bartender.

Slocum sipped the beer, savoring every swallow, and let his

earlier worries slide, content to enjoy the moment. He was halfway through the mug when a voice at his left said, "Evening, Slocum."

Slocum turned to the mustached man in the derby hat cocked at an angle toward his right ear, and smiled. "Hello, Bat." He extended a hand. "It's been a long time."

Bat Masterson smiled back. "That it has. Dodge City. You find that fellow you were looking for?"

"I found him," Slocum said. He didn't elaborate. There was no need.

Masterson waved a casual hand to the bartender, made a signal with his index finger, and nodded toward Slocum's beer. A moment later the bartender placed a snifter of brandy before Masterson and a fresh mug before Slocum.

"Much obliged," Slocum said. "I'll get the next round."

"On the house," Masterson said with a wry smile. "Always did like to play it free and easy with Luke's money."

"Luke's here?"

"Owns a third of the place. He's sitting in on a high-stakes game going upstairs. Want to join in?"

Slocum shook his head. "Luke Short's high-stakes games are way out of my reach, Bat. Is the whole of the Dodge City Peace Commission here?"

"Missing a few. There's me, Luke, Charlie Bassett. Haven't heard from Wyatt or W.F. Petillon lately." Masterson inclined his head away from the bar. "I have a private table over in the corner, and I never did enjoy drinking standing up as much as sitting down. Join me?"

Slocum followed as Masterson threaded his way through the crowd, pausing from time to time to exchange greetings with acquaintances. The slender, narrow-shouldered man moved light on his feet. He didn't look at all like a gunman, except for the alertly intense eyes that observed all that went on around him, but Slocum knew the man beneath the derby could be a shooter any time the occasion arose. He couldn't call Masterson a friend, more of an acquaintance. They were two men who shared a mutual respect. Neither wanted the pleasure of facing the other in a gunfight.

Masterson had been in his teens in the Battle of Adobe

Walls, but some people still claimed it was Bat, not Billy Dixon, who fired the half-mile shot that dropped an Indian from his pony and broke the siege. Neither Dixon nor Masterson admitted to or denied having pulled the trigger on that legendary shot. It didn't matter to Slocum. And it sure as hell hadn't mattered to the Indian.

True to his nature, Bat's table was in a corner, walls at his back and two sides. No one could come up behind him, and from there he could see everything that went on in the White Elephant, including the comings and goings of men who strode up or down the carpeted stairs leading to the second-floor gaming rooms.

The two men idled away a time in small talk about the old days in Dodge and beyond, sharing news of acquaintances among both red and white men and their fates where known. Neither asked direct questions about the other.

During a brief lull in the conversation, Slocum asked casually, "Bat, do you know anybody named 'Bull' in Fort Worth?"

Masterson smiled. "Not more than a dozen. Not that it's any of my business, but are you looking for someone in particular?"

Slocum flipped open the tintype. "Her."

Masterson studied the faded picture for a moment, then shook his head. "Sorry, Slocum. Can't say as I've ever seen her. Pretty girl, though."

"She was when this was taken," Slocum said grimly. "I don't know what she'll be like when I find her." The heavy, carved mantel clock on the shelf beside the back-bar mirror read twenty minutes to two. He took his leave of Masterson, idly wondering how Luke Short was making out in the big game upstairs, and left the White Elephant.

Slocum was within a block of the wagon yard when he heard the excited babble of voices and a woman's scream. A young man hurried along the street, his face pale, eyes wide. Slocum reached out and grabbed the man's arm.

"What's all the commotion?" Slocum asked.

"Woman"—the young man's voice quavered, came in quick gasps—"nailed to the—back wall—wagon yard."

Slocum's heart leapt into his throat. "What's she look like?"

"Like—Christ on the cross—blond—"

Slocum released his grip and sprinted toward the wagon yard. He skidded to a stop, heart hammering, at the back of the crowd. Four feet up the side of the heavy log stable wall, a slender blond woman's thin body stretched arms wide, feet crossed, and naked, the light from the crowd's torches and handheld lanterns casting a ghostly glow against her white skin.

Slocum shoved his way to the front of the crowd, and pulled up short four feet from the body. The bile rose in his throat. Heavy spikes driven through both wrists and the insteps of the crossed feet held the pale body against the wall, dark droplets of blood oozing from the spike wounds. She was rail-thin, her dishwater-blond hair tumbled down across her face. Slocum steeled himself, crossed the final couple of strides, and swept the woman's hair aside.

Hanna's eyes were open, glazed in death, downcast as if staring at the spike nailed through her feet. Slocum swallowed back the bitterness in his throat. A small drop of blood trickled from a tiny puncture wound beneath her left breast. Slocum could only hope she'd already been dead when she'd been crucified.

"Good gawd!" a voice from the crowd said. "Why would anybody do somethin' like that—and to a woman?"

Slocum had a damned good idea why. It was a warning. From somebody named Bull. To anybody who might even think of talking to Slocum about Mary Connally.

A shout from the back of the crowd told Slocum the law had arrived. He strode away from the body, slipped around the side of the stable, and sagged against the rough logs.

It was his fault; he had killed Hanna just as surely as if he'd stuck a .44 in her ear and pulled the trigger. Somehow, someone had found out about his appointment with her. That had doomed her.

An ember of rage glowed in his gut, flickered into flame, pushed its way past the burning acid of guilt. Slocum realized he had been clenching his fist so hard the nails dug into his palm.

"Anybody know who she is?" The voice from around the corner of the building held the tone of authority.

"Name's Hanna," a shaky voice replied. "One of Miss Esther's whores."

Slocum took a deep breath to steady his rage and frayed nerves. A man who acted in anger made mistakes and got himself killed. Slocum had learned how to control that anger, that raw fury, to turn it into a weapon as deadly as the Peacemaker he wore. He strode away from the wagon yard, deliberately keeping his pace casual and measured. He reached the end of Seventh Street and turned onto Main, heading south by southwest, jostling his way through the crowd that thickened and grew more boisterous as he moved deeper into the Acre.

Somebody, by God, is going to pay for this, Slocum vowed as he walked. Somebody called Bull. There was little doubt in Slocum's mind. Hanna had said Bull would kill her "if he knew." Bull obviously knew. Hanna's death also meant that word had gotten around the Acre that Slocum was looking for Mary Connally.

He could only hope that that didn't also cost Mary her life. A new sense of urgency lengthened Slocum's strides. He knew he had to find her. What he didn't know was just how long he had before it was too late. Any savage who would do something like that to Hanna . . .

Slocum couldn't let himself finish the thought.

He turned in the trash-cluttered alley between Ninth and Tenth, the scent of urine and rotting garbage thick in the narrow passageway between buildings. The weak light from the streets didn't penetrate here; all it did was deepen the shadows to the color of printer's ink.

Slocum barely heard the soft voice from behind: "Your right, Slocum. Two o'clock."

Slocum caught a faint glimpse of movement in the shadows, the glint of pale light on a long tube; he flexed his knees, whipped the Peacemaker from its shoulder holster, and slipped the hammer as a bright muzzle flash bloomed from the tube. A cloud of buckshot tore into the wall two feet in front of

Slocum. He heard the solid whack of his slug against flesh almost simultaneously with the heavy bellow of the shotgun. A second shadow twitched an arm's length from the shotgun. Slocum dropped to a knee. A shorter lance of flame sent a ball humming above his head. Slocum kept both eyes on the spot where the handgun muzzle flash had come from, let the muzzle fall into line a couple of feet to the left of the flash, and stroked the trigger.

A man grunted and spun from against the wall, silhouetted for an instant against the faint streetlights at the end of the alley. He half spun, broke into a shambling run, and went to his knees after three steps.

The whole incident lasted but a couple of heartbeats. Slocum sensed the slender man's presence beside him, and glanced at Bat Masterson. "Obliged, Bat. They'd have had me cold."

Masterson shrugged, casually lowered the hammer of the snub-nosed revolver in his fist, and slipped it back into a pocket. "My pleasure. Never did like to see a man cut down from ambush. Didn't think I'd need to back your play, but what the hell. One of them could have gotten lucky. You're as quick with that Peacemaker as I've heard, it seems."

Slocum grunted as he and Masterson strode the few feet to the two men lying in the street. "It was closer than I'd have liked," Slocum said. "Shoulder rigs slow me down." He kept the hammer back on the Colt as Masterson knelt by the shotgunner and struck a match. The man was dead, a neat round hole at the base of his throat. Slocum didn't need to look at the other side to know what it looked like. A 240-grain soft lead slug though the spinal cord at shoulder level tended to stop a man fast and make a hell of a mess where it came out.

"Know this one, Bat?"

Masterson shook his head. The second man was still on his hands and knees, a Smith & Wesson Schofield revolver in the dirt before him, now mostly covered with vomit. The man groaned as Slocum tucked a boot against his side and toppled him onto his back. Slocum's slug had taken him low in the belly, most likely turned a kidney to mush on its way out above his hip.

"God's—sake—help me," the square-jawed, heavy-shouldered man gasped. "I'm—gutshot—get me—doctor."

Slocum said casually, "Maybe. If you tell me why you two tried to bushwhack me."

The man twisted his head. Then his body convulsed as he retched. Nothing came up. His stomach's contents already lay in the street. "Mon—money," the stocky man said between heaves. "Lots—money. Damn, I—ain't never—had no luck—"

"How much? Who set you on me?" Slocum asked.

There was no answer. The man had passed out from the pain and shock. A few shouts sounded from beyond the alley.

"If you're open to suggestions, Slocum, I would recommend we withdraw from the field before somebody gets too curious about the gunshots and decides to check them out."

Slocum nodded reluctantly. "I'd sure like to have a little palaver with the gutshot one before he dies, but I suppose you're right." He turned back up the alley, ejecting the spent rounds and thumbing fresh loads into the Peacemaker as they walked. Neither man spoke again until they were a good three blocks from the alley.

Slocum glanced at Masterson. "Mind letting me know why you were were behind me in that alley?"

Masterson shrugged again. "I had a feeling there was mischief afoot. Saw those two across the street watching you when you left the White Elephant. I knew you could handle it, but thought I'd tag along a bit, just in case."

"I'm grateful you did, Bat," Slocum said earnestly. "I owe you one."

"May I inquire as to where you were headed when the shooting started?"

Slocum's jaw tightened. "To a whorehouse. To squeeze some answers out of somebody."

"It would be my pleasure to lend a hand," Masterson said.

"No, Bat. I appreciate the offer, but you've done enough. I already owe you for stepping in here. No offense, but this is my fight. No need for you to get your knuckles skinned in it."

"Fair enough," Masterson said. He touched his fingertips

to the brim of his derby. "Keep your hair on, Slocum. See you around." The slightly built gunman watched Slocum stride away, his steps controlled but purposeful. "I'd hate to be the one who has to face that man right now," Masterson muttered aloud.

8

Slocum shouldered his way past three men who stood in the doorway of Miss Esther's Boarding House for Young Ladies, ignoring their mutters of protest.

He had neither hurried nor dallied about during the short walk, and paused but once—to pick up a palm-sized chunk of broken concrete from a pile of rubble. He cradled the rough chunk in his left hand now. He strode straight for the end of the bar.

The big bartender glanced up and scowled as Slocum crossed the room. He moved to the end of the bar, his scarred hands clenched into fists.

"That's far enough, mister," the bartender said.

Slocum didn't speak or break stride. He just kept coming.

"All right, that's the way you want it—"

The bartender swung a looping haymaker toward Slocum's head. Like many big and heavily muscled men, he was slow. Slocum ducked the awkward swing and drove a knee into the bartender's groin. The big man grunted in pain and doubled over at the waist. Slocum swung his left hand in a sharp, choppy arc. The concrete chunk in his palm cracked against the back of the bartender's head. The barkeep went down as if he'd been hit with a Sharp's slug.

Slocum dropped the concrete fragment, reduced to half its original size by the force of the blow, aware of the sudden silence that had dropped on the noisy crowd.

At Slocum's right, a young man rose halfway from his chair, his hand at his belt. Slocum shot him a hard glare and shook his head. The man meekly sat back down.

Slocum didn't knock. He shoved open the door to Esther's office, stepped through, and slid the heavy iron bolt into place behind him. It would take half-a-dozen men to break through the thick door now. He had Miss Esther all to himself for a time. Long enough.

The gray-haired woman behind the desk glanced up irritably, but her scowl of anger turned to a twitch of surprise, and then a touch of apprehension, as she stared into Slocum's eyes. "Get the hell out of my office or I'll have Dan throw you out."

"Your man's taking a little nap," Slocum said. "He may or may not wake up. Touch that six-gun in the drawer of the desk and I'll kill you, Esther. I'd hate that. I don't like to drop a hammer on a woman, but by God, I just might make an exception in your case."

The madam looked deep into Slocum's eyes, saw the hard, cold fire there, and quickly came to the conclusion the black-haired man wasn't bluffing. She moved her hands well away from the desk drawer. Her fingers trembled.

"You'd better get out of my office, mister. Right now, before I get mad," she blustered.

"Who killed Hanna?" Slocum snapped.

"Who—what—" Esther's face turned even whiter. Her hand went to her mouth. She didn't know, Slocum thought. Or if she did, she was a fine actress. "Hanna? Dead? What—when?"

"She was crucified, Esther," Slocum said calmly. "Big railroad spikes driven through both wrists and her feet, nailed to the back of the barn at the wagon yard. Whether she was dead or not when she was nailed up, I don't know."

"Oh, my God—" Esther seemed to fold into her chair, her shoulders slumped. It wasn't theatrics, Slocum now knew for sure. She *hadn't* known. And the news had shaken her to the core. Somehow, the realization deflated his rage a bit. "When?" she finally asked, her voice quavering.

"Tonight. I just came from there. On the way here, a couple of toughs tried to bushwhack me."

Esther seemed to recover a bit of her former bluster. "Obviously, they missed. Damn shame."

"They won't try it again."

The faint touch of defiance faded from Esther's eyes. "You killed them, didn't you?"

A couple of taps, then a hammering of fists, rapped against the bolted door. "Miss Esther, you all right?" a voice called out.

Slocum knew he was running out of time. There had been enough killing tonight. He pinned a hard gaze on Esther. "Any man—or woman—who pulls a gun on me is fair game," he said coldly. "You and your friends might want to keep that in mind. Now, who's Bull?"

Esther's body tensed in a sudden burst of obvious fear. Still, she tried. Slocum gave her credit for that. She had sand. But she lowered her gaze under Slocum's steady stare. "Bull? I don't know anybody called Bull."

"Miss Esther!" The door creaked against its frame as someone tried to heave it open. Slocum ignored the call and the growing murmur from the crowd outside the office.

"The hell you don't know him, Esther. You're lying through your teeth, and you're not quite as good at it as you think. I'll lay odds it was Bull who killed Hanna. Or had her killed. And sicced a couple of shooters on me. Tell me about him."

"I can't—don't know—" She suddenly raised her head; the expression in her eyes pleading. "Slocum, I can't tell you. I'd wind up like—like Hanna." The words stuttered between quavering lips.

"Esther!" A thump sounded against the door. Someone had leaned a shoulder into it. Slocum knew he had reached the end of this trail. He would get nothing from Esther. She was more frightened of this man named Bull than she was of him, and with good reason. Slocum couldn't and wouldn't harm a woman without more justification than she had given him. He'd have to do it the hard way.

He said softly, "Esther, I'll give you a bit of advice, and

not the friendly kind. The next time you see Bull, tell him this: If he has Mary Connally, if he's harmed her in any way, I'll find out. And I'll kill him. If you get caught in the cross fire, I'm not responsible for what might happen to you.''

Slocum strode to the small back door he had noticed in his previous visit to Esther's office. ''By the way,'' he said in parting, ''the first man who comes through this door gets a slug between the eyes. Might want to mention that to your friends out there.'' Slocum stepped into the cluttered alleyway behind the building.

Twenty minutes later he was back in his room, pondering the bottle of rye on the sideboard by the washstand. After a moment he shook his head, remembering a bit of long-ago advice from an Irishman with whom he had ridden in the Powder River country:

''Never drink in anger, auld sod. It but makes one's bile more bitter.''

Slocum was past angry. A cold fire burned in his gut. He heeded the Irishman's advice and turned in.

Slocum normally came awake instantly, senses alert and tuned to the sounds around him.

Today he woke groggy, sluggish, even a bit disoriented. A glance at the window told him why. The thin curtains were backlighted by a bright sun, his room bathed in a soft white light.

He had slept past the noon hour. Even though it had been near dawn before he'd managed to fall asleep, the realization irritated him. Out on the plains, where a man should be, he would have put twenty miles of trail behind him by this time of day. Instead, he had lain abed like a suck-egg hound.

And he didn't feel rested. Sleep, when it finally came, had been fitful and troubled; the sheets beneath him were damp with sweat despite the chill in the room. Several times during the night he'd dreamed. A dream of a thin blond woman nailed to a barn. That she had been a whore didn't matter. It was the nature of her death that lingered in Slocum's mind. Had she been shot, strangled, or her throat cut, it wouldn't have jarred him so deeply. Violent ends came to prostitutes in tough towns. But not that way. He forced the lingering scene from his mind. It was done. It couldn't be changed. And he still had a job to do.

His stomach rumbled, reminding Slocum he hadn't eaten in a long time. Touchy Toucherman would have closed his cafe hours ago. That left the hotel restaurant. The fare wasn't as good there as it was at Touchy's, but it was better than nothing.

He finished his meal, was into his third cup of coffee, and almost felt human again. But his sense of time and place still seemed to be warped. Missing a sunrise did that to Slocum. Being in a town, where it was so crowded a man would have to ride an hour just to have room to change his mind, made it worse.

He sighed and picked up the newspaper again. The *Democrat* was in fine fettle today. Almost the entire front page was devoted to railing against Dallas, the city some forty miles east across the Trinity River. There was no love lost between the two towns. Slocum felt a slightly disgusted amusement at the idea of the civic leaders of two cities being involved in a pissing contest over which was the best place to do business, live, raise a family—or gamble. According to the *Democrat,* there wasn't a fair poker game to be found in all of Dallas.

As usual, he found nothing in the paper that might give him a clue as to Mary Connally's whereabouts. Nor was there a mention of the crucified prostitute or the deaths of two men in a dark alley in the Acre. He hadn't expected either. He'd already concluded it took the *Democrat* a couple of days to catch up with such news. The constant flailing at Dallas took too much of the editor's time apparently.

Slocum glanced up as a hesitant shuffle of feet broke his train of thought. A young boy, perhaps nine or ten, with red hair, an impressive swatch of freckles, and oversized ears that stood out from his head, stood a few feet away, studying him as if trying to decide whether to approach a big man who looked mad at the world. Slocum gestured the boy closer.

"You Mr. Slocum?" the boy asked.

"I'm him." The question grated on Slocum's raw nerves.

It seemed everybody in town knew who he was now. Even jug-eared kids.

The youth held out a plain white envelope. "I was asked to fetch this to you." Slocum nodded his thanks and took the envelope. The boy cleared his throat. "Lady said there was a dollar inside I'd get paid for bringin' it, mister. Like she didn't trust me enough to pay me first before I brung it."

"What do you think of that?" Slocum asked.

The youth grinned. "I reckon she's a pretty smart woman."

Slocum pulled a silver dollar from a vest pocket and handed it to the lad. The boy took the dollar and all but ran for the door. Slocum opened the envelope, and a grin cut through the burr of irritation.

There was no dollar inside. The kid had slicked him out of a buck.

Slocum figured the lad would go far. Maybe even become a banker, embezzler, politician, or some other such creature of lucrative larceny someday.

He flipped open the note. The paper held a faint scent of rosewater. The handwriting was feminine, a free, flowing script, and expectedly brief and to the point:

"Imperative I see you. Have information. I'll send a hack for you at three o'clock. Alley behind the hotel." It was signed simply, "A.J."

Slocum pocketed the note. The idea of seeing A.J. McDonough again lifted his gray spirits a bit, despite the ominous tone of the message. At least he had time to get a bath and shave.

Slocum nodded his thanks to the hack driver and stood for a moment, studying the house on Bluff Street.

A.J. McDonough's home was a one-and-a-half-story building made of carefully fitted stone, with two kiln-dried brick chimneys sprouting from the Mexican-style baked-clay shingles of the roof. Compared to the sprawling three-story Southern plantation and Greek-style mansions up and down the street, A.J.'s house tended toward the modest side. She might be rich, he mused, but she didn't flaunt it.

At his back, the bluff fell away sharply toward the wooded

Trinity River below, little more than a sluggish stream now. When the spring rains came, A.J.'s home would be well above the reach of the floodwaters.

He strode up the flagstone walk flanked by massive oak and sugar maple trees. A squirrel fussed at him from an oak branch. Slocum stepped onto the covered veranda and reached for the brass door-knocker. The heavy door swung open before he touched it.

"Come in, Slocum," A.J. said with a faint smile. She wore a plain dark-gray housedress that seemed to deepen the gun-metal color of her eyes. "I'm about to crack the seal on a bottle of Tennessee's finest."

"Second best offer I've had all day," Slocum said.

"What was the best?"

"A note from a high-class lady." He removed his hat as he stepped into the foyer. The place might be austere on the outside, but inside it was no dugout. Expensive rugs covered most of the polished hardwood floors. A Navajo tapestry based on a sand painting hung on one wall. Slocum saw at a glance it was the real thing, not a crude Eastern reproduction. A pair of cut-glass-crystal gas lamps hissed softly on each wall.

"I'm glad Johnny Pockets was able to deliver my note," A.J. said. "Did he con you out of a quarter when he handed it to you?"

Slocum grinned. "No. A dollar."

She chuckled, the sound low and musical. "That's why we call him Johnny Pockets. Always working both ends of the track. He'll be an absolutely magnificent con artist when he grows up." She took Slocum's hat and duster and hung them on a mahogany hall tree in the corner. "But he's a trustworthy messenger. I feel perfectly safe sending confidential notes with Johnny. He can't tell anyone else what they say. He can't read."

Slocum checked the urge to sweep her into his arms and bury his face in the raven-black auburn hair. From the tone of her note, this was a serious meeting.

"What's the information you have for me?"

"It'll keep for a few minutes. Let's have that drink first." He followed A.J. through the main room with its heavily padded, almost masculine, furnishings, past the massive fire-place where embers gleamed red and orange. She opened the door to a smaller room.

"Forgive the clutter," she said. "I've been up to my butt in paperwork, as usual."

The room obviously served as an office. A sturdy mahogany desk, mostly covered with papers, dominated the room. Against the back wall, a short bar similar to the one in A.J.'s private railroad car gleamed under a coat of wax. She waved him to an overstuffed leather chair and busied herself behind the bar.

A moment later she handed him a glass and took her own seat in a smaller but equally soft chair separated from his by a low table on which rested a cut-crystal ashtray. She gestured around with her glass. "Welcome to my lodge, Slocum. This room is where I hide out when there's work to be done and deals to be cut."

She sipped at her drink and reached for a cigarette, ignoring the thin holder beside the ashtray. She tapped the ready-roll on a thumbnail to tamp the tobacco, lit the smoke, and squinted through the blue-white swirls at Slocum.

"It seems you've created quite a stir in Fort Worth," she said. "Those two men you shot in the alley were hired to kill you."

Slocum lifted an eyebrow. "How did you find out about that so soon? The shooting hasn't been in the papers, and I thought you didn't have any sources in the Acre."

"I said I didn't have *many* sources there," she said, "but the few I do have are fully trustworthy. And they, in turn, have sources." She sipped at her drink. "I was delighted to find those two men didn't get the job done."

"So was I."

"You don't seem overly surprised or concerned by the news."

"I suspected as much. They didn't act like common robbers. If it hadn't been for Bat Masterson, I might have walked straight into a load of buckshot. I had other things on my mind at the time."

A.J. nodded solemnly. "The prostitute who was crucified."

She shuddered slightly. "There's no good way to go, but that was particularly horrible."

Slocum winced. "It's my fault. She knew more about Mary than she let on. She was supposed to meet me later that night. I believe she was killed as a warning to others."

"Likely she was. But you shouldn't blame yourself for it, Slocum. Blame the man—or men—who did it." A.J. drew on her cigarette, a worried expression in her eyes. "There's a price on your head. Five hundred dollars."

"Lot of money," Slocum said. He sipped at his glass. As expected, it was prime whiskey. Smooth and mellow, but with a pleasant kick when it hit the belly.

"Enough to make a girl worry," she said. "Not that I think you can't take care of yourself." Her voice softened, but the concern remained in her steel-colored eyes. "There are people in Fort Worth who would kill their own mothers for that kind of money."

"The amount's not the question," Slocum said calmly. "The real question is, who's putting it up? Which brings up another question: Why? Assuming it's not the work of somebody out to get me for the pleasure of it, to settle some old score, another question follows—why go to so much trouble and expense over one girl when there are so many around?"

A.J. studied the ash on her cigarette for a moment, frowning. "I have a theory, Slocum. Unfortunately, I have no proof. At least none that I can take to the law, or the newspapers. Yet."

"Proof is for the law, A.J. Let's hear it."

She finished her drink, went to the bar, brought back the bottle, and topped off both glasses.

"It's far-fetched."

"Fetch it out. I'm open to anything."

She hesitated for a moment, then said, "Promise me one thing first, Slocum. That you'll move out of that hotel. They know where you're staying, and they're watching the place."

"The short man in the brown hat and sheepskin coat and the big one in the overalls and fur cap who take turns on watch?"

"You knew?"

"For a day and a half now."

She reached across the table and put a hand on his arm. "Then you know how important it is for you to go somewhere else. Someplace you'll be safe. Like here."

Slocum stared at her for several heartbeats, saw the pleading expression in her eyes, then shook his head. "I can't, A.J. It might put you in danger, and I won't allow that."

Her shoulders sagged a bit. "I was afraid you'd say that. All right, I know when I've met a man as stubborn as I am. So we'll compromise. Stay here for two days—one day, at least. Until we've had a chance to find out where Mary Connally is."

"I'd rather you didn't get involved," Slocum said. "You'd be taking quite a risk if the wrong people found out you were helping me, A.J."

"Dammit, I didn't put together a small fortune and take over a railroad without rolling the dice once in a while. I'm offering you my help. Take it, for Christ's sake."

Slocum started to decline again, but something in the set of her jaw and the look in her eye stayed his tongue. The simple fact was that A.J. McDonough wasn't the least bit afraid. He nodded. "All right. If you assure me it won't cause any trouble for you, I'll agree to that."

"No trouble I can't handle, Slocum. The fact is, I've wanted to put these men out of business for some time. What they're doing is"—she groped for the right word—"abominable." She leaned back in her chair and peered over steepled fingertips at him. "You've no doubt heard of the white-slave trade. Where women are abducted, held in captivity, and then sold into prostitution abroad. Europe, China, the Middle East. A girl like Mary—slender pretty, and most importantly, a blue-eyed blonde—will bring as much as fifteen to twenty thousand dollars in some of those markets. This isn't the first time it's happened here."

Slocum's heart beat faster. "There have been others?"

"I'm convinced there have been two others, possibly more, taken from the Acre here, and another in Dallas. Two in San Antonio, one more in Waco. All blond, all blue-eyed, all pretty—or would be pretty with a proper diet and medical attention. And all prostitutes who have no one to notice they've disappeared, or care.''

Slocum picked up his glass, swirling the amber liquid for a moment. ''And Mary Connally could be the next?''

''That would be my guess.''

''May I ask how you know these things?''

A faint smile touched her full lips. ''I know a lot about what's going on around here, Slocum. Information drives the world, not machines and money. I read every newspaper I can lay my hands on, from Boston to San Francisco, and I listen. A lot.'' A.J. took another sip from her drink. The smile faded. ''Also, I've taken something of an interest in young women who have had a much harder life than I. Perhaps it's a bit of guilt on my part, for climbing above what could have been my own fate in other circumstances. I'd like to think there's a touch of altruism there too. Women aren't cattle, to be owned, bought, and sold.''

Slocum nodded. He couldn't argue the point. But a deep philosophical and political conversation wouldn't help him find Mary. He tossed back the last of his drink.

''How long do you think I have left to find her before it's too late?'' he asked.

The frown lines between A.J.'s brows deepened. ''Not long, I fear. There's a ship, the *Orient Clipper,* leaving from Corpus Christi in a week. It makes one stop in San Francisco, then sails straight for Hong Kong. If I were to guess, that would be the ship Mary—and others—will be on.''

Slocum gnawed on that information for a moment, a warm spot that wasn't from whiskey growing in his gut. ''Any idea who's behind it?''

''In Fort Worth, three ring bosses. An unholy alliance, you might say. The supplier is Esther. The missing girls worked at her place the last time they were seen. Another leg of the triangle is a Chinese called Ho Chan. He runs the most popular opium parlor—hop house, I believe they're called—in town. It's he who gets the girls addicted to opium and other drugs until they're little more than walking dead, oblivious to their surroundings until it's too late.''

''And the third?''

"A black man who goes by the name of Dardus Freeman."

"Who also goes by the name of Bull?"

A.J. nodded. "How did you know that?"

"That's the name Hanna mentioned. She was going to tell me about Bull. And Esther almost peed in her pants when I mentioned the name. I don't think Esther's the type who scares easily, but she's obviously frightened to death of the man."

"With good reason. Bull Freeman is brutal and totally ruthless, Slocum. He's said to have killed half-a-dozen men with his bare hands. Only the Lord knows how many others, men and women, he's ordered killed." A.J. reached for another cigarette. "He's called Bull for a good reason. He's huge, one of the biggest men I've ever seen. Over six and a half feet tall, three hundred pounds, and very little of it fat. And he's got money to hire as many toughs or guns as he needs. Bull Freeman is dangerous, Slocum. Damned dangerous."

She paused to light the smoke, then continued. "He runs a couple of gambling dens and whorehouses here, one uptown, one in the Negro section. The uptown place caters to all races and is generally on the up and up, except that anybody who wins a great deal of money at his tables usually winds up dead or beaten—and in either case, robbed of his winnings. The place in the Negro section is strictly for darkies. It's called the Plantation. Freeman's way of thumbing his nose at the white race, I'd guess. Any white man who walks in there has a damn slim chance of walking back out."

A.J. paused for a moment, then grimaced. "Freeman hates white people. For some reason, he especially hates women, and young blond women in particular. He takes great delight in degrading them. Once they're addicted to drugs, he uses them himself for a while. Then he—he keeps them for a time longer. For the amusement of his black friends. Then he sells them."

Slocum's gut went cold. "The son of a bitch. When I take Mary out of there, I'll leave his balls nailed to the wall."

"Wait a minute, Slocum," A.J. said. "I don't know for sure he has her. As I said before, it's just a theory. By noon tomorrow, we just might know."

"How?"

"I've asked one of my employees, a tie-spiker on a rail repair crew, to check out the Plantation tonight. He's a good, solid man who just happens to be black as midnight. And completely reliable. Freeman doesn't know him. George will find out whether or not Mary is there. If she is, then we'll decide on the best way to get her out."

Slocum raised a hand. "Not we, A.J. By now, half the people in town probably know I'm looking for Mary. If they want to stop me bad enough to put a price on my head, and they know you're helping me, they could kill you too. Or worse."

"I'm not afraid of them, Slocum."

"From what you tell me, you should be."

"But you aren't."

"Afraid? No. I've gone up against enough bad men that I know them fairly well. That gives me an advantage. That doesn't mean I'm not cautious as hell. But this one time, I'm going to put my foot down. I'm bigger than you are and I care about what could happen to you. You've done more than enough already. When the time comes to get Mary, I don't want you anywhere around. I couldn't handle it if you got hurt on my account. Even without that, it's my job—and mine alone—to get her back. Agreed?"

A.J. nodded reluctantly. "You've made your point, and I respect it, Slocum. Agreed. But there are tough, ruthless men involved in this. If you get Mary out without getting killed in the attempt, they'll come after you. I don't doubt your ability for a moment, but one man against that crowd would be odds I wouldn't cover in any wager."

Slocum managed a wry grin. "I wouldn't fade the bet either, A.J. But I took on this job. I'll finish it."

A.J. drained her glass, stubbed out her smoke, and gazed at Slocum for a moment. The worried look faded from her gray eyes, slowly replaced by a hint of mischief tinted by a sultry glow.

"I hereby declare the business portion of this meeting concluded," she said. "Now the second half of the story. The main reason I asked you was on Mary's behalf. But I also had purely selfish and personal reasons. I've given my cook and housekeeper the day off. We have the place all to ourselves.

You're staying the night, of course—if you're so inclined.''

Slocum's anger melted under her coltish gaze. Another, more comfortable, warmth began to take its place. He nodded. "I am most definitely so inclined. Or I'd ask you to check to see if I still have a pulse."

Her laugh was throaty and musical. "I intend to check, Slocum. In my own way. But first, we eat. Get the necessaries out of the way before we get to the real necessaries, so to speak. Besides, I'm absolutely famished. My talents don't extend to cooking, but I did toss together a light dinner." She stood and reached for his hand. "It should be passable if you're hungry enough. Bring the bottle. I feel like good whiskey tonight, not wine."

9

Slocum leaned back in his chair, sighed, and smiled at A.J. McDonough, who was seated across from him at the small kitchen table. On a big platter between them lay the mortal remains of a fair-sized pullet, sacrificed to the oven and the gods of two stomachs.

"Looks like a chicken crawled up here and died," Slocum said. "I thought you said you couldn't cook, A.J. That was the best meal I've had in weeks."

She batted her eyes at him in mock embarrassment and flirtation. "Why, thank you, sir. My, my. Flattery will get you most anything with a shy little violet like myself, you know."

"Shy? I hardly think that applies to you." Slocum swirled the remaining whiskey in his glass and peered over the rim at her. "Pardon the crude expression, Miss McDonough, but even though you're obviously all woman, I truly believe you've got more balls than any man I've ever met."

Her steel-gray eyes twinkled with delight. "Now *that* is sincere and much appreciated flattery. Especially coming from you." She hefted the bottle, drained the last couple of shots into their glasses, and stood. "Bring another jug from the bar while I clean up the wreckage here, please. Then we'll have a smoke, a couple more drinks, relax in the main room, and let dinner settle for a spell. There's no hurry—well, maybe a little urgency—but anything worth having is worth waiting for a few minutes. Besides, I don't move well on a full stomach."

101

Slocum nodded in agreement. He didn't make love as well on a stretched gut himself. And, he had to admit, with A.J. he enjoyed the anticipation. He hadn't felt that way toward too many women. But then he'd never met many—make that any—women quite like A.J. He realized his belly wasn't the only thing feeling stuffed.

By the time he'd found another bottle of the brand they were drinking and brought it back to the kitchen, A.J. had most of the dishes cleared away. He opened the bottle, topped off her glass, and gave her a quick kiss on the side of her neck. "Can I lend a hand?"

"I've got it under control, Slocum. Quit trying to get me all hot and bothered, and have a seat. I'll be with you in a minute."

Slocum settled into his chair at the kitchen table and filled his glass. Firing up a cigarillo, he watched her at work. Her movements were fluid, no energy wasted, even when she lifted a hand to brush back a strand of stray hair. There was nothing delicate about A.J. McDonough, Slocum mused, but there was no doubt about her being a woman. The gray housedress she wore clung to a figure that was near enough to perfect that any minor flaws just made her all that much more desirable. The dress clung to her long, muscular legs. Slocum was content for the moment just to watch her.

By the time he'd shortened the cigarillo by an inch, she had hung her dish towel on a peg beside the kitchen cabinet. She came to him, leaned a hip against his shoulder, and held out her half-empty glass. He topped it off. "Make yourself comfortable out in the main room, Slocum," she said with a smile. "I'll join you shortly."

Slocum sat on a plush leather couch in the expansive main room, nursed a drink, and listened to the sound of running water from upstairs. He didn't care for a lot of things that progress had brought, but one of the exceptions to his disdain toward civilization was indoor plumbing. It was becoming more common these days, even in frontier towns smaller than Fort Worth. He ran a hand across his chin, and felt no scratchy stubble. It hadn't been that long since he'd shaved.

The sound of water rushing through pipes stopped.

The ornate grandfather clock in a corner hadn't ticked many times before he heard the voice from the stairs:

"Hey, cowboy. Buy a girl a drink?"

He glanced up, and his breath caught in his throat.

A.J. stood at the top of the landing, her left hand resting on the polished mahogany banister. She still wore the gray house-dress, but nothing underneath. She hadn't bothered with the buttons. Erect nipples tipped her impressively full breasts. She cocked a leg. Slocum caught a quick glimpse of the dense triangle of hair above her thigh.

He finally found his tongue. "My pleasure," he said, "especially when it's her whiskey to begin with."

She chuckled and tossed her head. "Bring the bottle up here. We'll be more comfortable in my room. That couch is nice, but I wouldn't choose it for a field of combat."

"Oh. We're going to fight?"

Her grin bordered on the outright wicked. "Close-range. Extremely close, friend. Get off your butt and bring the jug."

Slocum picked up the bottle, and glanced at the shoulder rig holding his Peacemaker that lay on the table beside him.

"Bring it along," A.J. said casually. "We'll both feel better if it's within easy reach."

At the top of the stairs, he paused as she took the bottle, then followed her a few steps down a carpeted hallway. She nudged a door open with a hip and flashed a warm smile at him.

"My chambers, sir."

Slocum stepped into the room and took it in at a glance. It was more than comfortable. It was downright luxurious. An oversized four-poster bed dominated half the space, a small pedestal table at one side of the carved headboard. Polished brass gas lamps, turned low, cast a soft glow over turned-down blankets and pale-blue sheets that had the sheen of silk.

Heavy damask drapes covered a window in the far wall. A small couch and overstuffed chair sat beneath the window, sharing a low table. The thick rug on the floor matched the drapes. The rest of the furniture was solidly built, obviously hand-crafted of the finest hardwoods, and seemed to glow under a thick layer of wax. A faint scent of rosewater misted the air. A.J. knew how to live comfortably, Slocum again thought.

"Like it?" A.J. asked as she pushed the door closed with her rump.

"Nice furnishings." He turned to face her, conscious of the growing tightness in his groin. "But the nicest furnishings just walked in behind me."

Her gunmetal-gray eyes went smoky, a soft smile tilting the corners of her full lips. "Slocum, you're a sweet-talking son of a bitch, but you're not going to get any until you put the gun down." She nodded toward the table beside the bed. "I'll pour while you're doing that."

He folded the shoulder holster with care and placed it on the table beside the bed, grips turned toward the pillows and within easy reach. He turned as A.J. approached, took both drinks from her hands, placed them beside the holstered Colt, and pulled her into his arms.

For some time, he was content to just hold her. To feel the firm softness and warmth of her, the clean smell of her hair. He could feel her heart pound against his chest, hear her breathing quicken. He nuzzled the soft curve where her neck met her shoulder, brushed his lips across the dark skin there, heard her soft sigh. She pushed more firmly against him, her hands moving across his back. Then she raised her head and kissed him, first softly, then with a growing urgency. Her tongue flicked against his. Slocum finally broke the kiss, put both hands on her waist, and pushed her back a foot or so.

Her fingers reached for the buttons of his shirt. He reached up and caught her hand. "Not just yet," he said, his own breathing shallow and rapid. He sat on the edge of the bed. His eyes were at the level of her belly button. "Just stand there a minute."

He released her hand and pushed aside the thin cloth of her unbuttoned dress, exposing her breasts and the dense black triangle of hair where her thighs met. The faint, musky scent of woman caressed his nostrils. Slocum reached a hand up and stroked the smooth swell of her left breast; her breath caught in her throat as his palm brushed across her swollen nipple. Then he slipped his hands to her waist, pulled her to him, and kissed her below the navel. She shuddered at the touch of his lips on her skin.

"What—what—" Her words were husky, breathless. Slocum stroked her stomach with the flat of his tongue, then flicked its tip back and forth, tracing a path down her belly. "Oh, my God," she whispered. She pushed her shoulders back and hips forward as Slocum's tongue moved past the edge of the thicket of crotch hair, down the front of her thighs, back up the warm skin toward the heat so near his face. Her breath came in jerky, ragged gasps. She shuddered again; her legs seemed to spread of their own will, opening her to him.

Her whimpers turned to a deep, soft moan as Slocum's tongue inched upward, stroked the hot, damp crease of her outer lips. He took his time, toyed with her a moment despite the growing ache at his own crotch. Then he forced her labia aside with his tongue and stroked it gently across her swollen clitoris. She cried aloud at the touch; her hips pressed against his face, her legs spread wider. Slocum flicked his tongue against the swollen nub of tissue. Her back arched. A low moan started deep in her throat, her head thrown back, hands on the sides of his head, holding him against her. Then she shuddered again, every muscle in her body convulsed, and her cry broken into a small series of puffed exclamations.

Her orgasm seemed to last for several seconds before her muscles slowly went slack. Slocum moved his tongue away from her crotch, and back up her belly, then felt her weight suddenly collapse against him.

"My God, Slocum," she gasped, "Nobody ever—did that—to me before—"

"I hope you didn't mind."

"Mind? Christ, no! It was—hell, I can't describe it—it was—different. Unlike any sensation I've ever had . . ." Her voice trailed away for a moment, but her breathing quickened again. "And it's made me horny as hell." She slipped her hand to Slocum's crotch, stroked his painfully swollen shaft. Her eyes widened in mock astonishment. "Good Lord, Slocum, I do believe you've got a problem. A nice problem. Either get out of those clothes now, or I'll tear them off you."

By the time Slocum had stripped, A.J. had stretched out on

the bed. The light from the gas lamps danced over her dark skin. Slocum stood for a moment beside the bed, staring at her, feeling the ache in his testicles.

"What are you doing?" she asked.

"Just looking. A.J., you are the most flat-out beautiful woman I've even met."

She ran the tip of her tongue across her lips. Her gaze flicked to his crotch and back to his face. "Like I said, Slocum, you're a sweet-talking son of a bitch. Come here."

Slocum leaned back against the pillow, spent, completely relaxed and content, a cigarillo in his right hand, his left arm underneath A.J.'s neck.

He sighed in lingering disbelief. Even after her first orgasm standing beside the bed and all the natural juices that triggered, A.J. had still been tight. After his first one and her third—or fourth, he wasn't sure which, and he didn't think either of them were keeping track—he'd started to roll off her, thinking he was used up. But she'd started working those inside muscles again, and the first thing he knew, the second explosion shook him, deeper and more intense than the first one.

Finally, they'd separated and stretched out side by side, both too sated and exhausted to even reach for a glass of whiskey.

"One thing, Slocum," A.J. said, her voice drowsy, "don't go thinking this means we're engaged."

"What?"

"Just wanted to make sure we had everything straight. You're a fine-looking man and a hell of a good fuck, and there's a lot you could teach me in bed. But I'm not hunting a husband, so you can relax about that. This doesn't mean we have any hold over each other. No strings. No regrets. Agreed?"

Slocum didn't reply for a couple of heartbeats. He wasn't sure what to say; the notion had never entered his mind. It still took him aback a bit to hear A.J. lay it out so plain. Finally, he managed a nod. "Agreed."

She worked up the energy to inch her way up to a sitting position, lean back against the headboard, and light a cigarette. "We're a lot alike, Slocum. You and me," she said as she shook out the match. "We know what we want, and we go after it, and we don't quit until we've got it. And we're both loners, in our own way." She puffed a perfect smoke ring. It drifted toward the ceiling, gradually losing its shape until it became a faint gray haze. "When your job here is done, you'll ride on. And I'll go back to doing what I do best. Making money."

Slocum admitted to himself that she was right. They couldn't be a long-haul team, even if they wanted to be. What they had now was enough. For both of them.

She reached over Slocum, brushing her breast across his lips in the process. He couldn't resist the temptation. He licked the nipple as it went by. And again when it came back. The nipple was hard again.

"Lecherous bastard," she said with a soft chuckle and a warm smile as she settled back on her side of the bed, handing Slocum a drink when he'd inched himself up against the head-board enough to sit.

They drank for a moment in silence before A.J. finally spoke. Her tone was solemn. "Slocum, I think I told you on the train that I don't spread my legs for just any man. I don't want you to get the idea that I'm some sort of wanton slut."

He shook his head. "Never crossed my mind, A.J.," he said honestly. "I've seen class. You've got it. In spades."

"But I'll never forgive you for one thing."

"What'd I do?"

She sighed heavily. "Spoiled me. After you, I'll probably never want a man again. I wouldn't want to chance the disappointment."

"Mighty kind of you to say so, ma'am, but I doubt that. There'll be somebody come along who fits you just fine."

She tapped the ashes from her cigarette into the ashtray she'd placed on her stomach. She shook her head. "I doubt that, Slocum."

"Why? You're still young, you're the prettiest woman in nine states and three territories, and you're intelligent."

She half smiled. "Thanks for noticing. The intelligent part, I mean. Most men find that threatening in a woman. No, Slocum, I seriously doubt I'll ever marry. It's the dark side of having money. I'd never be sure whether the man wanted me, or just access to my bank accounts.''

"Did you wonder that about me?''

"Not for a minute. I know you'd rather have money than not have it, but that's not the driving force in your life." She stubbed out her smoke, moved the ashtray from her belly to the floor, and finished her drink. She linked her fingers together, raised her arms above her head, and stretched. The arch of her back lifted her perfectly formed breasts. Her dark nipples were still erect, glistening from the strokes of his tongue.

"Damn," A.J. said.

Slocum's brows arched. "What's the problem?''

A slow smile lifted the corners of her full lips, dimpling her cheeks and deepening the small crow's-feet wrinkles at the corner of those smoky gray eyes.

"I thought I was done. Now I've got that tingle again.'' She lowered her arms and rolled atop him.

Slocum came awake instantly, the Peacemaker in his hand and cocked before he'd fully sat up on the bed. Beside him, A.J. also sat bolt upright. The bang of the brass door-knocker seemed overly loud in the quiet of the house.

A.J. didn't speak. She rolled out of bed, slipped into the gray housedress, and buttoned it as she strode toward the door in her bare feet. Slocum stepped into his pants, looped the shoulder rig loosely into place, and followed a step behind.

The banging on the door became loud enough to hurt Slocum's ears as they went down the stairs. He touched A.J.'s elbow and inclined his head. She nodded in understanding. She waited a few seconds until Slocum moved to the side of the door away from the hinges, holding the Peacemaker at shoulder height, the muzzle toward the ceiling. He nodded as the pounding started again.

"Coming!" A.J. called out. The knocking stopped. Slocum heard a horse snort outside, the creak and clank of harness leather. She swung open the door.

"Amos! What—''

The drayman stepped inside, and started as he saw Slocum standing against the wall with a gun in hand.

"It's all right, Amos. He's a friend. What's happened?"

"It's George, ma'am. He's been hurt. I'm afraid it's pretty bad."

"My God," A.J. said, her hand at her mouth. "How? Where is he?"

"He was beaten, ma'am. His boy found him an alley down by the Plantation. Little George came to me. We got him to Doc Whitley's office. I thought I'd better let you know. He may make it. He may not."

"Wait, Amos. Give us a minute to get dressed, then take us to him."

Twenty minutes later, the man named Amos pulled the team to a stop before a two-story stone building, lights from the lower floor weakening against the coming dawn. The horses' breaths sent puffs of steam against the sharp late-winter air.

A.J. clambered down from the dray before Slocum could offer her a hand. The oversized leather bag around her shoulder, with her Colt Sheriff's Model .45 inside, swayed against the side of her coat as she strode rapidly toward the door. A newly painted sign above the door read simply, "Adam A. Whitley, M.D."

Whitley glanced up and nodded brusquely as A.J. and Slocum stepped into the examining room, now awash in flat white light from half-a-dozen gas lamps along the walls. Another gas lamp hissed beside the waist-high table on which a thick-shouldered black man lay, his shirt stripped away. The black man's face looked like a slab of just-skinned beef.

"How is he, Adam?" A.J. asked, her tone apprehensive. It was the first time she had spoken since the brief conversation with the drayman.

Whitley cut a quick look at her and Slocum, then expertly threaded a curved needle. "Not as bad as I'd feared when Amos brought him in. He's had a terrific beating, A.J. As near as I can tell at this point, he has a broken jaw, fractured collarbone, and three broken ribs. His skull was exposed. Likely he has a concussion, but I don't think the skull was cracked." Whitley swabbed an oozing section of scalp, worried the flap back into place, and went to work with the needle.

Slocum thought Adam Whitley a touch on the young side

to be a doctor, not even thirty yet. But it was obvious the tall, lean man knew his business. The needle did its work with quick, smooth efficiency. The sight made Slocum wince inwardly. He'd had to stitch up a few of his own wounds, and those of others, from time to time. He knew it hurt like hell.

Whitley finished with the scalp, switched to a straight needle, and went to work reattaching an ear that had been partly torn away. The black man moaned softly. Whitley paused, reached for a syringe, and eased it into the man's arm. The low moaning sound eased within a few seconds as the morphine took effect. The Negro's eyes fluttered open, then finally came into hazy focus on A.J.'s face.

"Sorry—ma'am—I didn't—get the—job done." The words were soft, slurred, and barely audible. "When I—asked about—white girl—they jumped me."

A.J. put a hand on the black's thick forearm. "Hush now, George. You shouldn't be talking."

"On the contrary," the physician said without looking up from his work. "It's probably the best thing he could be doing right now. It'll give me an indication if there's a major concussion, or perhaps any brain damage. Do you know where you are, George?"

"Yas—yassuh. I knows."

"How many children do you have, and what are their names and ages?"

George struggled through an impressive string of names and ages. Slocum quit counting at seven. The man's words became weaker as the effects of the morphine deepened. George turned an increasingly fogged gaze back to A.J.

"Didn't have—no chance—to fight much. Marked one—of 'em up some—busted nose, couple teeth—big nigger—" The dark brown eyes slowly closed. Slocum thought the man had passed out, but his lips moved. "Didn't—see her—but reckon she's there. Back room—two big men—moved in front of it—soon's I—asked about the girl." His eyes opened again. "Reckon I won't be doin' no rail work for a spell."

A.J. squeezed the thick forearm. "Don't you worry about a thing, George. You won't miss a payday. I'll see that your family is well cared for until you're back on your feet." She turned to Whitley. "What's the outlook, Adam?"

"He should make it," the doctor said. "As best I can tell, there were no major internal injuries. But he's absorbed a lot of punishment. I'm concerned about possible brain injuries. I'll want to keep him here for a few days, where I can keep a close watch on him and make sure we have no unexpected complications."

A.J. nodded. "Keep him as long as you feel necessary and do whatever it takes, Adam. I'll pay whatever it costs. He's a good man."

Slocum listened to the exchange and studied the black man on the table. George had apparently lost consciousness, either from the effects of the beating or the morphine. It was probably for the best. Slocum was surprised the man had even survived. George had taken as brutal a beating as Slocum had ever seen that left a man still living.

"There's nothing you can do here, A.J.," Whitley said, leaning over a sink as he scrubbed the blood from his hands with a soaped brush and something that smelled sharp in the nostrils. "My nurse will be coming on duty in a half hour. She can keep a close eye on George until I've taken care of some other patients. You might as well go on home and get some rest."

"Doc," Slocum said as Whitley toweled off his hands, "can I talk to you for a minute?"

Whitley nodded. "I've got a bit of time." He nodded toward a small office opening off the examining room. The office was jammed to the rafters with books, glass cabinets containing medical equipment, vials, pharmaceutical jars, and wrapped packets. "What can I do for you?"

"I think I'm about to get into something I don't know the first thing about," Slocum said. "I've had some experience at sobering up drunks, but I've never dealt with anyone addicted to drugs. How would I go about helping somebody like that?"

"That depends," Whitley said solemnly, brows furrowed. "What drugs?"

"I'm not sure. Maybe several. Let's assume the worst. A combination of some sort."

Whitley studied Slocum with interest. "Obviously, the patient isn't you."

"No. She's a prostitute."

Whitley's frown deepened. "Many of the women in that particular line of work are addicted. I suppose it's the only escape that makes things halfway tolerable for them, considering the life they lead. Quite a number of them commit suicide every year, especially those working the Acre." He paused for a moment, running a hand along his jaw. "Helping someone like that is difficult. Does she want to quit?"

"Probably not. I haven't seen her yet."

"Then the problem just got more difficult. Weaning a person who doesn't want to be weaned is a tough job. If you could bring her here, say, for at least a couple of weeks?"

"I can't do that, Doctor," Slocum said. He studied the young physician a moment and decided he could trust him. "I've come to Fort Worth to get her and take her back to her parents, whether she wants to go or not. In short, I'll kidnap her if I have to. What has to be done will have to be done on the trail, away from any towns."

"No medical help?"

"Not where we're going. There's one more complication. When I get her out, there may—probably will—be men hunting us. Men who want her back."

Whitley sighed. "Then you've got more than one problem. Getting a person to stop taking drugs, even when they want to stop, is a challenge. To force them to stop against their will is almost impossible. For both parties."

"I've got to try, Doc."

Whitley was silent for moment, thinking. Finally, he said, "Let's assume the worst. That we're looking at venous injections of pure cocaine. It's normally a powder, but there's a way to heat it until it turns liquid, and then inject it directly. If the patient is also using opium and morphine—and the combination hasn't already killed them—it's even more difficult."

Slocum checked the stir of impatience in his gut. He had a lot to do and not much time to do it in. "I'd appreciate any suggestions, Doc. Like I said, this is one bear I've never fought."

"Very well. First of all, you're going to have to build up her physical strength while weaning her off the drugs. People like her don't eat. Within a few weeks, they're near starvation, but they don't feel hunger. They just want the next pipe or needle, nothing else. The physical deterioration leaves them susceptible to illness and infections that wouldn't be a threat to a healthy person."

That, Slocum thought, would explain the difference between Mary Connally's tintype image and the responses he'd had from people who thought they might have seen her.

"Some physicians believe abrupt withdrawal is the only way to get someone off drugs," Whitley said, "but I think there's a more humane—and, in the long term, more effective—way. I would recommend a slow tapering off. Give her just enough at first to ease her discomfort and dull the pangs of her addiction. Gradually decrease the dosage until, after a time, she no longer has the physical need for drugs."

Whitley strode to a heavily stocked cabinet and studied the contents. Over his shoulder, he said, "To be perfectly honest with you, getting her free of drugs is only half the battle. A bruised and broken body can be mended. We haven't figured out yet how to fix a bruised mind. But first things first."

A few minutes later, Slocum stood alongside A.J. and the hack driver outside the doctor's quarters, a package wrapped in brown butcher paper and tied with string tucked under his arm.

A.J. stared into Slocum's eyes for a moment. "You're leaving now, aren't you?"

"Yes, A.J. I have no choice."

Her eyes seemed to mist a bit, but she merely nodded. "Is there anything else I can do?"

Slocum started to shake his head, then hesitated. "There is one thing." He tore a blank page from his expense tally book, scribbled the colonel's address on it, and handed it to A.J. "I would appreciate it if you would send him a wire when I get Mary safely out of town. Just say something to the effect that we're headed home, but it will be quite a while before we get there. And one other thing—take care of yourself. If there's trouble, I don't want you hurt." He ached to take her in his arms. But not in front of the hack driver.

A.J. had no such reservations.

She came to him, embraced him, and kissed him gently. Then she stepped back. "I'll stay out of the way, Slocum. I hope all goes well for you. And her. If there should be something more I could do, just send a wire or note. And if you get back to Fort Worth someday . . ." Her voice trailed away.

"You'll be the first to know, A.J., and that's more than a promise. It's a threat." Slocum paused at the dray long enough to fetch his rifle, then touched his fingers to his hat brim and strode away. The emptiness in his gut seemed to grow with each step. A.J. McDonough was a hell of a woman.

But he still had a job to do. The trick was to stay alive in the process.

10

Slocum crouched behind an oak barrel at the back of the saddle shop, the scent of lye-based tanning fluid sharp in his nostrils as he studied the alley leading past the rear door of the Commercial Hotel.

Trash, dust, and an occasional wisp of powdery drifting snow swirled and eddied before the freshening north wind that whipped around the buildings in the flat gray light of dawn. Slocum blinked against the dust and ignored the bite of the wind against his cheek, waiting and watching. There was a lot to do and little time to do it in, but a man who got in too big a hurry usually got himself dead.

A flicker of movement a few yards away caught his attention. Bull Freeman's boys had finally realized that the hotel had two ways in and out. They now had someone watching the back door as well as the front. The man waited in the recessed rear doorway of a small store, shoulders hunched, one hand holding a frayed Army-issue greatcoat closed at his throat. The earflaps of his fur cap were lowered against the cold, and he wore heavy leather gloves. The watcher was medium height and stocky. He wasn't very good at his job. His attention was more on his own misery than the hotel's back door.

Slocum stepped across the narrow alley, putting himself on the same side as the sentry. He carried his Winchester rifle across his right shoulder, upside down and butt forward, fingers locked around the stock behind the receiver. Keeping close to the walls of buildings, he eased his way toward the man.

The picket, his broad face grooved in a frown of misery and boredom, didn't see or hear Slocum's approach. Slocum was within arm's length before he stopped.

"See anything?" Slocum asked softly.

The man started at the sound, half turned toward Slocum— and caught the full force of the brass butt-plate of the Winchester in the forehead. The jab was short, but with all of Slocum's weight and muscle behind it; the crack of rifle butt against bone seemed as loud as a pistol shot in the alley. The blow knocked the man's head from beneath the fur cap. The sentry dropped without so much as a grunt.

Slocum stood for a moment, stared down at the man, and considered belting him with the rifle butt again, then realized it wouldn't be necessary. He was already dead. The depression in his skull was half an inch deep, a narrow crescent shape in a mirror image of the butt-plate of the Winchester. Slocum shifted the rifle to the crook of his elbow, propped the body against the side of the doorway, and pulled the fur cap down low over the dead man's eyes. Anyone passing by would think he was asleep, probably passed out drunk. If Freeman's men kept up their usual watch rotation, it wouldn't be time to change sentries for another five hours.

If nothing went wrong, Slocum thought, it should be time enough. He sauntered across the street and went in the back door of the hotel.

He fumbled with his room key for a moment, unaccustomed to having to lock things up, stepped inside—and found himself looking down the impressive black bore of a rifle barrel that seemed to reach halfway across the room.

Jeremiah Toucherman quickly lowered the rifle. "Howdy, Slocum," he said pleasantly as he hooked a thumb on the heavy scroll hammer and eased the weapon from full cock.

"Touchy." Slocum nodded in greeting, waiting a moment for the ball of ice in his gut to thaw. Having a .50 Hawken pointed at a spot between your eyes tended to chill a man.

"How'd you get in here?" Slocum asked as he toed the door closed behind him.

The weathered, balding little man shrugged. "Weren't no problem. Swiped the hotel house key when the desk man wasn't lookin'."

Slocum shrugged out of his coat. "Not that I mind seeing you again, Touchy, but I'd like to ask what you're doing in my room."

"Waitin' to see who come in, mostly. Been one of Freeman's boys, I'd of put a .50-caliber hole in him. Glad it was you showed instead. Droppin' the hammer of this cannon in a room this small'd deafen a man for a month." He put the long rifle on the bed and reached for a heavy crock jug. "I brung some coffee. Should still be warm enough—you want a cup?"

Slocum did. The mug steamed in his hands; the coffee was more than warm. Touchy hadn't been in there all that long. Slocum took a couple of swallows, put the cup on the table, and pulled the package the doctor had given him from beneath his shirt. His gear was still in the corner where he had left it. He wrapped the package in a spare shirt, then in a sheepskin-lined vest to further cushion it, and stowed it carefully in his saddlebag. He shucked the shoulder-holster rig, belted his regular gunbelt around his hips, and went back to his coffee.

"I bought that mule last night, Slocum. Two of 'em."

Slocum glanced up, a hollow spot in his gut. "It's time?" was all he could manage.

Toucherman shrugged. "Doc Whitley says I've got two, three months, tops. Before the heart quits. Or the kidneys go. Whichever happens first." The old frontiersman's tone was without emotion, as though he were discussing the weather. "Figured if I start now, I can make the Rockies about greengrass time."

Slocum didn't offer condolences. He couldn't think of anything much to say. Dying was a fact, just like living. It happened to everybody, sooner or later.

After a moment, Toucherman lifted an eyebrow. "Slocum, I ain't one to horn in on a man's business, but if you got no objections, I'd admire to ride along with you a ways when you get the gal back.''

"You know I'm going after her?''

"Said you was. Won't be easy. Bull Freeman's a mean son. Keeps some men around near as mean as he is, and can hire 'em even meaner. You're gonna be a busy man today, hoss.''

"How'd you know it was today?''

Toucherman shrugged again. "Feelin' in the bones. It's huntin' weather out there. You're a huntin' man. You know where she's at, and I figure you're gettin' some tired of town life.''

Slocum frowned. "I'm not absolutely certain she's in Freeman's place, Touchy. If I'm wrong . . .'' His voice trailed away.

"You ain't. She's in there. Back room, just right of center down the hall past the door behind the bar.''

"You've seen her?''

Toucherman shook his head. "Not up close. But the darkie I buy ham from has. Told me she's in there when I asked kinda sharp-like. Made me promise I wouldn't tell his old lady he knowed anything about the inside of the Plantation. Anyhow, I thought maybe you wouldn't mind company. 'Sides that, I don't like ol' Bull and his type much. How about it?''

Slocum didn't have to think any longer about the proposal; he wasn't so proud that he wouldn't welcome any help offered. An extra gun could be the edge he and Mary needed to stay alive. He nodded. "I'd welcome your company, Touchy. I'd hate to see you get killed riding with us, though.''

Toucherman snorted. "You think I'll fret on that? Hell, Slocum, I'm dyin' anyway. Six months, six days, or six hours, don't make that much difference. Flat on my back on a buffalo robe or goin' down from a slug don't make no difference neither. Dead's dead.'' A grin twitched the former mountain man's lips. "Matter of fact, I'd kind of like to have myself one more shinin' time 'fore they put them pennies on my eyes.''

Slocum extended a hand. "Touchy, I'm obliged. I can't think of anybody I'd rather ride the trail with.''

"Me neither, hoss. Just promise you'll lead my mule if I

can't make it on my own.'' He released Slocum's grip. ''Lord, I sure am gonna like seein' the plains and the mountains again.'' A wistful, faraway look flickered in Toucherman's eyes. ''God's country, Slocum.'' The old man abruptly turned serious. ''Now, let's get some figgerin' done. You're gonna need good horses, supplies. My pack mule's stout, so we won't need another pack animal. We'll need a saddle and trail clothes for the gal. I'll take care of that part—'' He raised a hand when Slocum started to interrupt. ''Hear me out. Now, you gotta stay out of sight, on account of ever' mother's son who packs a firestick's gonna be watchin' for you. Leave the stockin' up to me, and lay low till it's time to go get the gal.''

''And if I can't?''

''You'll get her. Hell, if you don't, I'll have plenty of grub and some fine ponies for the ride west.''

Slocum pulled a fold of bills from his pocket. Toucherman shook his head. ''We'll settle up later, once we're outta town. Not that it makes no difference. I got more money'n I need anyhow. Where and when you want to meet up?''

Slocum thought for a moment. ''Three hours give you enough time?''

''I'll make 'er do.''

''You know the Plantation layout. At nine o'clock, start riding down the street from the east end, leading the horses. When you're a couple blocks away, I'll go into the Plantation and get Mary. That should put you out front by the time we come out. It won't take but a few seconds to mount and ride if the horses are right outside. We'll be needing to make some fast tracks.''

''I'll be there, Slocum. You don't worry about nothin' 'cept gettin' the girl.'' He nodded toward the gear in the corner. ''Leave the saddle and other stuff. It'd just slow you down. I'll pick it up when I get the ponies. See you in three hours. Don't get yourself killed.''

Before Slocum could say anything else, Toucherman shouldered his long rifle and left. He didn't make much noise in the process. Slocum realized the old man was wearing moccasins. High-top, Southern Cheyenne style.

Slocum waited a few minutes, then strode to the window

and eased the curtains aside with the barrel of his rifle.

The front of the building was still being watched. Slocum toyed with the curtains until the slightly built man across the street reached inside his coat, staring at the window. Then Slocum let the curtains fall back into place. They would think he was still in his room, at least for a time. They wouldn't be looking for him at the Plantation if they thought he was here.

Slocum would take any edge he could get, no matter how slight.

Getting Mary out wasn't going to be a picnic on the church grounds, but keeping her out could be even chancier. Even with Toucherman's help. The horses would buy them time and distance. Freeman would have men watching the railroad depot, stage station, all the major roads out of town. But city folks were predictable. They expected others to be the same. It should take them a while to figure Slocum had left town on horseback, even longer to cut their tracks away from heavily traveled roads and trails. If Slocum, Toucherman, and Mary could make the first forty miles, into the rough post-oak hill country to the northwest—

The grandfather clock downstairs chimed. Slocum had two and a half hours.

He pulled his spare Peacemaker from the saddlebag, chambered a sixth round in the cylinder, and tucked the weapon into his waistband. A man never knew when another six shots might be the difference between living and dying. The Peacemaker was one hell of a fine weapon, but it did take a few seconds to reload. He shouldered his rifle and let himself out the back door.

Slocum slouched against the side of an abandoned barbershop, his coat collar turned up, hat pulled low over his eyes, hands in his pockets, trying to look like a saddle bum in the throes of a hellacious hangover.

He felt about as inconspicuous as a bishop in a whorehouse. He hadn't seen another white face in the last hour.

At least the weather was some help. The north wind that blew stronger by the moment was developing a bite like a loco wolf. Sleet pellets and an occasional puff of fine snow flurries swirled the trash and dust in the street. The few blacks who had passed by did so in a hurry, humped against the cold, and so far had paid no mind to the white man in the alley. Slocum could only hope his luck held for another quarter hour.

From beneath his lowered hat brim, he studied the building across the street. It wasn't going to be easy.

The Plantation was a one-story affair made of weathered clapboard, sixty feet long. It didn't look at all like its namesake. Twisted bois d'arc posts held up the porch in place of stately, carved columns. The ends and edges of warped porch planks curled upward or sank beneath the weight of neglect. Whatever Bull Freeman spent his money on, Slocum thought, it wasn't property improvements. It was hard to believe the Plantation was one of the biggest profit-makers in town.

Worst of all, there were no side or back doors, not even a window. Slocum had worked his way around the building before settling down to watch the front. The Plantation's few windows were all on the street side, narrow openings with panes so dirty and stained a man couldn't see through them; Slocum could detect only shadowed, shapeless movements inside.

The single door eliminated any chance to slip in and back out unseen. This would have to be a straight-ahead frontal charge. But the one entrance might even work to his advantage, provided he got out of there alive. If it made it tough for him to get in, it would also make it worrisome for Bull Freeman and his people to get out. If they came through the door after him, they'd risk running right into a slug. And they'd know it.

He had gotten one break, thanks to the late-season norther. There were no guards posted at the door. Or maybe it was just too early in the day for Freeman to be overly concerned about it. Even an establishment open around the clock had its quiet times. This was one of them.

Even on the streets, few people were about. The crowds wouldn't start milling for another hour or two, and the Plantation crowd not until around the noon hour, when they'd recovered enough to feel spunky again.

The clock ticking in his head told him he wouldn't have to

wait much longer. His nerves quieted at the thought. A relaxed calm flooded through him, a quirk of personal nature that left his muscles loose and heightened his senses. It was a quirk he had embraced and cultivated over the years. It had carried him through numerous tight spots from Civil War battlegrounds to challenges in frontier saloons from men who wanted to make a name by taking down the fast gun called Slocum.

This wasn't the terrain he would have picked for a show-down. But he had something else that gave him an edge, at least in theory. This was the last place anybody would be expecting him. He had the element of surprise.

At the far end of the street, a small man, hunched in the saddle aboard a mule and leading four other animals, came into view.

It was time.

He had about five minutes to get in, grab Mary, and get out before people started to wonder why an old white man leading saddled horses and pack animals would be waiting outside a saloon and whorehouse frequented by blacks.

Slocum loosened the Colt in its holster, stepped into the street, ignored the surly stare from a passing Negro man, and strode quickly to the front door of the Plantation. The door swung open at his touch, a hinge creaking in protest.

His luck held. Sort of.

There were half-a-dozen men in the Plantation. Three hud-dled near a coal-fired stove to his right. Two more—big, burly men with no visible necks—stood at the end of the bar, talking with a tall, gray-haired barkeep. Blood still seeped from the nose of one of the big men; one of his eyes was swollen almost shut. He was the man George had said he'd marked some before he was beaten into the dirt, Slocum figured.

All conversation stopped. Twelve dark eyes glared at Slo-cum in suspicion and thinly disguised hate. The big man with the busted nose stepped forward.

"We don't allow your kind in here, whitey," the no-neck said. "Go drink with your own."

Slocum leveled a steady gaze at the big man and ignored the challenge. "Bull around?" he asked calmly.

"He ain't here. Now, get out."

"Damn shame," Slocum said. "I sort of wanted to kill the bastard. You take one more step, mister, I guess you'll have to do instead." At the corner of his vision, Slocum saw the tall bartender edge a step to the left. "Reach for it, barkeep, and you'll be dead before you can blink," Slocum said.

"You got a lot of balls, whitey," the no-necked man said. "Gonna be my pleasure to rip 'em right off—" His words ended in a surprised squawk as the muzzle of Slocum's Peacemaker pointed straight at his Adam's apple.

Slocum let him squirm for few heartbeats. "Gentlemen, there's no sense in anybody getting killed. I just came for the girl, and then we'll be on our way."

"What girl you talkin' about, whitey?" the no-necked man asked.

"The blonde in the back room." Slocum cut a quick glance at the other men. "Shuck your handguns. Now. Barkeep, get over here with the others. You too, big man, or I'll splatter your neckbone all over the back wall."

Handguns thumped to the floor. For a moment, Slocum thought one of the men—a tall, whip-lean man wearing faded blue pants with a faint yellow stripe down the legs—might chance it. He looked like a shooter. The others just looked like town toughs. But the lean man lifted a Schofield from beneath his waistband and let the weapon drop.

Slocum flicked a quick gaze around, saw what he was looking for. A heavy oak door, iron strap held in place by a heavy padlock, stood at the end of the bar. Most town saloons bought liquor in quantity and kept what they weren't using at the time under lock and key. He inclined his head toward the barred door. "Over there, gentlemen."

When the surly and somewhat embarrassed men stood beside the door, Slocum nodded to the barkeep. "Open the padlock," he said.

"I ain't got the key—"

"I said open it. Now!"

The tall man fumbled in a pocket, and pulled out a heavy brass key. Metal chittered against metal as his trembling fingers struggled to insert the key in the lock. It opened with a heavy thunk. Behind the door was a storeroom stacked high with crates.

"Inside, gents," Slocum said, motioning with the muzzle of the Peacemaker. As the others filed into the cramped space, the barkeep held out the brass key. Slocum shook his head. "Keep it. You can't open the lock from inside anyway."

Slocum ignored the mumbled, angry threats as he closed the door and snapped the heavy padlock back into place. The men inside weren't going anywhere for a while.

He holstered his handgun and strode through the doorway that opened off to the side of the bar. He didn't bother to knock when he reached the first door on the right. He tested the knob, found it unlocked, and pushed the door open.

He knew then why nobody had recognized Mary Connally.

The girl in the bed looked at him without expression, the pupils of her eyes dilated over gaunt cheekbones. Her blond hair was lifeless, limp, and dirty; the room reeked of stale sex, unwashed bodies, and a scent new to Slocum. He glanced at the table beside the bed. A medical syringe lay beside a packet, a candle flickering above a blackened spoon.

Mary Connally stared at Slocum without truly seeing him. She slowly pulled back the covers and spread her legs. The fine blond hairs at her crotch were matted and crusted. Bruises marked her sunken belly, her sharply defined hipbones, and legs so thin they were little more than bone. Small breasts sagged against her rib cage. Puncture marks, some healed, some still in the raw, red stage, traced the course of her veins on both arms, even the tops of her feet and insides of her ankles. A single drop of bright red blood not more than a few minutes old pooled atop a vein in the crook of her thin left elbow.

Slocum's spirits sank. The bastard had her good. The emaciated shell of what once had been Mary Connally bore no resemblance to the healthy, glowing young girl in the tintype. Slocum knew now that getting her out of here would be the least of his troubles.

"I didn't come here for that, Mary," Slocum said. "I came to take you home. Get dressed."

She stared blankly at him, her mind somewhere off in a drug-induced fog. She didn't move.

Slocum stepped to the bed. His gut churned at the odor. It was obvious that not so much as a damp rag had touched Mary's body in days, maybe weeks.

He slipped an arm under bony shoulders and hauled her to her feet. He would have liked to be more gentle, but there wasn't time for tenderness now. He glanced around, saw no clothing—not even shoes. He swept two soiled, smelly blankets off the bed, wrapped them around her as best he could—then tossed her across his shoulder like a sack of flour and headed for the door.

The blankets weren't going to help much, Slocum knew. She would be a mighty cold young woman until they could reach a place where he'd feel safe dressing her properly for a long ride. Slocum doubted her brain would feel the cold in her current state, but her flesh would. On top of everything else, he had to worry about frostbite.

He heard the banging and thumping from inside the storeroom as he crossed the main saloon floor. At least Bull Freeman's men weren't going anywhere until somebody found out what happened and went for a key. Now, all he had to do was get her in the saddle, somehow keep her there, and cover as many miles as he could.

Toucherman's eyes narrowed as Slocum emerged from the building, the limp bundle over his shoulder.

"Girl don't look so good, Slocum," Toucherman said. "Think she'll stand up to the ride?"

Slocum hefted her into the single-rig saddle aboard a leggy brown gelding. The saddle was only slightly larger than a kid's rig, with a high cantle and prominent swells on the pommel. Mary instinctively locked her hands onto the saddlehorn.

"I don't know, Touchy," Slocum said honestly as he tucked the blankets around her as best he could. The clock in his head kept ticking. Finally satisfied that she wouldn't fall from the saddle, he started to toe the stirrup of his own rig on the back of a blue roan.

"Slocum!"

The yell from across the street brought Slocum's head around and a quiet curse to his lips.

A slightly built young man stood twenty feet away, one side of his face scraped raw and only now beginning to show signs of scabbing and scarring, his left arm in a sling—and his right hand on the butt of a revolver tied low on his thigh. The fall when Slocum had thrown him from the Texas & Pacific train hadn't killed him after all.

"Not now, Charlie," Slocum said. "I haven't got the time."

"You're taking the time, damn you! I owe you, Slocum, and now I'm going to pay you back. You're good at sneak-punching a man from the blind side. Let's see just how damn good you are with that six-gun!"

11

Slocum glared at the young gunman for a moment, then turned back to his mount and started to toe the stirrup.

"Damn you, Slocum! Face me like a man this time, or I'll put one in your back!"

Toucherman spat. "Looks like he ain't gonna go away, Slocum. Might as well kill the little bastard quick. I'd like to put a mile or so 'tween us and Fort Worth 'fore Bull finds out what we done."

Slocum sighed in disgust, flipped the reins to Touchy, and stepped away from the horses. There was no sense in taking the risk of getting a horse, or one of the riders, hurt if Charlie did manage to get off a shot. Slocum turned to face the young outlaw. The young ones were the most dangerous. A man never knew how quick their reflexes might be. And it had never dawned on them that they might get killed. The young thought they would live forever. One thing didn't change, though. The young ones were also dumb. A real shooter would already have emptied a chamber into him without saying a word.

"All right, Charlie. Let's get it over with—"

The kid was fast. His six-gun had cleared leather before Slocum's first slug caught him just above the belt buckle. Charlie grunted aloud, staggered a half step, and tried to raise his revolver. Slocum took his time. His second shot kicked a puff of dust from Charlie's shirt pocket.

The wiry gunman didn't go down. He stared at the pulse of blood from the hole through his heart, then at the handgun that suddenly seemed to weigh fifty pounds; he couldn't begin to lift it. The weapon slipped from his fingers.

Slocum holstered his Colt, strode to the snorting blue roan, and swung into the saddle.

"Tough little bastard," Toucherman said, staring at the man, who still stood, swaying slightly, in the street. "Don't reckon he knows he's dead yet."

Slocum shrugged as he snugged up the reins. "He made his choice. It turned out to be the wrong one. Forget him, Touchy. Let's ride."

He glanced back once, just before they turned the corner and headed northwest. Charlie had dropped to his knees. Touchy was right, Slocum thought; tough little bastard.

For more than an hour, Toucherman taking the point, Slocum divided his time and energy between holding Mary Connally in the saddle, keeping her covered with the blankets as best he could, and glancing back to check on their backtrail.

He saw no sign of pursuit. That didn't mean there was no one back there. Visibility dropped rapidly as flurries thickened into a heavy white blanket of snow. The wind had dropped. Within a half hour, their tracks would be covered. Slocum silently offered up thanks to the gods of winter.

He felt the shudder against the flesh of his forearm wrapped around Mary's almost painfully thin waist. Her lips had taken on a slightly blue tint, her cheeks as white as the snow that nestled without melting on dirty blond hair. Slocum didn't have enough hands to keep her blankets wrapped, keep her in the saddle, and still control both his mount and hers.

Her legs and shoulders were exposed to the frigid air. He glanced at her bare feet, which had been splashed with icy water in the crossing of the Trinity. Her flesh was the color of chalk tinged blue. But her face was still without expression, eyes dilated; Slocum didn't know where her mind was, but it wasn't on her physical suffering. The drugs in her bloodstream still blocked all feeling.

"Touchy," Slocum called, "we've got to stop for a few minutes and get this girl warmed up and dressed!"

"Planned on it!" Toucherman yelled back. "Live-oak grove in a creek up ahead, half a mile on the right! Decent cover there!"

Slocum sighed in relief as Toucherman reined in a few minutes later, deep in the copse of wind-twisted live-oak trees with trunks as thick as a man's waist. The year-round leaves caught most of the snowfall. On the north side of the small clearing, the tangled limbs of a deadfall piled high to form half of a natural lean-to shelter. The air felt a few degrees warmer deep inside the grove.

Toucherman leaned in the saddle, untied a canvas-wrapped bundle and blanket roll from behind the packs on the spare mule, and tossed them to Slocum. "Should be everything you need in here, Slocum. Had to guess at the fit. Reckon we can chance a small fire to get the gal warmed up and proper dressed." The wiry old man lifted his face to the skies, let the dusting of snow settle onto his weathered cheeks, and smiled. "Gawd, if this ain't a plumb fine day. All she needs is a few pine trees and a mess of mountains, and I'd figger I'm home." He lowered his gaze to Slocum. "While you're tendin' the gal, I'm gonna scout the backtrail a ways just to make sure."

Slocum knew Toucherman didn't expect to see anything on the backtrail. The snow fell even heavier now, fat flakes that came almost straight down, with only a slight stirring of wind. A man couldn't see fifty feet in this weather. Touchy just wanted to ride, to feel free again. On the other hand, Slocum figured, if there *was* anyone behind them to be seen, the old mountain man would spot him.

Slocum dismounted, tied the blue roan and pack animals to the lower limbs of a live oak, and helped Mary from the saddle. He almost had to pry her fingers from around the saddlehorn. Moments later he had her seated, her back against the thick trunk of a fallen tree, blankets wrapped around her from toes to chin. Their gazes caught for a moment. Slocum thought he saw a flicker of some emotion in her blue eyes. The expression quickly winked out.

By the time Slocum laid the small, smokeless fire, Mary showed signs of thawing out—at least physically. The shivering that had wracked her body the last couple of miles stopped; her cheeks took on some color, and her lips were no longer blue.

Slocum realized, almost with a start, that the pupils of her eyes were less dilated now. Whatever she had put in her blood was beginning to run its course. It was obvious she still had no idea where she was, or with whom. And didn't care.

Slocum opened the canvas-wrapped pack, studied the contents, and nodded in satisfaction. Toucherman had chosen well, even if he hadn't seen Mary in her current emaciated condition. The clothing would be a bit on the large side, but that was better than too small.

The package contained two sets of cotton long-handled drawers, a pair of heavy corduroy pants, suspenders, two flannel shirts, a heavy wool scarf, fur hat with earflaps, a hip-length buffalo coat with the hair still on. And best of all, a pair of knee-high moccasins lined with rabbit fur, and two pair of thick wool socks. A pair of lined leather gloves were tucked inside the moccasins. Mary might not be in step with the latest women's fashions, but at least she wouldn't freeze.

She didn't fight him, but didn't help either, as he struggled to get her dressed. It was like putting clothes on a drunk, stuffing limp arms and legs into layers of clothing. Touchy hadn't thought to buy any feminine undergarments, but that wouldn't matter—at least not until Slocum got Mary cleaned up a bit. Slocum winced at her body odor, resolving to get her bathed and cleaned up at the first opportunity. The moccasins were the last item. Slocum tucked the corduroy pants legs into the tops and laced the footwear into place. Touchy had even bought a canvas ground sheet and three flannel blankets for a bedroll for the girl.

Slocum decided there would be time for coffee before they had to ride out. The battered pot from the pack had reached a full boil when a voice from almost within arm's length startled Slocum.

"Nothin' out there but snow, hoss."

Slocum hadn't heard Toucherman approach. The mountain man and plainsman obviously hadn't lost his ability to move like a sore-footed cougar, despite his years in the big city.

Slocum tossed a handful of snow into the pot to settle the

grounds, then filled three tin cups. Toucherman nodded his thanks, sipped at the scalding brew, and sighed in contentment.

"Nothin' better'n camp coffee on a fine day like this," the old man said. "You make a fair cup, Slocum."

Slocum tried for a couple of minutes to get some coffee down Mary, then gave it up. She kept turning her head away from the cup, lips tightly clamped. Getting her fed and some flesh back on her bones was going to be a chore, Slocum thought wearily.

Toucherman stood at the edge of the clearing, sniffing the air and sipping from his cup. "Snow like this is the best friend a man on the run can have. Or his worst enemy," Toucherman said. "It ain't gonna last but till maybe sunup tomorrow. Noon at the latest. I smell a thaw comin' on."

Slocum nodded. He sensed the same change in the weather, and Touchy was right about snow. Fresh snow covered tracks as long as it fell. When it stopped falling, there was no way to move through the ground cover without leaving a trail a blind man could follow. And even if he didn't feel it himself, Slocum knew better than to question a mountain man's notion of what the weather would do.

"Reckon we best not hang around here too long, hoss," Toucherman said. "We can make a few miles before the snow stops." He squatted on his heels beside the small fire. "Been a spell since I been in the post-oak country. Nigh onto twenty year, best I recall. You savvy the lay of the land out there?"

"Some. Tracked a renegade Kiowa through most of it sometime back."

"Find him?"

"Yes."

That was a good enough answer for Toucherman. He didn't ask for any details. He glanced at Mary. "Know a spot where we can hole up a couple days, maybe three? We got to get that gal back on her own feet and amongst the livin'. Don't reckon she even knows yet what happened or where she's at. Or maybe she just don't care."

Slocum thought for a moment. "There's a place not many white men know about, little less than a day's ride from here. I think I can find it again." Slocum finished his coffee and peered over the rim of the cup at Toucherman. "Touchy, when the drugs in the girl wear off, we've got a problem. It might get messy."

Toucherman nodded solemnly. "Seen a couple people like that come back down hard. You're right; it ain't pretty. But I reckon we can handle it. Won't be near as hard on *us* as it is on *her*." He tossed the dregs from his cup, stood, took a deep breath, and lifted his face to the fat snowflakes. "Hoss, I'd done forgot what real air smelt like, and I reckon the Great Spirit done smiled on me this day. I ain't seen a sure-enough snow like this all the time I been away from the Rockies."

Toucherman was right, Slocum mused; this far south, the snows were mostly light—maybe three, four inches—drifted like hell, and then melted fast. This snow was more like what the Powderhorn country up in Colorado caught. Thick, heavy flakes, little wind. But the air didn't seem especially cold. Not like it got in the high country, when the limbs of trees exploded and a man's bare hands froze on exposure in a matter of minutes. Toucherman, his face still turned to the sky, all of a sudden looked twenty years younger, Slocum thought.

The mountain man lowered his head and grinned at Slocum. "Time to piss on the fire and get movin', hoss. Best take advantage of this here snowstorm while we got it."

Slocum rode point, breaking trail through snow that now was halfway up to the leggy blue roan's knees. Mary's bay trailed behind on loose lead, followed by the pack animals, and with Toucherman bringing up the rear.

Slocum held the blue roan to a slow walk, partly to save the animal's energy—breaking trail through even a foot or so of snow sapped a horse's strength in a hurry—but mostly because landmarks were hard to find in the post-oak country.

One rocky, juniper-studded hill looked much like the one just ahead and the one just behind, especially in heavy snow. He could barely make out Toucherman's shape, a blurred gray form that shifted into and out of focus beyond a blanket of white less than twenty yards behind Slocum's mount. And Slocum hadn't been through this country in years. If he missed the saddle-back hill by fifty yards, any chance at holing up with some degree of comfort and concealment would be lost.

"What—where?"

Slocum barely heard the flat, expressionless voice behind him. He turned in the saddle.

Mary Connally wasn't back in the world yet, but she was beginning to get there. A touch of blue showed around the black pupils of her eyes. Her head moved slowly from side to side, but Slocum doubted she actually saw—or comprehended—what she was looking at. He dropped back alongside her.

"How do you feel, Mary?" he asked.

Confusion flickered across her pale, drawn face. "Who— you?"

"My name's Slocum. I'm taking you home, Mary."

She stared at him blankly. "Home? To Bull?"

"No. To your real home. Don't worry. Bull isn't going to hurt you again."

"But Bull's got—my medicine." The raw edge of fear tinged her words. "I got to—have my—medicine." A slight shudder rippled through her body. "Where's my medicine?"

Slocum put a hand on her forearm. He felt the tension in the small, thin muscles. One part of Hell might be behind her, Slocum thought, but another part was coming up. Fast.

"Just hang on a while, Mary," Slocum said reassuringly. "We'll be in a safe place soon. I have some medicine that will help you."

Need twisted her drawn features. "Give it to me. Now."

"Not for a while yet. Let's wait until we're out of the storm, all dry and warm, and when you really need it."

Mary sniffed aloud, wiped her nose on her sleeve, and slouched deeper in the saddle. Slocum had no idea how long the drugs left in her bloodstream would last. Or, for that matter, exactly what she would do when she finally understood what really was happening to her. For the moment, at least, she seemed to have quieted. The blank expression dropped back across her face.

Toucherman reined in alongside. "She back with us now, Slocum?"

"Partway. I don't think she has any idea what's going on."

Slocum saw his own concern mirrored in the mountain man's eyes. "Can you keep her with you a while, Touchy? I've got to keep my mind on where we're going. If I miss that saddle-back hill, we're in trouble."

Toucherman took the reins to Mary's brown. "I'll keep an eye on her. Snow's thinnin' out a touch."

Slocum squinted into the white curtain and realized the old man was right. He could see farther now. The flakes still came down thick, but they were smaller, and beginning to swirl on a slight stir of air. The faint breeze seemed undecided where it was from and where it was headed. It didn't smell like a norther; Slocum sensed it would build, blow from the west, and pile the lighter snow into drifts before it stopped.

By then, they had to find cover. He waited as Toucherman led the girl's horse back to the end of the short train, then kneed the blue roan forward.

Slocum almost missed it in the swirling snow; the wind had kicked up in the last hour and spun the finer flakes into growing drifts and near-blinding snow squalls. He had begun to fear he'd ridden past the saddle-back hill before the distinctive shape flickered into view just off his left shoulder.

Now the hill was to his back, again hidden behind the white veil. He let the blue roan pick its way up the shallow draw, little more than a swale between two hills. He turned to glance back over his shoulder. Mary rode hunched over the saddle-horn. Even from this distance Slocum thought he could see her shiver. Despite the wind and snow, it didn't seem all that cold; only a few degrees below freezing, Slocum figured. Most likely, Mary was beginning to feel the true fires of the damned, like a drunk with a raging hangover—only worse.

Toucherman rode relaxed but alert beside Mary, his long rifle sheathed and swung across his back by a sling, obviously ready to grab her if she started to fall. The mountain man was whistling softly. Slocum could hear a few notes from time to time. Toucherman was a good whistler. The snowstorm had peeled away a lot of years from Touchy, Slocum thought. He hoped it had skinned away some of the aches and pains too. Several times he had seen Toucherman wince, flex his back, and run a hand across his kidneys when he thought no one was looking.

The snow had brought more than a fresh spark of life to Toucherman.

And it had covered their tracks. Slocum felt confident that not even Al Seiber, good as the old German scout was, could pick up their sign an hour after they'd passed. If Bull Freeman came after them, he'd be starting from scratch and with no idea which direction they'd gone. The storm had bought them time, and time was what they needed most.

Slocum breathed a sigh of relief as the blue roan rounded a bend in the draw. A few yards ahead, a rockfall lay at the base of the west wall below a clump of junipers clinging to the top rim. A stand of tall willows battled for space with a copse of live oak and chinaberry.

He could only hope the narrow entrance to the cave hadn't been blocked by rock slides in the last few years.

The draw between hills had deepened rapidly since they'd made the turn north from the saddle-back. It was almost a canyon now, fifty-to-sixty-foot-walls of loose, rocky soil flanking the bed of the dry creek they followed. The walls of the small canyon shielded the trail below from the wind. The snow swirled only slightly here. Slocum noticed the snowfall was thinning rapidly.

Toucherman had called it, Slocum thought. Within a few hours the snow would stop entirely.

He reined the blue roan to a halt and waited until Toucherman and Mary rode up.

"This is it," Slocum said, nodding toward the trees. "Another half mile and we'll be there. The next hundred yards or so, we walk and lead the horses until the trail opens up a bit."

Mary's shoulders quivered almost constantly now. She started to wipe her coat sleeve across her nose. Slocum caught her arm, then handed her his handkerchief. "My—medicine," she said, her tone pleading.

"It won't be long now, Mary. Better get down now. Can you walk?"

He didn't think she heard the question. Toucherman dismounted as Slocum helped the girl from the saddle and slipped an arm around her waist to steady her.

"Lead on, hoss," Toucherman said. "Let's see what's behind them trees."

Slocum breathed a sigh of relief as, all but carrying Mary, he stepped through the last twisting bend of the trail. The deep, narrow cut through which they walked abruptly widened. The secluded canyon was as he remembered, maybe a pistol shot wide and a rifle shot deep. The walls weren't high, but they were steep. Loose soil and rocks on the nearly vertical walls meant not even a man on foot could descend—at least not without raising enough racket to wake the dead and leaving himself exposed to gunfire in the process.

The tops of tall, dry buffalo grass poked through the snow, almost knee-deep on the canyon floor. A spring-fed stream trickled, unfrozen, from the east end, only to disappear back into the earth fifty yards from the pass through which they had come. Chinaberry, post-oak, willows, junipers, and cottonwood trees nestled against the north wall.

Slocum had to study the north face for a few moments before he spotted the twisted juniper with one dead limb curled over its back, like a big wooden scorpion's tail, twenty feet up the steep wall.

"Nice little spot here," Toucherman said as he stopped beside Slocum. "Good grass and water. Was it a tad bigger, like a couple sections, a man could raise some fair hosses here. Where we pitch camp?"

Slocum pointed toward the scorpion-tailed juniper. "Behind that tree is the opening to a cave. We'll have to leave the horses down below and pack our supplies up on foot. Maybe chase out a bear or two, but I think you'll find it comfortable enough, Touchy."

A half hour later, Toucherman stood inside the narrow opening and surveyed the cave, illuminated now by a single cottonwood torch in Slocum's hand.

"Mighty nice," Toucherman said. "Sure never expected nothin' like this in the post-oak country."

"Surprised me too when that Kiowa I was tracking led me

to it. You usually don't find caves this size except in limestone country."

"This where you caught up with him? The Injun?"

Slocum nodded. "He got careless." Slocum noticed the old mountain man was breathing a bit hard and kept flexing his left fist after he had put down the packs he carried. "You all right, Touchy?"

"Sure. Just a little short of wind. Too much town livin', I reckon. Let's get settled in, hoss. Damned if this don't look better than the fanciest hotel in Denver. Plumb cozy."

"You sound a little disappointed, Touchy."

"Was hopin' we might have to mix it up with one of them bears. Ain't had me a good tussle with a bear since that ol' silvertip grizzly up in the Yellowstone took a dislike at me."

Slocum eased the shivering, sniffling Mary to a seat on a rock slab that protruded from the cave wall forming a natural bench. "The bear win?"

"Yep," Toucherman said, a twinkle in his eyes. "Sumbitch et me plumb up. But not until after I'd gnawed off half his haunch. Damn good scrap. You get a fire started and tend the gal. I'll fetch some more packs."

Slocum started to object—he wasn't sure the old man was up to any heavy work like lugging loaded packs uphill—but Touchy was gone before he could say anything.

Getting a fire going didn't take long. An armload of dry, cured wood still waited where Slocum had left it on his last visit, as did the half circle of stones along one wall of the cave. The wood burned hot, but fast. He'd have to gather more soon. The warmth of the blaze quickly took the chill from the air of the cavern. The heated rocks and exposed sandstone wall would soak in heat from the fire and retain it well after the wood was consumed. The faint wisp of smoke drifted up and back toward the narrow fissure at the rear of the cave. Slocum didn't worry about a passing horseman spotting the smoke. It would dissipate through the limbs of the juniper above the fissure.

His work with the fire finished, Slocum went to Mary. It was the first time he'd had a good close look at her in hours. It wasn't reassuring.

She sat humped over, shivering violently and moaning aloud, arms clamped across her abdomen. Sweat dotted her forehead. She seemed unaware of the steady flow of mucus from her nose.

She drew herself into a ball as Slocum touched her shoulder, then looked up at him through squinted, watery lids. "My— my medicine—you promised—"

"In a minute, Mary. Let me get your coat off first."

"No. It's—it's freezing—in here." Sweat matted her dirty blond hair to her cheeks and forehead. "Cold—"

"Mary, listen to me," Slocum said firmly. "What you're feeling now is coming from inside you, not outside. It's going to get worse unless I give you your medicine, and I won't do that until you decide to cooperate. You help me and I'll help you."

Her teeth chattered as an especially violent shudder wracked her slim body. She nodded weakly, and didn't fight Slocum as he peeled off her coat. Beneath the heavy jacket, her sweat-soaked shirt clung to her skin. Her flesh felt clammy to Slocum. He draped one of the soiled blankets taken from her room in the Plantation across her shoulders and said, "All right, Mary. I'll get your medicine now."

Slocum felt her gaze on him as he strode across the cave to the pile of packs and rummaged in his saddlebag. When he turned, a brown pint bottle in his hand, Mary was struggling to roll up the sleeve of her shirt to bare an arm.

Slocum shook his head as he pried the cork stopper from the bottle. "No, Mary. This doesn't go in your arm. You drink it." He held it to her lips, let her take a swallow, then had to pry her fingers from around the bottle. "That's enough for now. It'll start to work in a minute," he said reassuringly.

Her only response was a quick shudder and a grab at the bottle.

"Damn," Toucherman said from the mouth of the cave, his words coming in short bursts between gulps of air, "the gal's got it bad, ain't she?"

"I'm afraid so, Touchy. You sure you're all right?"

"Like I said, just a bit winded." He placed the packs beside the others piled along the wall. "Had these little spells before.

It'll pass. Don't fret it none.'' Toucherman turned to study the girl more carefully. "I'll rustle up some coffee and grub. We gotta get some vittles down that girl.''

Slocum stowed the bottle back in the carefully wrapped and padded package in his saddlebag, knowing as he did he'd have to move it, keep it someplace where Mary couldn't get to it when his back was turned. The doctor had given him three pints of tincture of laudanum. Handled right, it might be enough to ease Mary's pain until her body could rid itself of the need for stronger stuff. If she got hold of it and drank it all at once, it would kill her. Which, he thought to himself, might be what she would be wanting before this was over.

Slocum glanced at Toucherman, kneeling beside the yard-wide pool in a back corner of the cavern. The water was fresh and clear, the pool fed by a steady trickle down the cave wall from a fissure halfway up. Slocum figured the seep was part of the spring that fed the stream down below.

Toucherman scooped up a palm full of water, sipped at it, and grunted in satisfaction. "Good stuff, and plenty of it," he said as he filled the coffeepot, then a pan not much bigger than his cupped hands. "Man couldn't ask for more. 'Cept maybe a couple mountains, some pines, and an old bull elk buglin' in the distance.''

A few minutes later Toucherman had the coffee on to boil and was shredding strips of jerky into the pan. "Don't reckon the gal's gonna be up to solid food for a spell. If we can get some of this here broth down her, though, it'll be a start.''

Slocum studied Mary as Toucherman worked. The laudanum seemed to be taking effect; her eyes had a dreamy look to them, and she no longer clamped her arms across her belly. She leaned back against the smooth cave wall, her breathing shallow but measured. The shivering had almost stopped, but she was still sweating heavily.

It was, Slocum knew, going to a mighty long couple of days.

12

Slocum's eyelids felt as if they'd been sprinkled with grit, and he might as well have been carrying a fifty-pound sack of flour across his shoulders.

He was, he concluded, definitely earning his pay from the colonel.

For three days, or so it seemed, he had been on his feet constantly. When he wasn't keeping a hawk's eye on Mary Connally, which was most of the time, he spelled Toucherman on lookout atop the saddle-back hill. From there, a man could see just about anything that moved for miles.

Mostly, lookout was Toucherman's duty. The old mountain man didn't mind. If anything, he thrived on the fresh outdoor air. There seemed to be a new spring to his step, a new glint in his eye, and the leathery skin of his face had gone a shade darker from the sun and wind. The shortness of breath had passed, as had the ache in his left arm.

The old man, whose heart and kidneys were going, looked to be in a lot better shape than Slocum.

Slocum knew it wasn't purely the lack of rest that had ground him down. Many times he had gone for longer stretches without sleep and hadn't missed it all that much. When a man was the hunter or the hunted and closing in on action, the body stayed fresh and alert. What had worn him down here was something else. He found it hard to stomach what was happening to Mary.

He took some comfort in the fact that she seemed to be getting better. The sweats, chills, belly cramps, the tears of pain kept coming back. But at least now they seemed less severe, with more time passing between the bouts. Mary spent less time hunched over with her hands across her gut, cursing him for not giving her the "good medicine." The medicine that Bull Freeman kept her pumped full of.

The laudanum helped; after a swallow, she calmed down a bit, for a while. But the supply was running low. If she didn't manage to climb that hill out of her own private Hell soon, it would only get worse. Without the dulling effects of the laudanum, there was no telling what she might do.

Slocum endured her verbal, and sometimes even physical, outbursts stoically. He knew it wasn't Mary Connally ranting and raving. The harridan he saw before him was being forced to break free from the one thing she'd come to live for in her days in Hell's Half Acre.

At least he'd managed to get her cleaned up.

The morning after their first night in the cave camp, Slocum had heated a pan of water, found a sliver of soap and a rag, and started undressing Mary while she was still under the influence of her latest dose of laudanum.

Toucherman cleared his throat and wandered outside, clearly uncomfortable with the idea of seeing Mary naked.

Slocum's heart sank even further when he had her stripped. She was little more than skin and bones. The needle marks tracked on her arms, legs, and ankles were in various stages of healing. Her breasts were small, seemingly withered and sagging, her thighs not much thicker than his biceps, her hipbones prominent and sharp.

He felt no stirrings of want, need, or desire as he scrubbed the semen crust from her crotch and thighs and cleaned her vagina as best he could. His knowledge of medicine was pretty much limited to patching gunshot wounds and setting broken bones, so he could only hope the rank odor from between her legs wasn't some sign of disease. Only the Creator knew what she might have been exposed to in Bull Freeman's back room.

He became aware of her gaze on him as he wielded the wet rag between her legs.

"Give me some more medicine—a lot more—and I'll fuck you anytime you want," she said. The dulling effect of the laudanum didn't cover the urgent craving in her words.

Slocum's reply was soft and sympathetic. "No, Mary."

"Because I'm a whore? I bet you've had whores before."

"I have. That was different."

"What's the difference? Pussy's pussy."

Slocum winced at her words. He'd never heard any woman, even the coarsest prostitute, use language that crude. "It's hard to explain, Mary. I just can't, and won't."

He managed to catch her wrist before her small fist reached his jaw.

"You son of a bitch—is it because I've fucked niggers?"

The bitterness of her tone jarred Slocum a bit, but not as much as the fact that she even remembered. When he'd first seen her, he'd figured she didn't have the foggiest idea of what was going on around her, what she was doing, lost in the between-worlds haze of drugs.

He released her wrist. "No, not that either." Slocum scrubbed her belly, the bony rib cage, the small, sagging breasts. Her nipples remained soft despite the exposure to air or dampness of the washrag. "It's not what you've done, but what you've had done to you. Those days are over for you, at least for now. What you do with the rest of your life after I take you home is up to you."

"You don't think I'm pretty enough?"

Slocum looked her straight in the eye. "I think you are. Or you once were, and will be again."

Her tone turned even more sharply sarcastic. "What's the matter? You like boys instead of girls?"

Slocum fought back the quick flare of anger in his gut, reminding himself that this wasn't Mary Connally talking at the moment. He shook his head. "It won't work, Mary. You're not getting any more drugs for now." He smiled at her through the aggravation. "When you're back on your feet and healthy again, and feel the need—the real need—for a man, ask me. If you don't hate me enough to rip my guts out by then."

That night, Slocum awoke from one of his infrequent naps to find Mary kneeling at his side, her trembling fingers fumbling with the buttons of his trousers. He caught both her hands in one of his own and held them in a firm grip. "Mary, I said no earlier, and I meant it."

She was sweating again, the expression in her eyes wild but somehow cold at the same time. "I'll suck you off, Slocum. I'm real good at it. Just give me some more medicine—"

"It isn't time yet, Mary. You can hold on another hour."

She dissolved into tears of desperation and hunger. "I can't, Slocum. I just can't."

He released her hands, put a reassuring palm against her cheek, and smiled. "Yes, you can. It won't be easy, I know. But you can do it."

"You son of a bitch!" She jerked away from him and stumbled back to her blankets, shivering violently now, sweat dripping from her chin, her nose running. "Why—do you—hate me so much, damn you?"

"I don't hate you, Mary. I'm trying to help you."

"Goddamn—pissy way—of showing it."

Slocum knew his brief rest was over for that night. It was going to be a long hour, and even after her next dose of laudanum, he'd have to keep a close eye on her. A person who craved something that much would kill for it. And he knew that, if she had any idea where she was or in which direction Fort Worth lay, she would try to break away and go back to Bull Freeman and his needle.

And Slocum wasn't sure she didn't know which way to ride.

The day after that was less of a fight, but still no picnic. He managed to get some of Toucherman's rich broth down her, along with half a biscuit, and this time it stayed down. She made no move to seduce Slocum in an attempt to get at the laudanum, which he kept in the pack he used as a pillow.

One thing was for damned sure, Slocum realized. He'd never given nurses the level of respect they deserved.

Slocum woke with a start from a fitful doze, his hand on the butt of his Peacemaker.

"What is it?" Mary sat erect on her bedroll, a blanket clutched over her breasts, a note of alarm in her voice.

"A rifle shot. Some distance off."

"I didn't hear anything."

Slocum got to his feet. "Stay where you are, Mary." He strode to the narrow cave entrance and stood for a long time, studying the countryside as best he could through the brush that hid the cavern opening.

The snow was gone now; Toucherman's nose for the thaw had been on the money. In its place, the damp earth and mild breeze carried a distinct scent of the coming spring. Already, patches of green were beginning to show in the meadow below. Slocum's blue roan, visible through a break in the brush, had his head up, nostrils flared, ears pricked toward the southeast.

Slocum concentrated on the horse. If a threat developed, the blue roan would see or smell it long before the man. A good horse was better than a mongrel as a watchdog.

Almost two hours passed in silence before a solitary figure, a bundle draped across the withers of an accompanying mule, ambled through the pass and into the meadow.

Slocum relaxed and glanced over his shoulder at Mary. She still sat on her bedroll. "It's Touchy," Slocum said. "Looks like he's brought fresh meat."

"Oh. I guess I'd better get dressed." Mary reached for her shirt and pants beside the bedroll, surprising Slocum; until now, she hadn't cared whether she was clothed or naked. He sensed that was a good sign.

Slocum waited until she'd dressed, then said, "Mary, I'm going down to help Touchy. Promise me you won't try to get into the medicine?"

She smiled and nodded. "I don't need it, Slocum. I feel much better now." She had some color back in her cheeks, Slocum noticed. Some of the weight of responsibility dropped from his shoulders. He wasn't yet sure he could trust her, but he had to find out sometime. It might as well be now.

He met Toucherman at the bottom of the trail to the cave.

"Couldn't pass up a chance at some fresh meat," Toucherman said with a grin. "Young whitetail doe, rollin' fat. Should make mighty fine eatin'. She didn't have no fawn."

That was like a mountain man, Slocum thought. He wouldn't leave a baby to starve except to save his own life.

Slocum almost asked Toucherman if he'd seen signs of human life, then realized how dumb the question would be. If Toucherman even thought there might be someone about, he would never have touched off that Hawken.

Slocum shouldered the doe. The carcass didn't weigh a hundred pounds field-dressed. It had been a clean shot, he noted, a single .56-caliber ball through the neckbone. Very little wasted meat.

"How's the gal?" Toucherman asked as he stripped the tack from his mule and turned the animal loose.

"Doing better. I think she may be over the worst of it." Slocum sighed. "I sure as hell hope she is."

"You do look a sight tuckered at that, hoss. Like you been rode hard and put up wet. Get your belly full of good, fresh meat and a full night's sleep, you'll perk up some. I'll watch the gal."

Slocum started to object, then changed his mind. Toucherman seemed able to go on little rest—in fact, in the last couple of days the old man had seemed to be gaining strength—and Slocum was even more tuckered out than Touchy knew. He started up the trail, the doe draped limply over a shoulder.

Mary was fully dressed, adding wood to the fire, when the two men entered the cave. Slocum noticed that her fingers didn't tremble, and she wasn't sweating. She looked up with a shy smile of greeting. A flush spread over her cheeks.

"I would have put the coffeepot on," she said a bit apologetically, "but I'm afraid I've forgotten how to make it."

"No problem, missy," Toucherman said expansively. "Slocum here makes a passin' fair cup, even if it don't have as much kick to it as a real man likes. Lace-drawers coffee, but it'll do in a pinch." He knelt beside the doe carcass and pulled a long, heavy-bladed knife from a beaded sheath at his waist. "We'll have us a big feed tonight."

"Good," Mary said, startling Slocum, "I'm absolutely famished. Anything I can do?"

Toucherman put her to work. Slocum sank onto his bedroll. His lids closed.

Slocum wasn't sure how much time had passed before he came awake at Mary's light touch on his shoulder, but he felt a bit refreshed. The scent of broiling venison and Dutch oven bread set his mouth to watering.

"Supper's ready, Slocum," Mary said softly. Her fingers seemed to linger on his shoulder for a moment, then fell away.

Slocum and Toucherman ate like field hands. Mary finished one plateful of beans, bread, and venison chops, and declared herself unable to eat another bite. Slocum wasn't surprised. A person who had gone so long without eating real food couldn't hold as much.

After they'd finished, Mary helped Toucherman clean up the utensils. Not once did she glance at the pack where the last bit of laudanum waited. Slocum knew then she had reached, or at least was near, the top of that hill she'd had to climb.

Slocum went outside for a smoke and to breathe in the fresh, clean night air. There was no moon, but a solid blanket of stars overhead cast a faint light over the meadow below. Toucherman's two mules stood head to tail, asleep. Slocum's blue roan, Mary's brown, and the packhorse grazed peacefully along the banks of the stream. Even the air was still. An owl hooted in the distance, getting a reply from the grove beneath the cave, and a coyote yelped in the distance.

It was, Slocum mused, the finest night he'd seen since he'd boarded the Texas & Pacific for the ride to Fort Worth. The notion brought A.J. McDonough to mind. He wondered what she was doing tonight, if he would ever see her again—

"Slocum?" The soft, shy voice at his side broke through his reverie.

He turned to the girl. The faint starlight emphasized the pale, gaunt face, the cheekbones and chin sharp and angular, the narrow, bony shoulders. "Yes, Mary?"

"I—I can't go back. Back home, I mean." Starlight glistened from the tears on her cheeks. "I can't—face them. Not what I've become."

"Not what you've become, Mary," Slocum said softly. "That's in the past. It's what you're going to be in the future that counts."

"They'll despise me—when they find out—"

Slocum put a hand on her shoulder. "They won't. They

can't. Your father wouldn't have sent me after you if they didn't still love you, Mary. The colonel blames himself for losing you in the first place.''

A sob caught in Mary's throat. ''I never could do anything to please him, Slocum. All I ever wanted from him was a pat on the shoulder, a hug or a kind word . . .'' Her voice trailed away.

Slocum dragged at his cigarillo and let the smoke trickle from his nostrils. ''Your father is a stern, hard man, Mary. The war did that to him. He had to be, to be one of the best commanding officers in the Confederate Army. But he's mellowed with the years. He knows he made mistakes, and the one he regrets most is not giving you what a young girl needed. He wants to make it up to you, Mary. For what it's worth, I know the man is serious about that.''

''But—how can he—and Mother—even want me back now? A common whore, addicted to drugs—I'm not worthy of them, Slocum. My God, you can't imagine the humiliation—''

Slocum unconsciously pulled her closer, hoping to somehow comfort her. ''No, I can't. But I've done some things in my life I'm not especially proud of myself. I've learned to live with them. So can you.''

She hiccuped a sob. ''How can you be so sure?''

''I can't,'' Slocum said honestly. ''I'm not you, Mary. But after what you've been through in the past few days, I think you're strong enough. You've been through Hell in the past few years. Now you have a chance to turn that around, to have a good life. And as far as your parents knowing about the men, they already do.''

''Oh, my God, no! He'll never forgive me!'' She grabbed his arm. ''Don't you see now why I can't go back?''

''It isn't a matter of him forgiving you, Mary. It's a matter of *you* forgiving *him*. The colonel himself told me that. It's the only time I've ever seen him cry.'' Slocum paused for a moment, studying the girl; tears ran freely down her cheeks. ''Regardless of how you remember your father, it takes a strong man to recognize his own failures and admit his mistakes. That doesn't come easily to a man like the colonel. He knows now he failed you—as a father—and he's asking for a second chance. The only thing he wants before his days run out is to have you back.''

Slocum took a final drag of the cigarillo and ground the butt beneath a boot heel. ''Your folks don't know about the drugs. I have no intention of telling them. If you think they should know, that's up to you.''

They stood in silence for a long time, Slocum staring off into the distance, the girl with her head lowered, wiping her eyes from time to time with the back of her thin, delicate hand.

Mary finally broke the lengthy silence. ''Slocum, I don't know if I can do it—if I can face them again, knowing the shame I've put them, and myself, through.''

Slocum nodded sympathetically. He had faced a lot of tough decisions in his life, but nothing as outright terrifying as what awaited Mary. After a moment, he sighed. ''It's a heavy load, Mary. But you have to do it. You have to take the chance. Could your life then be worse than what it's been up to now?''

''I—suppose not.'' She seemed to have cried herself out; her voice was soft and sad against the whisper of the gentle night breeze. She suddenly gasped, shuddered, and bent over at the waist, clutching her belly. Slocum knew the symptoms well by now.

''Do you need another sip from the bottle, Mary?''

She shook her head and, through gritted teeth, said, ''No. It'll pass in—a minute—''

Slocum put a gentle hand on her shoulder. For some reason he couldn't explain, he felt a warmth of pride in his chest. ''Mary, I don't think you realize just how strong you really are.''

She slowly straightened, her clenched lips softening. ''I'm not strong. I'm weak. I'd like to go to bed now. And you could use a good night's sleep too.'' She started to turn back to the cave entrance, then paused.

''Slocum.''

''Yes?''

''I overheard you and Mr. Toucherman talking. Is it true that he—Bull—is probably going to come after me?''

''Yes,'' Slocum said softly. ''I'd bet on it.''

She squared her shoulders and looked him in the eye. "Promise me something, Slocum. If it looks like he's going to get me back—shoot me. I won't go back to that life."

"He won't get you back, Mary. Touchy and I will see to that."

"But if—"

"If he gets past us, Mary, yes. I promise." He took her elbow. "Let's get back inside. It's getting late."

Toucherman rode in just before noon, his mule sweating and nostrils flared. Slocum met the mountain man at the bottom of the trail.

"Trouble, Touchy?"

Toucherman was already loosening the cinch on the mule. " 'Nuff to last a spell, Slocum. Thought I seen a fire about an hour 'fore sunup. Checked it out. Bull Freeman's out there. He's got ten men with 'im."

Slocum swore softly. "Look like they'd cut any sign on us?"

"Just a matter of time, Hoss. The son of a bitch has got Will Gallagher with him, and that bastard's the best tracker ever drew a breath. What you reckonin' to do now?"

Slocum turned toward the trail up to the cave. "Get the hell out of here," he said over his shoulder.

"Was hopin' you'd say that, hoss," Toucherman said. "Smart man knows when to stand and when to run. I'll saddle the mounts."

Slocum's breath caught in his throat every time a horse coughed or snorted; he winced at each creak of saddle leather or clink of bit or curb chain.

Less than three hundred yards away, on the other side of the saddleback hill, eleven dangerous men rode north. On Slocum's side, two men and a girl headed south.

The two groups would be opposite each other at this moment, Slocum figured. And if Will Gallagher heard or even suspected his quarry were just on the other side of the hill, he'd check it out—and Slocum didn't kid himself about their chances of living long. Not against those odds.

Slocum had weighed the odds and decided to roll the dice anyway. He counted on Gallagher putting all His concentration on following the tracks that led from the saddle-back to the cave hideout. And he hoped that Gallagher would figure that if the searchers flushed them, they'd try to make a run for it to the north or west.

So Slocum had done the unexpected.

If they got past the saddle-back safely, they'd have time to put a few miles behind them before Gallagher sorted out the tangle of tracks, figured out what had happened, and came after them again. And the wiry little tracker would do just that. Gallagher stood barely five feet tall in his boots, didn't weigh 110 soaking wet, and could track one snowflake through a blizzard. The man was damned good at his job. Maybe the best in the Southwest. Slocum knew they weren't going to shake Will Gallagher for long.

He was just hoping to buy time. And distance.

Slocum glanced over his shoulder. Mary rode tense in the saddle, her face the color of chalkstone, the reins in her left hand and her right fist squeezing the saddlehorn. Pure terror showed in her blue eyes and the set of her shoulders, but Slocum was sure she wouldn't panic. She had more to lose than any of them.

Toucherman was astride his mule behind the pack animals, the butt of the Hawken rifle resting against a thigh, muzzle pointed skyward. He was alert but relaxed, head cocked, listening as he rode.

Slocum had been a bit surprised when Toucherman dug in the packs and strapped on a handgun just before they left the meadow below the cave. Slocum didn't even know the old mountain man owned a short gun. It was an old Colt's First Dragoon cap-and-ball model, the first offspring of the Walker, and it might have seen action in the Mexican War with the First Texas Volunteers. Slocum knew Touchy wasn't a *pistolero*. Few mountain men were, staking their lives on their long guns and preferring the big knives for close-in battle. But if Toucherman carried a six-gun, it was a good bet he knew how to use it.

Slocum's heart skipped a beat as the nicker of a horse on

the far side of the hill reached his ears. The animal probably had caught the scent of the horses just beyond the saddle-back; the breeze quartered from Slocum's right front. Slocum could only hope the men on the other side would ignore the horse's signal of greeting to its own unseen kind.

He raised a hand in the signal to halt, lifted himself in the stirrups, and listened intently. The saddle-back narrowed here, near the southern end of the hill. Bull Freeman's boys would be less than a hundred yards away. Slocum thought he heard muted voices, but couldn't be sure.

The soft, barely audible call of a bobwhite quail sounded from behind him. Slocum turned and caught Toucherman's eye. The mountain man's hands fluttered in Plains Indian sign language. Then a finger pointed toward a rock deadfall at the base of the south end of the saddle-back.

Slocum mouthed a silent curse. Toucherman's hand sign said one rider trailed the others—and had dropped back to come around this side of the hill. Slocum nodded in understanding, held a hand palm out in the signal for Toucherman and Mary to stay still, then stepped from the saddle and ground-hitched the blue roan.

There was only one thing he could do. Take down the outrider, and do it without alerting the other pursuers that anything was amiss on their flank.

He covered the twenty yards to the rockfall as quickly as he could without making noise. He found his spot, a yard-wide opening between two junipers alongside the game trail. Most men tended to take the easiest route. The game trail was it.

Slocum pulled his belt knife, tested the keen edge of the six-inch blade with a thumb, and grimaced. He had never been fond of knife work. It was messy, had to be done face to face or body against body, and the thought of cold steel slicing into flesh made the hairs on his forearm prickle.

But he had no choice. A gunshot was out of the question. Only a few heartbeats passed between the time he pulled the knife and when he heard the sound. The clink of shod hoof on stone seemed loud in his ears. . . .

13

Slocum knew he would only get one chance.

Miss that, and Bull Freeman's men would be on them. And it had to be done in almost complete silence.

He worried less about taking the rider than he did about controlling the man's horse. If the animal shied at the wrong instant, or broke free afterward to run loose, and caught up with the other mounts in Freeman's posse . . .

Slocum pushed the thoughts from his mind as the hoofbeats neared, all his senses and concentration on the job at hand. He shifted the knife to his left hand, the edge of the blade almost touching his forearm. The horse and rider came into view as they rounded the rockfall. The sorrel moved at a slow walk, head carried low, ears flopped. The horse obviously was ridden down, which played into Slocum's hands; a tired mount was less likely to sense his presence.

The rider looked as tired as the horse. He rode slumped in the saddle, paying little attention to his surroundings as he rolled a cigarette, the tobacco sack dangling from his teeth. He looked to be in his late thirties, lean and stubbled, his nose and cheeks pink from sun and wind. A town man, Slocum thought. He waited, his breathing steady and heartbeat regular. The horse and rider were only a few feet away now. Slocum instinctively shifted his weight to the balls of his feet, knees flexed.

The rider came alongside Slocum, hands cupped around a

152

match flame as he lit his smoke, his chin down; the horse plodded along little more than an arm's length away, unaware of Slocum's presence. It was now or never.

He uncoiled from the half-crouch and leapt forward; his right hand closed on the slack reins as he swiped the blade upward, backhanded, felt the slight jolt as his forearm knocked aside the rider's cupped hands. The blade whipped across the rider's throat. For an instant there was no blood, only a thin, clean slash angling from the man's left collarbone to below his right jaw. A half-grunt gurgled from the man's lips. The startled horse tried to bolt, but its head snapped around as the reins tightened in Slocum's grip.

Then the blood came. Crimson pulsed and spurted from severed arteries in the rider's neck; the abrupt twisting of the horse as the reins snapped tight tumbled the man from the saddle. He fell on his back, hands lifted to his throat, his mouth opening and closing. No words, only a muted gurgle and soft whistle, came from the severed windpipe.

Slocum knew it would take a couple of minutes, maybe more, before the man died. He crouched beside the writhing form, pulled the revolver from the man's holster, unloaded the weapon, and placed it in the nearest juniper. He checked his blade, and saw the cut had been so quick and clean as to leave no blood on the knife. He sheathed the steel, then turned his back on the dying man and led the horse back to where Mary and Touchy waited on the far side of an abutment to the saddle-back hill.

Mary's eyes went wide, her face whitened even more, as Slocum came into view. Slocum glanced back at the sorrel, and noticed for the first time the distinct splash of crimson across the horse's withers and the empty saddle.

"See you got him," Toucherman said.

Slocum nodded, a queasy feeling in his gut. Using a blade always left him uneasy once it was over; killing a man with a knife was so damn personal. And messy.

Slocum's blue roan rolled his eyes and snorted at the scent of blood as Slocum mounted, the reins of the dead man's sorrel in his hand.

"Maybe that bought some time," Slocum said. "Even if it

didn't, it cut down the odds some. With luck, they won't even miss their outrider for a while. We can make a few miles before they figure out what's happened.''

Toucherman inclined his head toward the sorrel. ''What you think we'd ought to do with the pony? Cut his throat?''

Slocum shook his head. ''I can't do that to a horse, Touchy.''

''But you did—to a man,'' Mary said haltingly.

''The horse wasn't hoping to kill us, Mary. The man was. We'll keep the sorrel with us until it seems safe to turn him loose. We don't want him running back to his buddies in Freeman's cavvy.''

''Won't they know anyway when they find the dead man?''

''Touchy and I'll drag him back into the brush and wipe out the sign on the way past, Mary,'' Slocum said.

Toucherman's brows furrowed. ''We'd best get a move on, hoss. I'd as soon put some country between us and ol' Bull before sundown.''

Slocum didn't call a halt until the sun rode a handspan above the southwestern horizon.

For the first couple of hours, he hadn't bothered to even try to hide their trail. Then he'd done his best. He laid false trails and switchbacks, crossed over such hardpan and solid rock as could be found in the sandy, shale-covered hill country. They'd cut a flowing creek, little more than a foot deep in most places, and put the horses into the chilly water. Slocum and Mary rode downstream, leading the dead man's sorrel, while Toucherman went upstream leading the pack mule.

Slocum knew his tactics wouldn't slow Gallagher down long. The weathered little tracker had seen every trick in the books and invented a few of his own. All Slocum could hope was that it took Gallagher just long enough to sort it all out to buy them some country. And if the other mounts in Freeman's bunch were as ridden down as the dead man's sorrel, they wouldn't be gaining any ground.

The dead man's sorrel was all but down as it was, Slocum thought. The gelding was game, though. He stumbled at almost every step, and his knees buckled on the steep downgrades and upslopes of the difficult trails they had taken.

Slocum reined in at the base of a rock-strewn hill that stood slightly higher than the surrounding countryside. Its flat top would be as good a lookout point as a man was likely to find on the western edge of the rolling post-oak hills.

Toucherman, scouting ahead, had found the campsite. Slocum surveyed it and nodded in satisfaction. In this country, it was as good as a man had a right to hope for. Centuries of wind and water had scooped a chunk out of the southeast side of the flat-topped hill, leaving their backs protected by an almost perpendicular wall of exposed rock and shale. The front side offered a reasonably good field of fire. Dried buffalo grass knee-deep to a horse flanked the cut, providing good forage for the animals. A spring-fed creek ran nearby, its water shallow but sweet and cold.

Slocum knew it would be the last good camp they'd have for a while.

As he swung down from the blue roan, Slocum noticed the faint pinkish tint in the lather oozing from beneath the old A-fork saddle on the sorrel. A muscle twitched in his jaw as he stripped the tack from the beaten-down horse. Raw, bloody sores weeped on both sides of the sorrel's back, a foot behind the withers.

Mary noticed it too as she stepped down, a bit stiffly, from atop the tall brown. She stroked the sorrel's neck as the horse nuzzled beneath her armpit. "Poor thing," she said. Her tone took on a hard edge. "All of a sudden, I don't feel too badly about the man you killed, Slocum."

Slocum snorted in disgust. "Any son of a bitch who deliberately rides a sore-backed horse half into the ground deserves to have his throat cut. I don't feel so bad about it now myself."

He became aware of Mary's steady gaze. "You're a strange man, Slocum." When he didn't reply, she said, "Is there anything we can do for him? The horse, I mean?"

Slocum tossed the worn-out saddle aside. "Get rid of this piece of junk, for starters. Rub the sores with cooking grease tonight. It may not speed the healing, but at least it'll ease the sting a bit."

"You care more deeply about animals than I'd thought, Slocum," Mary said.

"As a group, I prefer animals to people," Slocum said solemnly. "I hate to see anything mistreated when it can't fight back."

"Even drug-sodden whores?"

Slocum leveled a steady gaze on her. "We're going to get one thing straight right now, Mary Connally. You will not now, nor or at any time in the future, refer to yourself that way. Or I will turn you over my knee and paddle the everlasting hell out of you. Understood?"

She flushed and said, "Understood," then fell quiet as Toucherman rode in, his gray mule hardly having broken a sweat despite the miles.

"All clear on t'other side of the hill . . ." The old mountain man's voice trailed away as he stared at the sores on the sorrel's back. "Jesus. Any son of a bitch who'd ride a sore-backed horse—"

Mary suddenly giggled.

"What's so funny, missy?"

"It's just that—well, I seem to have heard that identical comment just a few minutes ago. It seems I'm in the hands of better men than I thought." She gave the sorrel a parting pat on the neck. "Now, gentlemen, if you two will tend the horses and mules, I'll get supper started. It's time I began pulling my weight around here. I must warn you, though. I've never had much in the way of talent around a skillet."

Jeremiah Toucherman leaned back against his bedroll, belched loud enough to almost spook the horses, and patted his belly. "Damn, girl," he said, "I thought you told us you didn't know to cook. That was mighty tasty."

Mary's cheeks colored a bit. "It's nice of you to say so, Mr. Toucherman, even though we both know I can't hold a candle to you when it comes to cooking."

Slocum said, "Mary, Touchy's right. It was good."

Toucherman stood, stretched, and picked up his Hawken rifle. "I'll take first watch."

"Touchy, you should get some rest," Slocum said. "I'll stand watch."

"Hoss, you got to learn not to argue with your elders all the time," Toucherman said, rummaging in a pack. "It's too damn nice a night to waste. Cool enough to get a man's blood pumpin'. Stars out all over the place. I sure as hell ain't gonna fritter it away sleepin'." He pulled a pair of binoculars from the pack. The case was stamped "USA."

"Where'd you get those, Touchy?" Slocum asked.

"Won 'em playin' five-card stud with a foot-soldier sergeant sometime back. Handy as hell. Eyes ain't quite what they usta be. Man takes his help where he finds it." With that, the mountain man disappeared into the night.

Mary sat for several moments, a few bites of food still left on her plate, staring toward the spot where Toucherman had been. "Slocum, he's dying, isn't he?"

"Yes."

"Then, why isn't he back in Fort Worth? There are doctors there who could at least make his passing easier when his time comes, maybe even give him a little longer to live."

Slocum dragged thoughtfully at his cigarette. "I'm not sure I can explain it, Mary, but to men like Jeremiah Toucherman, it isn't the length of life that matters. It's the way what's left of that life is spent that counts."

Mary fell silent for a moment, then sighed. "I think I understand. Isn't that what you've been trying to tell me? That it's true for all of us?"

"Yes."

After a moment, she asked, "Why is he with us?"

"Because we're going back to the mountains. Touchy wants to meet his Maker in the high country. He asked me to lead his mule for him if he didn't make it that far." Slocum downed the last of the coffee from his cup and put on a fresh pot. Touchy would be needing a cup when he came back from standing first watch. "Let's get the camp stuff cleaned and stored, Mary. It's time to turn in."

Slocum awoke near midnight and lay motionless for a moment, alert, his hand on the grips of the Peacemaker, senses tuned to identify whatever out-of-the-ordinary sound had brought him from a dreamless sleep.

It was a muffled sob.

Slocum glanced at Mary, barely visible in the reddish glow of the dying campfire embers. She sat on her bedroll, bent at the waist, arms across her belly. A low moan, more like a whimper, sounded from her clenched lips.

"The craving again, Mary?"

She nodded, the faint firelight glistening on damp cheeks. "I thought—it was over. But when I start thinking about—about facing them, it—comes back. The need to—forget. To just float—away from everything."

"There's still some of the laudanum left."

She shook her head. "This will pass in a few minutes. Dammit, Slocum, you have no idea what kind of hold the stuff can have on a person."

Slocum said softly, "No, Mary, I don't."

"Back in the cave—when I—did what I did—offering to do anything for you to get the drugs. I was serious, Slocum. And I'm ashamed."

"Don't be."

She shuddered once, then slowly straightened and drew in a deep breath of the chilly night air. Her breath left a puff of steam when she exhaled. "I'm all right now," she said. "It's passed. Jesus, Slocum, I'm so damned—weak. I didn't have to become what I became, and then I didn't even have the courage to kill myself. Like so many of the other—girls—did."

"Maybe they were the ones who lacked courage, Mary, not you. They took the easy way out—" He broke off his comment as Toucherman strode into camp.

"They're out there, hoss," Toucherman said as he squatted by the coals and poured himself a cup of coffee. "Campfire about five, six miles back. The trick with the creek slowed them down some, but it didn't lose them."

Slocum stood and reached for his rifle and jacket. "We didn't expect it to, Touchy. I'll take the watch now. Get some rest. Tomorrow's going to be a long day."

"What you plan to do now?"

"For a while, quit trying to lose them. Just put as much distance between them and us as we can."

Toucherman sipped at his coffee. "There's one way to put 'em off our track, Slocum. Put that son of a bitch Gallagher down. It'd be my pleasure."

"If it comes to that, so be it." Slocum shouldered his rifle and strode toward the narrow, twisting trail that led up the side of the flat-topped hill.

By the first light of dawn, the two men and the woman were four miles from camp, headed northwest.

Slocum had changed his plans during his hours on the hilltop, but not solely because Freeman's bunch were so close behind.

He'd changed the route because of Toucherman. The wiry mountain man never complained—in fact, he seemed to be having the time of his life—but Slocum had glimpsed the furtive grimaces on the leathered face, noticed that Toucherman flexed or shook the fingers of his left hand more often. And noticed the times when simple movements left him wheezing for air.

Slocum sensed he didn't have that much time to get Jeremiah Toucherman to the mountains.

They would ride northwest to Tascosa and board a train for the short trip to Raton and the southern Rockies. The idea of Toucherman spending a few hours of his last days cooped up on a crowded, smoky train caught in Slocum's craw. But if that was the quickest way to get him to the mountains, it was worth taking a chance that Freeman wouldn't have men on the train.

After he got Touchy to the mountains, Slocum could take the long, slow way back to the Crooked River country. He needed to be certain Mary had broken free of the grip of drugs. He was reasonably sure now she would make it; she still didn't eat as much as he would have liked, but already it seemed that her cheeks had filled out some. Before he turned her over to her parents, Slocum wanted to fatten her up a bit.

The notion brought a wry smile to Slocum's lips. He couldn't remember ever thinking of a woman as if she were a beef to be fattened for market. He made himself a mental note never to mention such a thing to her. Women tended to be a might bristly about such things.

Toucherman's mule pulled alongside Slocum's blue roan. The old-timer had his pipe between his teeth, the fragrance of burning tobacco pleasant in the crisp early morning air.

"Just wonderin', hoss," Toucherman said. "Whichaway you plan on ridin'?"

"West by northwest," Slocum said. "Through the Copper Breaks country to Tule Canyon, up the Palo Duro, top out on the Staked Plains. Then north across the Panhandle to Tascosa. From there it's a short train ride to Raton Pass."

Toucherman thought for a moment, then nodded. "Sounds good to me. The Sangre de Cristos ain't nothin' like the northern Rockies, but by God, they're mountains. Tough ride, though. Rough country up through the canyons, then just miles and miles of nothin' but more miles once we top out on the Caprock." He paused to tamp the pipe and relight it. "Hunted buffalo up on the Staked Plains and Canadian River country many a time, back when we still had a mess of shaggies around. Long ways between water holes between Palo Duro and Tascosa. Reckon the girl can handle it?"

"I think so, Touchy. She may be tougher, in her own way, than either of us. And if it's tough for us, it'll be worse for the people chasing us. We've got rested mounts and plenty of supplies. They're on tired horses, and I doubt they outfitted for a long haul. Probably expected to catch us quick, get their business done, and head back to Fort Worth. We'll find out just how bad they want the girl back. Could be they'll give up trying to catch us."

"Suppose they don't quit and just keep a-comin'?"

"Then they go down."

Toucherman grinned. "Spoke like a sure-'nuff plainsman, hoss." The grin faded as abruptly as it came. The old man glanced back at Mary. "Don't know why, but I kinda got fond of that little gal. Sure would hate to see Bull to get her back."

"He won't, Touchy," Slocum said, his tone tight. "We'll see to that. Speaking of good horses, I never did pay you for the mounts—"

Toucherman interrupted with a wave of his pipe stem. "Don't fret it none, hoss. Nothin' to buy out here, and where I'm goin', I don't need money." He leaned back in the saddle and drew in a deep breath. "Smells mighty fine out this mornin', Slocum. Reckon spring's done sprung on us. Be warmin' up fast now."

Slocum sniffed the clean, cool air. Toucherman was right; it did smell like springtime. The sun stayed out longer every day, and the afternoons were downright balmy when the wind wasn't blowing. The horses sensed it too. There was more of a spring in their step, and the blue roan humped up in the mornings, feeling his oats. But the horse didn't try to buck hard—just crow-hopped a bit, enjoying himself and limbering up his muscles.

"Have new grass in a few days, hoss," Toucherman said, "but there'll still be snow on them shinin' mountains when we get there, by God." The old man checked his mule, then dropped back to his usual position behind Mary and the pack animals, where he could watch their backtrail. Slocum kneed the blue roan into a fast walk. It was a long ride from here to the Canadian, he thought.

Slocum reined in at the base of the game trail that twisted up the steep slope out of Tule Canyon, and tried to shake the sense of unease from his gut.

The chill wasn't because of the shadows in the chinaberry grove. Riding through acres of scattered bones tended to give a man the shimmytwitches.

A couple of hours ago they had ridden across the killing fields where Colonel Ranald Mackenzie's Fourth Cavalry troopers had slaughtered the big pony herd captured in the raid on Quanah Parker's Quahadi Comanche camp a few miles north. Horse bones, bleached white by sun and weather and scattered by scavengers, still lay in profusion in the canyon meadow.

Slocum hated the idea of shooting down horses, but he admitted Mackenzie's order had been sound. Left with no winter supplies and afoot—which meant abject poverty to the Comanche, who counted their wealth not in money but in horses—the Indians had had no choice but to give up, ending the campaign that had become known as the Red River War. The massacre of the Indian ponies had been the end of the wild Southern Plains tribes. And with few lives lost in battle on either side.

Mackenzie might—or might not—be crazy, Slocum thought, but the soldier chief the Comanches called Bad Hand knew how to fight Indians. Leave them with no horses, no supplies, and no hope.

Mary's eyes had gone wide and her face had paled as they picked their way through the valley of bones. Despite the warmth from the spring sun on their backs, she'd shuddered when Slocum told her what had happened there. She hadn't mentioned it again.

Now Mary reined in alongside Slocum. The pack mule, its load considerably lighter now, was trailing along under loose lead. All the animals, including Slocum's blue roan, dropped their heads to crop the tender green shoots of young grass on the canyon floor.

"How are you holding up, Mary?" Slocum asked.

She sighed. "My rump's a little sore, but otherwise I feel better than I have in months." She glanced around. "Will we camp here? For a short time anyway?"

Slocum lit the last of his cigarillos. He had been saving it for a few days. When it was gone, he'd be back to Bull Durham roll-your-owns until they reached the nearest settlement. And that was still a long ride away. "We'll wait and see what Touchy has to say before we decide."

A frown creased Mary's pinkish-tinged forehead. Like most fair-skinned people, she sunburned easily and never seemed to tan. "He's been gone a long time. I hope nothing's happened to him."

Slocum shared her concern, but tried not to let it show. Toucherman's "little spells" had seemed to come on more frequently with the passing days. Touchy never complained, but Slocum sensed an urgency in the old man—as though Toucherman knew his time was running out and he was still a long way from the mountains.

"He'll be along soon. Meantime, let's step down and rest

a bit. Loosen the cinch so your horse can breathe easier.''

Slocum slacked the latigo on the blue roan and watched as Mary stretched, rubbed her haunches, and squatted in the shade of a big juniper. She was on the way back to health, even if she still had a ways to go, he thought in satisfaction.

Despite the eight long days in the saddle since they'd left the post-oak country, Mary had put on a bit of weight; her cheekbones were less prominent now, her arms and legs beginning to show muscle instead of a thin covering of white skin over small bones. She was back on her feed too, eating almost as much as Slocum and more than Toucherman, whose appetite seemed to fade even as Mary's grew.

The saddle horses and pack animals were still in decent shape. Slocum had kept the pace steady, neither dawdling about nor in a hurry, alternating at a walk and trot, taking rest breaks a couple of times a day to conserve the animals' strength. If it came to a horse race, Slocum was reasonably sure they would win. He and Toucherman had thrown every trick they knew at Will Gallagher back in the rugged Copper Canyon brakes southeast of Palo Duro. Slocum didn't delude himself that they'd lost Gallagher completely. The man was just too good a tracker.

He did figure they had at least gained ground. It would take even Gallagher a while to sort out the signs. Freeman's men were on mounts that weren't getting any fresher. Altogether, it wasn't enough of an edge to suit Slocum, but it would have to do.

Time seemed to stop here in the pleasant, still air of the chinaberry trees, but Slocum's cigarillo was down to a couple of inches and the shadows had noticeably shifted. And still there was no sign of Toucherman. Slocum's gaze constantly swept their backtrail and the winding canyon floor, occasionally flicking toward Mary.

She leaned against the trunk of a chinaberry tree. Her fingers nervously twisted the reins in her hand. She caught his gaze. ''Shouldn't he be back by now?'' she asked.

Slocum tried a reassuring smile, and wasn't sure he'd pulled it off. ''He'll be along when he gets his scout finished, Mary. Don't worry about Touchy.'' He ground out the cigarillo butt beneath a boot heel. "How did it happen, Mary?"

She glanced at him, momentarily confused, then understood the question. Her shoulders slumped and a pain flickered in her pale blue eyes. "It's a long story."

"You don't need to tell it all. Or any of it even. You don't have to."

She sat silently for a moment, gathering her thoughts, then sighed. "I should have realized what I was doing, Slocum. But it didn't dawn on me at the time I was simply running away from home when I agreed to marry Matt."

"You didn't love him?"

She winced. "I—don't know. He was young, strong, and handsome in a rugged sort of way. And he was—attentive to me. Maybe that's what drew me to him. I thought I loved him, but now I'm not sure. Maybe I was just using him." Her voice trailed away for a moment, her eyes misty. Then she squared her shoulders with an obvious effort.

"Maybe it was just curiosity. About the physical thing. Until I met Matt Kehoe, I'd never slept with a man." She blinked the mist from her eyes. "Anyway, we went to Laredo, where Matt had a job waiting on the T6 Ranch. We hadn't been married four months when—when the horse fell on him. We buried him the next day. I didn't have the money for a marker. . . ." Her voice trailed away again.

Slocum patiently waited out the extended pause. He knew it was hurting her inside to talk about it.

"After Matt died, I thought the ranch would keep me on, maybe as a cook. They didn't. The owner wasn't a generous man. He didn't even pay me the two weeks' wages Matt had coming."

"I'm not surprised to hear that," Slocum said. "I know him. Dan Inverness never felt a thing for another human being in his life. It's like him to just kick a young widow off the place and cheat her out of money due at the same time. Go on."

Tears welled in Mary's lower lids again. "I don't know what I was thinking, Slocum. Or even that I was thinking at all. It seems so—so unreal now. As if it happened to someone else. I knew I couldn't go home." Her Adam's apple bobbed as she swallowed, her voice soft and thin now. "So the short version is, a teamster offered me a ride to San Antonio. The first night out of Laredo, he—he asked me if I'd sleep with him—for money. I sensed that if I didn't agree, he'd take me anyway."

She paused again, shuddered slightly. "Slocum, I didn't know what I was getting into. I spread my legs for him and took his money. Maybe I was punishing myself; I don't know. That was the beginning of it. My life as a whore. I never felt a thing, Slocum. Not even with Matt. I'd heard how wonderful it was supposed to be, and it wasn't." Her face flushed. "I don't know why I told you that, Slocum. It's just—well, I guess I wanted to. To maybe help you understand why."

Slocum nodded solemnly. "I understand. At least as well as a man can understand."

"Thank you. Anyway, I went downhill from there, all the way into the outhouse pit. Into one whorehouse and then another. You know, the girls are expected to act like they enjoy it. The drugs helped. Just cocaine once in a while, at first, to help me with the playacting. Soon, I found I was spending most of my money on drugs. It's a trap, Slocum, a vicious circle. I needed the drugs to get me through the nights, and needed to get through the nights to earn enough money for the drugs.

"I just thought I'd hit bottom, though. It wasn't until Bull Freeman took me in, so to speak, in Fort Worth that I hit the full depths. He supplied the drugs, all I wanted. And all I had to do was lie there in a fog and spread my legs for any man who came into that room, and I'd get all the drugs I wanted. . . ."

Her voice trailed off as shudders wracked her shoulders. Tears tracked across the sunburned skin of her cheeks. Slocum instinctively moved closer and put an arm around her, an awkward attempt to comfort her.

"It's all right now, Mary. That life no longer exists for you. If you're strong enough to resist going back to it—"

"I reckon she is, hoss."

Slocum started at the words from the depths of the chinaberry trees.

"Damn, Touchy," Slocum said, half irritated, "don't you know you shouldn't sneak up on a man like that? Could get you killed."

"Don't get your drawers in a wad, hoss," the former mountain man said with a grin. "I learnt sneakin' from the Crows, and there ain't no better sneakers nowhere." The grin faded. "Looks like we still got us a problem."

"They're on us again?"

"Like stink on wolf droppin's. Will Gallagher's a son of a bitch, but a hell of a tracker. I'd say we're gonna have to pick us a spot to make a stand, hoss, on account of them boys back there ain't goin' to ride off and leave us be." Toucherman paused to stuff and light his pipe. "Bull Freeman ain't with 'em anymore."

Slocum raised a questioning eyebrow.

"Bull and that tall buffalo soldier buddy of his broke off from the rest of the bunch. Headed north. Could be gone for supplies, new horses, maybe more men." He puffed the pipe into a full boil. "Ol' Bull sure must want this girl back somethin' fierce."

"Maybe it's more than that now, Touchy," Slocum said softly. "It could be he wants me as much, or more. I can't say for sure, but there's a better-than-average chance he's made this whole thing personal."

Toucherman nodded. "Likely. Bull don't like to be bested by nobody. 'Specially a white man. Well, hoss? What's your druthers? Keep runnin' or stand and fight?"

14

Slocum stood for a moment, staring toward the southeast, thinking. Then he turned to Toucherman. "We'll stand," he said.

Anticipation flickered in the frontiersman's eyes. "'Bout bygod time, hoss. I been gettin' somewhat agitated toward them jaspers follerin' us. Take 'em here?"

Slocum shook his head. "There's a better spot. You know that west side canyon across from the rock formation that looks like a monkey in the Palo Duro a few miles up?"

"Been past the spot once," Toucherman said. "Don't rightly recall the lay of the land."

"It's a good place for an ambush. Two ways in and out. The bottom of the canyon's fairly open. A man on each side with a rifle could do a lot of damage to anybody down below. We'll sucker them into a trap."

"You mean just shoot them down from ambush?" Mary asked, her sunburned face pale.

"That's exactly what I mean, Mary. There isn't another way."

She seemed to shudder slightly. "It just seems so—cold and heartless, killing a man like that."

"Maybe, but it's a damn sight more efficient and safer than just riding up to them and telling them to go away and leave us alone. As to it's being cold, do you think it would be more

167

heartless than what would happen to you if we don't stop them first?''

She shook her head. ''No. I suppose not.''

Toucherman frowned. ''Might not be that easy, hoss. Will Gallagher's mama didn't raise no fools. That damned little rattler can spot a bushwhack spot from two days off.''

''That's the first order of business,'' Slocum said. ''We have to take him down.'' Even as he said the words, Slocum tasted the bitterness in his throat. Gallagher wasn't a shooter. Just a tracker. But he was the head of the snake that followed them. Cut off the head and the rest of the snake just wriggles around.

Toucherman dragged at the pipe again, his eyes cold and narrowed to little more than slits. ''Be my pleasure to let the hammer down on him.''

Slocum raised an eyebrow at the hard tone of hate in Toucherman's voice. ''I didn't think you knew him all that well.''

''Better'n even he knows, Slocum. Gallagher led Custer's boys to Black Kettle's camp up on the Washita. My wife and boy died in that fight.''

Slocum nodded in understanding. ''Then you have the right. Just don't take any chances.''

''Don't plan to,'' Toucherman said. ''Gallagher won't know who killed him, but I damn sure will, and that's enough.'' He slid the long rifle from its sheath, checked to make sure the cap was still firmly in place on the nipple, and turned back to Slocum. ''Shinin' times again, hoss. And right here's as good a spot as any. You two get along. I'll catch up shortly.''

Slocum tightened his cinch, watched as Mary did the same, then spoke in little more than a whisper to Toucherman. ''Are you still having those pains in the chest, Touchy?''

''Some. But don't you fret it. I'll get the job done.'' The old frontiersman, his jaw set, glanced at the sun. ''You two better get movin'. Them boys ain't that far back. I'll be along in a bit.''

Slocum toed the stirrup, swung aboard the blue roan, and reined the gelding up-canyon, Mary riding alongside. After a hundred yards or so, Mary twisted in the saddle to stare back toward the slight figure climbing the wall of the canyon.

"Will he be all right, Slocum?" she asked.

"I'd bet on it."

"But—his heart."

"Is probably beating stronger now than it has in months," Slocum said. "That man is tougher than the mule he rides, Mary. He'll will himself to stay alive until he reaches the mountains. Like he said, he'll be along in a while."

She rode in silence for a moment, then said, "Slocum, what did Mr. Toucherman mean back there, when he said 'shinin' times'?"

"It's a mountain-man expression, Mary. It's hard to describe, but basically it boils down to the times when a man's living in danger, when Indians or a grizzly bear could end his life in a heartbeat. Or when he's half drunk at Rendezvous, or snuggled in beside a pretty Indian woman while the winter wind howls outside the lodge. I guess it just means the pure joy of living."

"And shinin' times can be even killing a man? From ambush?"

"Even that, Mary. Especially for a man like Touchy. And it's his right. He has to settle accounts with Gallagher, so the souls of his wife and son can rest in peace."

Mary fell silent again for some time. Finally, she turned to gaze at Slocum. "I think I understand now why you decided to make a stand here. It's because of Mr. Toucherman, isn't it?"

Slocum nodded. "He hasn't much time left, Mary. I intend to get him to his shining mountains before that time runs out."

"Why is that so important to you?"

"Because he's a friend. And because he's among the last of a dying breed. We'll never see his like again, Mary. Times are changing. In some ways for the better, and in some ways for the worse."

She smiled at him through the pain that showed in her blue eyes. "Like I said, you're a strange man, Slocum. I think there's a soft streak in you, one you take great pains to hide. I'll bet you even pet stray dogs."

"If I'm sure they won't bite."

"And if they do?"

"I bite back."

They rode another mile without speaking before Slocum reined in at a small spring. "Better fill the canteens here," he said. "When we top out on the west side of that canyon, we'll have a long, dry ride ahead."

Slocum was filling the last canteen when the sound reached his ears—the faint but throaty, rolling echoes of a distant shot from a big-bore rifle. Seconds later a volley of thinner cracks from smaller-bore weapons reached his ears, followed by another heavy rifle report.

Mary started, then glanced down-canyon. "That was him, wasn't it?"

"Yes. A Hawken has a distinct sound. Not like any other rifle I've ever heard."

"Do you suppose he's all right?"

Slocum lashed the canteen into place on the pack mule, then swung aboard the blue roan. "He'll be along soon. Let's go."

Slocum and Mary had waited only a couple of hours after reaching the narrow trail leading up the west wall and out of the small canyon off the Palo Duro when Toucherman rode in.

The wiry mountain man's gaze raked both sides of the canyon as he booted his mule into a shambling lope to the waiting pair. Slocum saw the soft look of contentment in Toucherman's eyes as he reined in.

"Any problems, Touchy?" Slocum asked.

"Nary a whit. Reckon the wife and boy'll rest easier now. Gallagher's been paid back. They're short a tracker now."

Slocum nodded silently. "I heard quite a few shots."

"Don't know where them boys got the idea a little pissant Winchester would shoot a quarter mile," Touchy said with a snort of disgust. "They shot hell out of the ground a hundred yards in front of me. I buzzed another ball their way just to quieten 'em down some."

"Mr. Toucherman, do you think they'll keep on coming—after what happened to the tracker, I mean?" Mary asked.

Toucherman glanced at the girl. "That's what we're countin' on. And they won't need a tracker to find this place. I didn't try no harder'n you two did to hide sign. Ten-year-old Kickapoo could foller the tracks to here, and Kickapoos can't do hardly nothin' right.'' His gaze drifted around the canyon walls one more time. ''Good spot to take 'em out, hoss.''

Slocum nodded grimly. ''We won't have a better chance.'' At least the odds weren't quite as long now. There had been eleven men, counting Freeman, on their trail. Slocum had put one down, Toucherman one. Freeman and the ex-cavalryman had ridden out. That cut the odds to seven against two. ''Mary, can you handle a gun?''

She shook her head, her eyes wide. ''I've never shot one.''

Slocum didn't change his outward expression, but sighed inwardly. It was a little late in the game to be trying to teach someone how to shoot. And if she panicked, she might turn a weapon on herself. He couldn't take the chance.

''If anything should go wrong, Mary, and they get past us, forget everything else and kick that brown as hard as you can. He can outrun anything those men are riding. Head north. In fifteen miles or so, you'll reach a railroad. Follow it and you'll eventually find a town. Understand?''

Mary nodded, her face drawn and pale.

''All right, Touchy, let's go to work,'' Slocum said.

An hour later, Slocum lay in a shallow notch between two boulders on the north side of the canyon. He had a good field of fire; there wasn't much cover in the exposed canyon floor. Across the way and a bit to his left, Toucherman sent a ''ready'' hand signal his way. Mary held his horse and Toucherman's mules on the flats beyond the west trail out of the canyon.

The next few minutes were going to be hard on her, Slocum knew. She was going to be very frightened, alone for the first time in months.

He heard the horsemen before he saw them, muted voices and the creak of saddle leather from the east end of the canyon. Slocum knew that they already were under the sights of a big Hawken percussion rifle. From Toucherman's post beneath a pair of big junipers, the mountain man could see the length of the canyon. Slocum glanced toward Touchy in time to catch his hand signal for patience.

The riders came into Slocum's view little more than seventy yards away and a hundred feet below. They moved cautiously, rifles at the ready. One of the men carried a double shotgun. Slocum altered his plan slightly. The shotgunner would have to be the first man down. Smoothbores could be trouble if that man managed to make it to the rockfalls at the base of the canyon walls.

Slocum lined the sights on the shotgunner's neck, waited a few seconds to make sure Toucherman had a clean shot at the last man in line, and stroked the trigger.

An instant after the muzzle blast of the Winchester, Slocum heard the distinct whack of lead against flesh. The rider's head snapped to the side, his hat hanging in midair, the shotgun tumbling to the dirt. He stayed in the saddle for two quick lunges of his spooked horse, then fell heavily.

As Slocum racked a fresh round into the chamber, he heard the deep, ear-thumping bellow of Toucherman's Hawken. The last rider in line lifted from the saddle as if hit by a boulder, and pitched over the rump of his horse.

Slocum dropped the lead rider with a single shot through the spine—three men down before the others could even react. Two men bailed off their mounts, dove behind a low, sandy mound of earth, and started firing wildly toward the dense cloud of smoke left by Toucherman's big rifle.

Slocum bit back a curse as the other two drove steel to their horses, and in two jumps were racing toward the west end of the canyon—straight toward the spot where Mary waited.

Slocum slapped two quick rounds at the spurring riders. He knew both shots missed. He took his time, allowed for a considerable lead, squeezed the trigger, and saw the lead rider flinch. Slocum knew instinctively the man wasn't hit hard. He fired as fast as he could work the action until the Winchester was empty. He couldn't see through the thick powder smoke, didn't know if he'd hit anything.

A slug whipped past his cheek, then another hit a couple of feet in front of him, kicking dirt and sand into his face as he thumbed cartridges into the Winchester loading port. Through a hole in the powder smoke, he saw one horseman spurring hard toward the west trail out—well out of range of Slocum's long gun. Another ball ripped past his head.

Then he heard the impact of lead on flesh, heard the cry of pain from one of the men below, then the thump of Touch-erman's old Dragoon six-gun. "Dammit, Touchy, don't worry about them," Slocum muttered, "stop that one out front—" The brim of his hat fluttered as another slug buzzed past his ear. Slocum's heart hammered against his ribs. He'd never get to the other man before the rider reached Mary. But he had to try. He snugged the stock of the Winchester against his cheek, lined the sights, and shot the man who had been firing at him.

Then Slocum was on his feet, sprinting along the rough shale of the canyon rim toward the trail out. His heart skipped a beat as he heard a rifle shot up ahead, then a faint, feminine cry. And nothing else except his own labored breathing.

As he ran, Slocum glanced to his left, saw a body lying astride the narrow trail out of the canyon. One of his wild shots had hit the second horseman. He rounded the last juniper clump at the end of the canyon and skidded to a stop. An icy fist clamped around his heart.

Sixty feet away, a big black man with no visible neck stood, his left hand tangled in Mary's hair. Sunlight glinted from the nickel-plated Colt Lightning revolver in his right hand. The muzzle of the six-gun rested against Mary's neck. Half-a-dozen strides to the left, a tall, lean black man in a cavalry-man's uniform stood, a Remington rolling-block carbine in his hands. The black hole in the rifle muzzle pointed straight at Slocum's shirtfront.

They had him cold.

And they had Mary.

A third rider sat hunched in the saddle, blood soaking the side of his shirt. He held a revolver in the hand pressed against his side. A few feet farther back, Mary's brown gelding lay, blood pulsing from the neck, the horse's hooves cribbing at the dirt in its death throes.

For a moment, no one spoke. Then the no-necked black man's lips twisted in a grin of triumph.

"You went to a hell of a lot of trouble for nothing, Slo-cum," he said. "We got her back. Toss that rifle aside and maybe we'll let you walk out of here alive. All I want I've got right here. I'd cost me a bundle, but I'll blow her head off in an eyeblink, you try anything."

"No—Slocum!" Mary's cry was little more than a rasping whisper. "You—promised—"

Slocum knew what she meant. That he'd promised to kill her before he'd let Bull Freeman have her back. But he let the Winchester slip from his fingers, trying to ignore the quick flash of horror in Mary's blue eyes. Slocum deliberately let his shoulders slump, as though accepting defeat, as he calculated his chances with the handgun still holstered at his belt.

The chances weren't good.

Even if the lean cavalryman couldn't handle a carbine all that well, he'd still get a slug into Slocum before he could draw and fire at both men. Freeman had to be the first one down, and Slocum didn't have that much of a target—just the oversized head, part of a shoulder, the arm holding the revolver. It would be chancy even without the carbine centered on his chest.

"All right, Freeman," Slocum said. "Looks like you've got all the aces." He stalled for time, trying to come up with a plan. "How'd you know where we'd be?"

The huge black man cut a quick glance at the cavalryman. "Enos, there. He chased Kiowas and Comanches in this country. Knew about the canyon. I rolled the dice and hit a natural, looks like." The muzzle of the revolver swung away from Mary's neck. "And you lost, Slocum. Let's take him, Enos—"

The cavalryman's head suddenly exploded, burst open like a melon in a cloud of reddish haze. The carbine bellowed, the shot wild; Slocum whipped his Peacemaker from the holster, cocked the weapon as it cleared leather, and let the hammer slip. It was a shot fired on pure instinct. Bull Freeman's head snapped to one side, the nickel-plated handgun spinning from his grip. He went down.

The blast of Slocum's Peacemaker had almost faded before the heavy, rolling report of a big-bore rifle. The man still on horseback seemed to become aware of what had happened. He tried to swing his handgun in Slocum's direction. Slocum drove a slug into the mounted man's chest. He tumbled over the rump of his horse, hit the ground, and lay still.

Slocum was at Mary's side in three long strides. He slipped an arm around her waist as her knees started to buckle.

"Are you all right, Mary?" Slocum asked.

She sagged against him, a sob catching in her throat, and nodded. He shoved her around behind him and stood over the downed hulk of the big black man. His slug had taken Freeman under the cheekbone, laid the flesh open, and torn off a chunk of ear. Freeman was unconscious, but still breathing.

Slocum lifted Freeman's .41 Lightning and tucked it beneath his own belt. He prodded the big man in the ribs with a boot toe. After a couple more jabs, Freeman stirred, moaned, and tried to lift a hand to his damaged face.

Slocum waited until the haze of shock retreated from Freeman's eyes. "You rolled the dice, all right, Bull. They turned up snake-eyes for you." He waited as comprehension flickered to life in the nearly black eyes, then gave way to fear, then to resignation.

"Get it—over with, damn you."

Over his shoulder, Slocum said, "Mary, you've earned the right to kill him."

"Slocum, I—I can't."

"Then I can." Slocum raised his cocked Peacemaker. "Bull, you've caused a lot of people a lot of hurt. Now it's time to pay." Slocum shot Freeman in the left knee. The big man was still screaming when Slocum put the next 240-grain lead slug through his right elbow. And the last one in the chamber into Freeman's gut, just above his belt buckle.

"Have a nice, slow time dying, you son of a bitch," Slocum said pleasantly as he thumbed the spent cartridges from the Peacemaker and reloaded. "I never met a man who deserved it more."

He checked on the rider he'd shot, saw the man's eyes had already glazed in death, and turned to Mary. He caught her as she all but collapsed in his arms. "It's over," he said softly as sobs began to wrack her body. "Bull Freeman will never bother you again."

"I—turned to run like you said, Slocum," Mary said between hiccuping sobs. "They—they shot my horse. The tall man."

"It's all right, Mary. We'll switch your saddle to one of their horses. For now, we'll ride double on mine. Let's see if we can find Touchy."

Jeremiah Toucherman lay slumped across the stock of the big Hawken, the barrel still resting in the X where the improvised shooting sticks—two juniper limbs tied with a length of rawhide thong—crossed.

Slocum's heart skipped a beat as he reined in, helped Mary dismount, then swung down. Toucherman's face was gray, his jaws clenched. But he was still alive.

"Howdy, hoss," Toucherman said, his voice weak and shaky, as Slocum knelt beside him. "Picked a—damn fine time—to have one of them spells, didn't I?"

"It worked out, Touchy," Slocum said. He motioned to Mary to lend a hand. They got the wiry little mountain man into a sitting position. Toucherman's left arm dangled at his side. "You hurting, Touchy?" Slocum asked.

The old man swallowed. "Some. Left arm mostly. Chest some. Spell come over me—durin' the fight. Had a hell of a time reloadin' with just one workin' hand. I hit that soldier feller?"

"Square in the head, Touchy." Slocum stared toward the west trail of the canyon. He could barely make out the huddled bodies from here. "That was one mighty fine shot. Over four hundred yards."

"Four-eighty, you step it off. Sorry I was so damn slow. Reckon we cut it sort of fine, didn't we, hoss?"

"Fine enough that I was fretting a bit," Slocum admitted. "Think you can ride?"

"Damn sure ain't gonna walk. Lead that lop-eared mule up here and boost me in the saddle. Don't forget my Hawken. That's a fine rifle."

"That's the last thing I'd forget, Touchy." Slocum glanced at Mary. "You'll ride my horse back to the mule, Touchy. The walk will do Mary and me some good."

Slocum all but picked up Toucherman bodily and put him

in the saddle, then reloaded and capped the Hawken, tucked it into the deerskin sheath, and handed it to the mountain man.

A half hour later, with Bull Freeman's alternate screams and pleas in their ears, Slocum boosted Mary into her saddle, switched from the dead brown to Freeman's raw-boned bay. Toucherman managed to heave himself aboard the mule. The old-timer seemed to be gaining strength.

"You up to a little ride, Touchy?"

"I'll manage, hoss. Whichaway we headin'?"

"Toward the mountains."

"Then, by God, I'm up to it." A faint grin lifted Toucherman's lips. "Damn good scrap, hoss. Shinin' times, sure 'nuff." He glanced at Freeman, who doubled over, moaning in pure agony. "You gonna finish off that big bastard?"

"No," Slocum said. "He doesn't deserve any pity or favors. He'll hurt bad and for a long time before he dies."

"Good. Was he much of a fighter, I'd lift his kinky scalp on the way out." Toucherman turned his head and spat. "He'd been a Injun, he'd been a damn Kickapoo." The old man turned to Mary. "You look a bit drawed-down in the flanks, girl. You okay?"

"I'm all right. Just—a little shaky yet." Her gaze flicked from Toucherman to Slocum, who thought he saw just the faintest shake of her head, the tears welling in her eyes.

Slocum knew he didn't have much time. It was a long way from here to Touchy's "shinin' mountains." The idea put a knot in Slocum's throat. But it wasn't far to Amarillo, and to the Fort Worth & Denver railroad stop. It could be chancy if Freeman had any men on the train. But it was worth the risk.

They'd reach the mountains a lot faster that way.

Mary and Slocum stood beside the idly chuffing locomotive at its Raton stop, neither knowing quite what to say as Jeremiah Toucherman pulled the cinch tight on his old mule.

The trip hadn't been easy for Touchy, Slocum knew. The mountain man hadn't complained, but Slocum knew he'd been in considerable pain over the last few hours. Toucherman hadn't spoken often during the lurching ride on the Fort Worth & Denver from Amarillo.

Doc Whitley had given Toucherman some pills for his heart, but could do nothing for his kidneys. They were failing almost by the hour. Slocum figured the frequent swallows Toucherman downed from the rye whiskey had helped deaden the pain some.

Still, the old man's face was serene and peaceful when he stepped from the rail coach at Raton and turned to stare at the Sangre de Cristos, bathed in the mild March sun and topped by the white snowdrifts of winter that lingered in the high country.

Toucherman was still staring at the nearby peaks, breathing in the crisp, clean air, a smile playing openly on his lips, as Slocum unloaded Touchy's mule and pack animal, and led them up to the old-timer.

"Shinin' mountains," Touchy said softly. "Like I said, they ain't the Tetons, but by God, they're *mountains*. I was afraid I wouldn't never see 'em again." Toucherman finally turned and offered a hand to Slocum.

"Much obliged, hoss. For bringin' me up here."

Slocum swallowed against the knot in his throat. "What the hell, Touchy. It was on the way."

Toucherman released Slocum's hand, then took Mary's small hands in his own and looked deep into her eyes, the smile still on his lips. "You'll be fine, missy. Just don't you worry your pretty head one bit. You got a long, shinin' life ahead of you, girl."

Tears flowed openly down Mary's cheeks as she clung to the small, wiry frontiersman. "Can we—go along with you a way, Mr. Toucherman?" she asked.

"No, honey. I got near as far as I'm goin' anyway. I can be way up in them mountains by sundown." Mary's shoulders shook in open sobs. "Now, missy, don't you be cryin' for me. I've had seventy-odd winters of a pretty damn good life, I ain't done one damn thing I wouldn't do over, and now I'm goin' home. Goin' to see my family, just like you."

Toucherman released Mary's hands and swung aboard the mule. The old man's face had some color now, and a brightness in the eyes Slocum hadn't seen since that first day in the snowstorm out of Fort Worth.

The mountain man touched his fingers to the front of the badger-skin hat he'd dug from somewhere deep in a pack. "Been some shinin' times, hoss. Keep your hair on."

"You, too, Touchy," Slocum said.

They stood and watched as the old man eased the mules across the twin iron rails, yanked at the pack animal's reins, and kicked his saddle mule into a trot toward the nearest snow-capped peak.

Mary's voice cracked a bit when she finally spoke. "I don't know whether to cry from sadness or joy, Slocum," she said. "I know he's riding off to die, but somehow—somehow, it all seems right."

"It is right, Mary." Slocum became aware he had his arm around Mary's trim waist, and wondered when he'd put it there. "The only sad thing about it is, he's the last of the breed. There aren't any more old-time mountain men—"

"Hate to interrupt you folks," the Fort Worth & Denver conductor said, "but you'd better board up. We're ready to roll." He glanced toward the small figure on the mule. "Your friend's not going on with us?"

"No," Slocum said solemnly. "He's going home."

"And you, Slocum?" Mary asked, "Where do you call home?"

A wry smile touched his lips. "Wherever I happen to be at the moment," he said.

15

Slocum rode relaxed in the saddle, enjoying the long, easy stride of the blue roan and the warm early April sun that bathed the Crooked River country.

A gentle south breeze rippled the green that blanketed the valleys between low, rolling hills. Sunlight danced on the clear, quick-flowing waters of streams lacing the valleys, fed by spring rains and snowmelt from the Cascade Mountains, bluish-gray on the far western horizon.

Here and there splashes of color—reds, yellows, different shades of lavender and purple—hinted at the explosion of wildflower blooms to come over the next few days.

They had been on Double C range for the better part of the day now. From time to time they rode past small groups of Shorthorn cattle wearing the colonel's brand. Early spring calves bucked, ran, and played among their mothers.

Colonel Wesley Connally had chosen well.

Slocum didn't think a man could have taken a pencil and drawn a better ranch than the Double C. Good grass and water, mild winters, occasional stands of timber, no heavy brush to complicate the business of gathering cattle.

He glanced at the girl beside him, astride the blooded sorrel mare he'd traded Bull Freeman's horse for during the week-long layover in Boise before starting the last leg of the trip. Getting rid of the horse, Slocum hoped, would put the last reminder of Mary's past to rest.

She had gained weight during the leisurely trip to Oregon, fleshed out in all the right places. She now resembled the young girl in the tintype Slocum still carried in his pocket.

And she had been damned lucky, considering where she had been. The doctor back in Denver had examined her thoroughly and found no disease other than the lingering effects of malnutrition. Physically, she was on her way back to complete health. Her face all but glowed under the slight, golden tan she had finally managed to acquire under the long days of sun and wind. Her hair was longer, lustrous and shimmering gold under the warm light of the sun.

What shape her mind was in, Slocum didn't know. Only Mary could know that. And there wasn't much Slocum could do about it anyway, except trust her. Talk to her when she wanted, leave her alone when she didn't. She had seemed to become quieter, more subdued and thoughtful, as they crossed into Double C land.

Despite the fact that Mary Connally was once again a pretty young woman with an admirable, if not remarkable, figure, Slocum felt no real stirrings toward her. It wasn't her past. It was just that she seemed more like a younger sister than a grown woman. And, he had to admit, A.J. McDonough was still fresh in his mind. All other women paled in comparison to A.J.

He idly wondered where A.J. was now, what she was doing. Skinning some poor sucker in a business deal probably. She might own half of Texas by now.

Mary reined the mare to a stop at the top of the rise overlooking the neat cluster of Double C headquarters buildings nestled in the grove of trees almost a mile away.

Slocum pulled the blue roan to a stop, let the animal drop its head to graze, and waited patiently.

After a while, Mary turned toward him, her knuckles white on the saddlehorn, lips drawn into a thin line, the expression in her blue eyes that of a wounded doe.

"Slocum, I—I can't. I can't face them. I can't bring such shame to them—their only daughter a whore and—taking drugs." Her voice trailed away, soft and hurt.

Slocum sat quietly for a moment, then smiled gently at

Mary. "I knew that girl you're talking about, Mary. She worked in Hell's Acre in Fort Worth." He pulled a cheroot from his pocket and fired the smoke. "Funny thing, though. I haven't seen that particular girl in quite some time. I wonder whatever happened to her."

Moisture glinted in Mary's eyes as she stared at him. "Damn you, Slocum—why do you always have to say the right thing? Even if you *are* lying through your teeth." She sighed heavily. "All right, let's go."

Slocum sat on the veranda of the sprawling main house, smoking and working his way into a bottle of the colonel's finest rye.

Mary needn't have worried about the homecoming.

Even Slocum had gotten a lump in his throat. After the initial reunion, he'd wandered outside, leaving Mary, the colonel, and her mother, Camelia, to sort through the rough edge of emotions.

The aging and rather broad-beamed housekeeper named Meg had brought Slocum the bottle, along with a wide smile. She had been crying too; she dabbed at the corner of her eyes with her apron, then went back inside.

The sun had dropped beyond the Cascades, leaving behind a wash of red and gold that gradually faded to successively deeper hues, to dark blue, and finally black, as the first stars winked on overhead. The smell of broiling elk steaks and baking bread drifted through the open front door and set Slocum's mouth to watering.

The door opened and Colonel Wes Connally stepped onto the veranda. Despite the fading light, Slocum could see the man's red-rimmed eyes. It was a bit of a surprise. Slocum had never considered the fact that Wes Connally, all five-feet-five and 140 pounds of erect, stern commander, might be capable of shedding a tear.

It didn't make the colonel stand less tall in Slocum's eyes.

Connally sat in the rawhide chair beside Slocum, tamped and lit his pipe, poured himself a glass of the rye, and sighed.

"Just thought you might like to know, Slocum," he said, his voice a surprisingly deep baritone for a man of his slight build. "Mary's forgiven me. For being a damned martinet instead of a father. God, all those wasted years when I didn't even seemed to realize I had a daughter. I don't know how a man can be such a total fool. But we're getting a fresh start now. This time, I won't screw it up. . . ." His voice trailed away.

The silence dragged on for a few minutes, but it wasn't an uncomfortable one. Slocum and the colonel smoked; occasionally one or the other would lower the level in the bottle of rye a touch. Finally, the colonel turned to face him.

"Slocum, I owe you more than you'll ever realize."

"Just doing what I was paid to do, Colonel."

Connally shook his head. "Money can't compensate you for what you brought back to me. If you don't have a child, Slocum, you can't imagine what it means. To lose her. Then to get her back." He stared at the remnants of the spectacular sunset for a moment, then stood. "Supper's ready. You'll stay here as long as you wish, of course. We have several spare rooms."

"Thanks for the offer, Colonel. But just overnight will be long enough. I'm afraid I might be somewhat in the way around here." Slocum half smiled. "No offense, but I think I've been around people enough here lately."

"No offense taken, Slocum. But if you change your mind, the offer stands." At the call from inside, Connally stood. "We'll settle accounts later. Dinner's ready. Hope you don't mind elk steaks."

Slocum lounged in the overstuffed arm chair in Connally's comfortably equipped office, a drink on the table beside him and his belt let out a notch.

It had been a while since he'd had a prime elk steak, cooked just right. The broad-beamed housekeeper set a heavy table. And a tasty one. Slocum felt as if he wouldn't have to eat for at least a week.

He lit a cigarillo as the colonel pulled a metal cash box from a Wells Fargo safe behind the big cherrywood desk overlooked by a massive stuffed bull-elk head with the biggest rack Slocum had ever seen.

The colonel lived well, Slocum thought, yet he hadn't been a happy man. Until now. Slocum hoped for all their sakes that the happiness continued.

There would be bumps along the way, just as there were still a few strained pauses in the conversation around the dinner table when someone was trying to decide whether or not to ask a question or how to phrase a comment. Mary was still nervous—and maybe a bit frightened—but she seemed to relax more with each passing hour.

Connally opened the metal cash box, lifted out a stack of bills, and counted out the substantial fee they'd agreed on before Slocum rode out.

"And your expenses?" Connally asked.

Slocum pulled the small notebook from his pocket and handed it to the colonel. "I've listed everything that applied—"

Connally waved a hand, cutting him off. "Just tell me the total, Slocum. If I thought you'd cheat a man, I'd never have hired you in the first place."

A minute later, Connally handed the stack of bills to Slocum, who tucked them into his leather wallet.

"Aren't you going to count it?" Connally asked.

Slocum flashed a grin. "Colonel, if I thought you'd cheat a man, I'd never have taken the job in the first place."

With the business end of their dealings wrapped up, Slocum and Connally chatted idly for a while, recalling old Civil War battles, the flashes of pure brilliance and total stupidity by leaders on both sides, and common acquaintances who had either fallen in battle or survived.

The colonel topped off their drinks, refilled his pipe, and raised a brow at Slocum as he shook out the match. "I didn't know you were acquainted with A.J. McDonough, Slocum."

For an instant, Slocum thought he caught a faint whiff of rosewater through the pall of pipe and cigarillo smoke. He smiled and nodded. "We know each other."

"McDonough kept us posted on your progress. The telegrams and letters were a week or two old by the time they got here, but they were a comfort."

"Sorry I couldn't do it myself, Colonel," Slocum said, "but

I didn't have much time to file reports, and no place to mail them if I could, up until we reached Denver and then Boise.''

Connally worked on the pipe for a moment, then said, ''I'm curious about one thing, Slocum, but if it's none of my business, forget I asked. Why did you take so long getting Mary back home once you found her?''

Slocum shrugged. ''She needed some time to get a few things straightened out.'' He didn't elaborate, and Connally didn't push the question.

After a moment's comfortable silence, Connally said, ''Oh, I almost forgot.'' He reached into a drawer of the desk and brought out a fat envelope. ''This came for you a few days ago.''

Slocum's heart skipped a beat as he glanced at the envelope. It had no return address, but Slocum didn't need one to recognize the elegant, sweeping penmanship. He started to tuck it into his pocket, then decided to open it on the spot.

The envelope contained half-a-dozen clippings neatly snipped from newspapers from New York to Fort Worth to Los Angeles. Slocum smiled in satisfaction as he scanned the clippings. A major white-slavery ring had been broken, and more than two dozen men were under arrest.

A Navy frigate captain had found several young women in the hold of a trading ship he had stopped and boarded off Galveston Island. The women had been chained to bunks. All were drugged. The trading vessel had been bound for the Orient and the Middle East. The law was still looking for one of the ringleaders, a man named Bull Freeman, who seemed to have vanished into thin air.

Slocum tucked the clippings into a pocket.

''Good news, Slocum?'' Connally asked.

''Yes, sir. You could say that.''

Slocum studied the one-page note written on paper with the Texas & Pacific Railway symbol at the top. ''Will be in San Francisco skinning a couple of businessmen who think they're smarter than they really are the last two weeks of April. Angelos Hotel, downtown. If you happen to be in the area.'' It was signed simply, ''A.J.''

Slocum slipped that note in with the colonel's money.

"Well, Slocum," Connally said after a moment, "sure you won't stay with us a few days?" He topped off Slocum's drink. "We have comfortable rooms, a good cook, and God knows you're welcome here anytime—I owe you more than I can ever repay for bringing my little girl home."

Slocum sipped at his drink and smiled. "Thanks again, Colonel, but I'll be moving on come daylight. It isn't all that far from here to San Francisco."